CREST

By

Robert Suret

ROB SURET

With thanks to:

My wife Christine for her patience and support.

My brother Christopher for keeping
me on the straight and narrow.

My son James for the excellent cover
design and technical advice.

About the author

Rob specialized in national multi-site operational management within the hospitality trade for 30 years. He began writing in 2018 to fulfil his lifetime ambition to emulate great British authors of the thriller genre. He has started a series of novels based around the character of Adam Crest, the first of which was launched in May of 2020. The sequel is expected to arrive at the end of 2020. Originally from the East Yorkshire, Rob has lived and worked in different parts of the country and settled in South Yorkshire with his wife and three children.

To keep up to date on Rob's work you can find him here:

Facebook - http://tiny.cc/izcwrz

Instagram - @suretrobert

CHAPTER 1

Friday 2.00 PM - 2019

Adam Crest leaned forward in his driving seat and frowned as he concentrated on the road ahead. He struggled to see through the rain lashing down at the windscreen on the storm darkened Friday afternoon in November. Passing under a railway bridge created a short sudden silence which emphasised the extreme conditions as he drove along the Reading road.

A yellow neon light appeared in the distance signifying the Shell garage. His stomach rumbled in anticipation of his lunchtime sandwich. Sadly this was often the highlight of his day. As a field-based middle manager, he would generally avoid the heavy traffic on a Friday afternoon. Before beginning his weekend, Adam favoured a peaceful afternoon at home, doing some 'admin' work on security provisions for Comm-Sec UK's national clients.

Turning right onto the garage forecourt he manoeuvred past a large black Mercedes with darkened privacy glass, parked near the forecourt's exit. He drove in and stopped as close to the shop as possible. Tilting the collar of his jacket, he braced himself against the rain, he was still going to get a soaking just reaching the shop door. Through the lashing rain, he noticed a figure doing much the same as him on the far side of the forecourt. Wearing a long black trench coat with a head of white hair poking out of the top, he was running back towards the Mercedes. Adam wondered why the driver hadn't parked closer, as the garage was deserted.

Wheels spun on the slippery wet road as the vehicle raced off.

Shaking the rain from his hair, he headed for the sandwiches fridge in anticipation. After some deliberation, he chose a ham and mustard.

'Hi Frank, just called in for the usual, it's bloody lousy weather out there,' he called towards the serving counter at the other end of the shop.

Adam and Frank Patterson, the fifty-something-year-old owner of the garage, had become good friends. They had engaged in idle chat every Friday for the past year or so. They also met for a lunchtime pint at their local, every Sunday.

He must be in the back office, thought Adam as there had been no reply.

'Just saying, it's absolutely filthy out there Frank,' Adam said a little louder.

Still no reply.

'Are you there, Frank?' he said, walking past the various sweets and magazine racks.

As Adam approached the counter, he noticed a pool of blood on the floor, tracking around the corner of the entrance to the serving area.

'Jesus Christ!'

He dropped his sandwich and dashed behind the counter, taking care not to stand in the oozing pool of viscous blood.

Frank Patterson's inert body lay on the floor. His eyes were closed, and his pallor was as grey as his hair. His white shirt was stained a scarlet red. To Adam's horror, a knife protruded from Frank's lower chest.

'Frank, can you hear me?' Adam said, but there was no response.

The hilt of what looked like an Arab ceremonial knife was expertly positioned slightly to the right of his lower chest. The blade horizontally in line with the bones of his rib cage doubtless slotting between them to most effectively enter Franks's heart. This was not the first time Adam had seen this type of weapon in use.

His armed forces' experience told him that the bright red colour of the blood rapidly oozing from Franks' body was undoubtedly arterial. If he wasn't already dead, he would not survive this attack. Adam grabbed the receiver from the telephone on the counter and rang 999.

'What service do you require?' Said the operator matter of factly.

'Ambulance,' Adam replied calmly,' a man has been stabbed in the chest and is dying.'

The operator sprang into action and as the call progressed, asked for Adam's name.

Instinctively Adam replied 'Kevin Williams.' The name was false. He had no intention of getting involved with the police and a messy murder case. Once he was sure that he could not do anything for Frank, he would disappear before the emergency services arrived.

He gave the operator details of the victim and the location, concluding with the garage's telephone number before ending the call.

Adams attention returned to Frank. His closed eyelids flickered, and a faint moan came from his lips. Adam moved onto both knees with difficulty, as his right leg was not in great shape. He leant forward, placing his right ear close to Frank's lips. The faint odour of fresh blood pumping out of Frank's chest, brought back bad memories for Adam.

'What is it, Frank?' Adam whispered, 'who did this to you?'

'Michelle knows everything,' Frank's voice was faint, 'speak to her. They mustn't get away with it.'

These were Frank's last words, and his final gasp was filled with bloody air bubbles as the dagger had punctured a lung.

'Dear God,' Adam said and wondered what Frank's words meant. *Who the hell was Michelle, and what did Frank mean when he said, 'They mustn't get away with it?'*

Standing up, he surveyed the immediate surroundings taking care not to touch anything. It looked as though nothing else had been disturbed including the till. His eyes returned to the hilt of the dagger. *Not the sort of weapon employed by the average drug addict carrying out a mugging,* he thought.

He stepped into the small office behind the servery. Once again, nothing seemed to be disturbed, including the small safe. Adam checked it was locked shut using a handkerchief to protect the handle from his prints. A CCTV recorder had been disconnected from the mains. 'Curiouser and curiouser as someone once said,' he murmured.

Suddenly blue lights were flashing through the shop windows.

Bugger, that was fast, he thought. Looking through the window he could see that it was a police car instead of the ambulance that he had expected. Not that it mattered now as Frank was beyond help. Adam returned to the customer side of the counter.

The shop door flew open, and a policeman yelled 'Are you, Kevin Williams?'

Adam had no choice but to continue the charade for now 'Yes, I called it in.'

'Where's the victim Mr Williams?' Demanded the police officer.

'Behind the counter.' Adam replied.

Both of the officers were wary of him. Adam could well be the attacker.

'Move away from the counter.'

The officers were cautious as they approached.

'I'm PC Sharpe, and this is PC Willis,' the older officer said, 'stand by the wall and don't move.'

PC Sharpe positioned himself in front of Adam whilst the younger man made haste to the back of the counter and immediately slipped in a substantive pool of Frank's blood.

He stood up then looked down at Frank's body and quickly exited the shop in some distress. PC Sharpe shouted after the rookie 'Sort yourself out and get back in here as quick as you can'.

PC Sharpe then took a look behind the counter and although not affected in the same way as PC

Willis his face darkened as he viewed Frank's demise.

'Well that is definitely Frank Patterson,' said PC Sharpe, checking for a pulse and finding none. His manner became subdued for a moment.

Adam remained silent.

PC Sharpe came back around the counter, taking care to avoid the well-smeared blood.

'Mr Williams,' said PC Sharpe having recovered his composure. 'Whilst we wait for the rest of the team to arrive, you'd better tell me what happened here. To begin with, tell me what time you arrived and carry on from there,' he said with notebook and pen in hand.

'I arrived just before 2 o'clock this afternoon intending to buy a sandwich whilst on my way home,' Adam began.

'Where do you live Mr Williams?'

'About a mile and a half away.'

'Address?'

'32, North Rise, Clements Estate, Lower Earley in the Clements Estate,' said Adam thinking quickly.

'What happened next?'

'I shouted hello to Frank, but there was no reply. I called again but still no answer. So I grabbed a sandwich and approached the counter.'

'This it?' He pointed his booted foot at the sandwich pack on the floor.

'Yes, it is.'

PC Sharpe bent down to inspect it.

'Please don't touch it, officer, as I am sure SOCO would like to take a first-hand look at it,' said Adam.

PC Sharpe quickly stood up and said rather testily 'Well, of course, they will Mr Williams.'

At this point, Adam thought that Sharpe was becoming annoyed at his over assertive manner. He hoped some more senior officers would arrive before these two destroyed the crime scene and in the process made things difficult for him. He needed as much forensic evidence as possible to support his claim of just being a visiting customer. His prints on the sandwich wrapper would go some way towards that.

'Tell me exactly what you saw when ......' PC Sharpe was interrupted at this point as his radio crackled into life. He snatched it from his collar and started walking towards the door saying 'Yes Sir …….. Of course, Sir.'

He was clearly talking to a superior, which could only be good news as far as Adam was concerned.

'Wait there, Williams. I'll be back shortly.' Adam

nodded.

A couple of minutes later PC Sharpe returned with, an ashen-faced, PC Willis and a more officious attitude, (if that were possible).

'Mr Williams, I'd like you to wait in the police vehicle with PC Willis until the inspector arrives.' PC Sharpe said in the sternest voice he could muster.

'Why can't we continue our conversation in here? Until the arrival of your superiors.' Adam wanted to make sure that there were no more disturbances to the crime scene.

PC Sharpe seemed to take this as a rebellious attitude and said 'That's not a request Mr Williams. Now, outside to the car please.' Both officers moved behind Adam and ushered him out of the shop.

Not wanting to create any further conflict and only too pleased to hear of the imminent arrival of some senior officers, Adam said 'That's not a problem officer.'

He got into the rear of the Police car, the door was then closed and locked. PC Willis got in the front and sat in silence, doubtless feeling unwell and a little embarrassed. PC Sharpe went back into the shop, once again talking on his radio.

Adam wondered what further damage Sharpe

might be doing to the crime scene, but at the moment there was little he could do about it.

Given time to think Adam considered the events of the last hour. *Franks attacker was most likely to be the white-haired man he had seen leaving the shop's rear, on his arrival. This was obviously an assassination rather than a robbery and carried out by a professional. But why on earth would anyone want to assassinate Frank Patterson and with an Arabic ceremonial dagger of all things? Frank's cryptic last words implied that he must have known something about his killer. The question is what and how involved do I want to get?*

It wasn't that long ago since he had managed to disentangle himself from an unpleasant time with military intelligence following 2 years in the SAS. He was content with a quiet life and didn't want to get involved. Despite that, he couldn't help feeling that his friend Frank could not have deserved to be murdered.

Adam made up his mind not to reveal to anyone either Franks last words or his own sighting of the mysterious white-haired man. He would stick to his story, which was also the truth. He was just an unfortunate customer passing through.

His thoughts were interrupted when a black Range Rover pulled up beside the Police car. Sharpe came hurrying out of the shop and went over to the driver's side window, which had been opened about two inches. All that Adam could make out was 'yes sir... no sir' from Sharpe. Then Sharpe rapped on Willis's window and said 'Let's have you.'

Willis responded by getting out of the car. The two of them had a quick conflab then came to Adam's door. Willis opened it.

Sharpe said 'Out you get Mr Williams. The gentlemen in the next car would like to have a word with you. Get into the front passenger seat of the Range Rover.'

'Who are they?' asked Adam.

'I will leave them to introduce themselves, Mr Williams. Just do as I've said.' Sharpe did not seem too happy about the situation.

Adam duly walked around to the passenger side door of the large 4x4 followed very closely by Sharpe and Willis. *Christ, they aren't taking any chances.* Thought Adam. Someone *has definitely put the wind up these two, perhaps I'm about to find out who.*

There was an audible click, the car door swung open 'Get in Mr Williams,' said a firm well-spoken male voice.

The blacked-out privacy glass made it so dark inside the car that he couldn't make out who was in the driver's seat or whether there was anybody in the rear.

'Who are you?'

'Never mind that for the moment Mr Williams. I just want to ask you a few questions. Now, please get in the car,' said the insistent voice.

Adam's senses were telling him not to. However, the use of the singular implied that the owner of the voice was on his own. Although Adam could easily have dispatched them if he wanted to, both Sharpe and Willis were standing inches behind him ready to encourage him into the car.

On balance, Adam decided that he would get in and hopefully clear everything up with whoever this was.

Sharpe closed the car door after Adam had entered.

Sitting in the comfortable front passenger seat, he tried to make out the features of his companion.

'Firstly, can you confirm that you are Kevin Williams of 32, North Rise, Clements Estate, Lower Earley?' asked the voice. Using erroneous information that he had obviously collected from Sharpe.

His intention had been to come clean regarding his ID once someone senior arrived. But there was still something *not quite right* about this, so he replied 'That's correct.'

As Adam's eyes grew more accustomed to the darkness inside the car, he turned to look at the man in the driver's seat and could see that he was slim and in his late 50's with dark hair and a thick moustache. He became aware of a presence in the rear of the car. Out of the corner of his right eye, he caught sight of a figure.

The figure was in the process of leaning forward out of the darkness when Adam suddenly realised that he had a full head of white spiked hair. Almost immediately he felt a sharp scratch to the back of his neck and only had time exclaim 'Ohhh no,' before passing into complete darkness.

CHAPTER 2

2017

Captain Crest had never been one for the sun-drenched beaches of the Mediterranean. On the occasional vacations, he much preferred the snow and ice of the ski slopes in Austria and Switzerland. He certainly was not enjoying having to lie on his belly at the top of a rocky outcrop with the insistent glare of the sun baking down on his prostrate body. It was over 45 degrees centigrade. Although his skin had long since become used to the relentless desert sun in southern Afghanistan, it was currently cooking inside a combat uniform including body armour. Adam knew that it was time for the intake of some electrolytes.

He lifted his head cautiously from the sights of the L115 sniper's rifle. It was pointing over the edge of the outcrop and towards the compound below, just short of 400 meters away. He had developed a love for the higher-calibre and slightly heavier weapon over the newer L129 which many preferred.

'Take over for ten will you Colin,' he said quietly to Trooper Colin Gooding lying next to him.

'Will do Sir.'

Adam swapped his snipers cap for the more protective helmet and shifted his weight onto his padded knee guards. Once away from the edge, he crawled to the shade provided by the higher rocks behind them. Grabbing a bottle of energy drink, he drained half of it then lay back in the shade to cool off a little.

As second in command or 2ic, Adam had 16 men in his troop, but only 3 were out with him today. SSM Hislop and Trooper Waring were back at the Armoured Personnel Carrier about half a mile away doing some longer-range surveillance.

They had been carrying out this surveillance operation for 2 days. Intel supported expectation was that some prominent members of the Taliban, yet to be named, were going to meet a major arms supplier at the compound below.

The hills of rock and sand near Now Zad formed a semi-circle behind the compound, and a long canyon-like entrance lay to the front. There was nothing else between here and Lashkar Gah except sand and dirt for 30 miles.

It was a bit open for a weapons trade-off, but it was reasonably remote. The Intel was graded A2, which meant it was an excellent source although details were unconfirmed. In Adams experience, this was about as good as it got.

All they had seen so far were women and children milling about which could well be a sign that something was going on. (The Taliban liked to have them around to use as a distraction or even a shield against attack.)

Putting his head back against the rock, he somehow managed to find a position where he could relax amongst the rubble. He lay there in the baking heat. *There must be an easier way to make a living,* he thought to himself. Resting in the peace and quiet, he allowed his mind to wander off mission and considered how he had arrived at this point.

He had joined the army at 22 almost immediately after graduating from Reading University with a BSc in Physics. He'd been a great success as a sportsman, representing the University in both Rugby and Cricket. A career in academia was not for him, though. He needed to find something much more physically challenging. His father had been in the TA for years, and it was his suggestion that pointed Adam in the Armies direction.

With a strong determination to succeed, he proved to be a first-class soldier, quickly rising through the ranks to Sergeant Major. Also proving to be an excellent marksman. Then came the call from the SAS and he was soon on his way to Hereford.

The last 2 eventful years had been spent progressing from Trooper to Captain during several tours in this superheated hell hole. However, he had recently lost two of his men. SQSM Mark Carlton was the victim of an IED which blew his head clean off. It ended up 25 meters away from his body. Adam would never forget the macabre sight of Marks head lying there, still in his helmet with the light of life gone from his cold staring eyes.

Becoming friendly with your colleagues was not recommended, but Adam was an amiable person. Mark and he had shared sports interests and a similar sense of humour. He had even met his sister, Claire, who was a bright, cheerful and attractive girl. He had every intention of asking her out when next on leave.

After Marks demise, Adam had managed to get some leave to go back to England and provide some little comfort to Claire and her mother. Unfortunately, as time passed, Claire became bitter regarding the SAS and shunned any further communication from Adam.

Only 3 months ago, his Staff Sergeant Tommy Grant caught a snipers bullet through the centre of his forehead during a recon expedition on Kandahar's outskirts. The two of them had started at Hereford together. Tommy had been in Adams troop for over a year. Adam could not get leave to visit Tommy's parents but intended to do so next time around.

Lifting his head, he looked at Gooding, who was the youngest of all of them and hoped that he would not have to make a similar visit to his parents or girlfriend.

Aware that he was becoming a little maudlin, he reminded himself that he was doing a job which he had chosen and for the most part enjoyed. There were plenty of occasions when he had taken men's lives in cold blood, having made 18 sniper kills in his career. *But that's OK because I am one of the good guys. Isn't it?* He thought to himself.

'Damn right it is,' he muttered with certainty. He took another swig from the bottle, got back on his belly and started his crawl back to the edge of the rock.

Swapping back his helmet for the sniper's cap. He took his rifle's stock into his shoulder, positioned his head with his right eye behind the Schmidt and Bender sights and said to Gooding.

'Anything happening?'

'No Sir, just the usual, 6 women and 8 children going about their day Sir.'

'Okay, carry on Colin.'

Gooding returned to his field glasses and continued to survey the valley below.

'Anything of interest at your end, Charlie?' Adam asked SSM Hislop via the radio on his lapel.

'No Sir. All quiet from the APC.'

'Okay, Charlie we'll swap round in one hour.'

'Will do Sir. See you at 14:00 hours.'

Adam returned to his surveillance of the area below. Consisting of a large single-story flat-roofed, whitewashed clay and stone building. It was set in a square with an open space to the side where the children played. There was a gated perimeter wall running along the front of the house and compound.

Suddenly Adam picked up the sound of a distant helicopter and without moving his head away from his sights said to Gooding 'Is that what it sounds like? Have you got eyes on it?'

'Nothing to see yet, Sir but it sounds like a small chopper,' said Gooding who had swung his field glasses around to view the entrance road to what was essentially a cul de sac canyon.

Gooding continued to scan the approach. As the chopper's sound grew louder, a large dust cloud came into view travelling toward the compound.

Adam kept his sights fixed firmly on the entrance to the front of the building. He was expecting some imminent activity.

'What have you got for me, Trooper?'

'Eyes on approaching targets Sir,' said Gooding with enthusiasm. 'One Mi-8 helicopter shadowing three trucks currently two clicks away.'

Adam pressed the button on his collar radio 'Charlie, we've got an Mi-8 chopper and three trucks heading towards the compound. You and Matt get yourselves down here as quick as you like, we'll need the RPG,' he ordered.

Almost seamlessly Adam changed the call to his OC Major Wallace Jones.

* * *

Major Wallace Jones was at his desk in camp Bastion with two very sweaty men in jeans and shirtsleeves sitting opposite. He had little time for civilians coming across from London to interfere with his operations. He had made that very clear to them, much to their discomfort.

'As you're here you can give me the ID photographs for the two targets, they weren't in the file with the original intel,' he said.

The two men glanced at each other nervously.

'I presume you have them?' barked Jones.

'Major Jones, as you're aware, this operation has been put together in a hurry. It is potentially very sensitive due to the countries and personnel that may be involved, behind the scenes, as it were,' said Rushton nervously but firmly. He seemed to be the more senior of the two men from Whitehall.

'Yes, yes, I appreciate all of that. But my men need to ID their targets for Christ's sake.'

'All that your team need to do is take out the leaders of each side of the exchange. I'm sure it will be very apparent who they are as they will be the ones carrying out the exchange,' Rushton said sarcastically.

'*What!* Don't be bloody ridiculous and do not presume to instruct me on how to carry out my operation,' said the Major now reaching boiling point.

The other man spoke quite softly but assertively, the Major couldn't remember his name, or maybe he hadn't given it.

'Major Jones, you have written orders from your superiors. They are from the correct government department and signed by the relevant senior government personnel. I appreciate you might expect such information, it does not state in those orders that targets IDs will be provided. You need to instruct your team to carry out your orders without further query. Is that clear?'

The Major leaned back in his chair, glaring at the man that he now realised was in charge. He was just about to reply when suddenly he saw Crest's call come through on his radio on the desk. He quickly grabbed it.

'Yes, Adam.'

'Looks like it's on, Sir. Three trucks and an Mi-8 approaching only one click away ….' he paused as he looked down at the building below. 'Oh bugger,' he said as he saw 10 Taliban fighters come hurtling out of the front of the building closely followed by 2 more men in formal looking dress. 3 of the Taliban stayed with the 2 men in white Thobes, but the rest of them disappeared from view around the compound's perimeters. *Where the hell did they come from?* Thought Adam.

Returning to his radio, Adam said 'We've got company, Sir. Seven Taliban fighters dispersed to protect their perimeter, they must have been inside the buildings all of the time. Let's hope that they don't know that we're up here. There are also two men in white Thobes. I need the target ID pics sending through now Sir.'

Charlie Hislop and Matt Waring appeared from the rocks behind. They dropped to their bellies crawling along the ledge towards Adam and trooper Gooding.

'Charlie, Matt find out where those seven 'Terri's' have gone, they've disappeared from sight and could be down at the base of these rocks, so look sharp. Colin get ready to confirm once the ID's come through on the tablet.'

Adam opened up the Getac tablet ready to receive the pictures of the targets from the OC.

The noise from the helicopter grew louder as it approached the compound. Adam zeroed his rifle sight on one of the figures in the white. After seeing their faces he spoke into the radio with some urgency in his voice 'Sir, I really need those ID pics. Things are starting to warm up. I think you should know that these two are not Taliban; they look like Saudis to me.'

'Okay, Adam.'

Major Jones clicked the radio off and looked sternly at the 2 men on the other side of his desk.

'Right you two what the hell is going on? My 2ic has just told me that we have two Saudis waiting to receive these weapons, assuming that is what is in those trucks.'

The quiet man calmly said 'Major Jones, those trucks *are* full of weapons. Your man *does need* to kill the two *apparent* Saudis. Along with whoever gets out of the helicopter and goes to greet them.'

'Are you saying that these are not Saudis? I'm sure even you will understand what sort of shit storm it will cause if they are,' the Major Warned.

'Carry out your orders. Major,' came the insistent reply.

Back on the hillside, the helicopter engines were becoming deafening as the sound bounced off the rocks. It hovered over the trucks coming to a halt in front of the compound and caused the Arabs to hold onto the folds of their white Thobes.

Adam pressed his radio 'Charlie, Matt have you get 'Eyes on' those 'Terri's' yet? I need to know that our position is still secure.'

'No, no sign of them. I need to get a better visual further around.'

'Okay, let me know, soon as.'

Adam clicked his radio again.

'Sir, I need those ID's now, or we're going to miss this one. We can't get eyes on the seven Taliban that are running around somewhere,' he shouted over the noise from the chopper.

Christ this is turning into a mess what the hell is wrong with the OC, thought Adam.

Then Major Jones voice came on the radio 'Listen carefully Crest, your targets are the two Arabs in Thobes and whoever gets out of the Mi-8 to greet them. I repeat three targets the two Arabs and the arms dealer. There will be no further ID information. Confirm on completion.'

'Will do, Sir.'

This was very strange, but Adam could tell from the OC's voice that there would be no point in arguing.

'Colin, get your sighting scope on the two Arabs and confirm distance and drop. The wind speed is a bit irrelevant.'

'Sir.'

Even though the helicopter had now landed, its rotors were still churning up the air. He would just have to deal with it.

Adam settled himself for the shot and looked through his sights centred on the first of the Arabs.

'Distance?'

'456 meters.'

'Drop?'

'138 degrees'

The sights were adjusted.

He was going for a closely grouped three-shot, a tricky thing to do but it wouldn't be the first time.

The European arms dealer walked towards the 2 Arabs, his mirrored shades glinting in the sunlight.

Adam slowed his breathing to an even steady pace in preparation, eye focused on the crosshairs centred on the first Arabs head.

Suddenly Charlie's voice was on the radio 'Sir, you have four 'Terri's' on their way up the rock face to your position, you've got three or four minutes at the most.'

'Okay Charlie. Gonna have to shoot and run, get yourselves back to the APC.'

Charlie and Matt had obviously spotted them from further around the hilltop. Adam still wondered where the other 3 'Terri's' were. But he had to focus on one thing only at the moment.

The third man had reached the Arabs. Adam's finger was poised to fire. In the background was the sound of a firefight going on further around the hilltop. He ignored the distraction.

The arms dealer, a white European, reached across to shake hands with the lead Arab. Gently Adam pulled the trigger, moved his rifle slightly to the left, fired again. Calmly he moved the rifle another couple of centimetres, anticipating the third target's movements and fired for the third time.

All three men dropped liked stones to the ground.

Adam immediately shouted 'Right, Colin. Go! Go! Go!'

But before Colin could even get to his feet, 2 of the Taliban fighters hauled themselves over the lip of the rocky outcrop. Colin launched himself from his haunches at one of them and sent him back over the edge of the 100 ft drop. The other one had time to plunge his dagger to the hilt into the centre of Colin's chest.

Adam drew his Glock and was able to shoot the 'Terri' in the head and chest.

Before he could get to Colin, the other 2 climbed over the lip on either side of Adam. He made his choice and turned to the man on the left and fired two shots into his face.

Aware that the other man was now behind him, he swivelled to the right to avoid the expected knife attack, launching himself backwards toward the rocks.

The Taliban fighter was quick enough to slide his dagger deep into the top of Adams right thigh just below his groin severing his femoral artery.

Adam hit the ground hard, and his skull crashed against the rock that had earlier provided some comfort as a headrest.

The last thing Adam could remember was the sound of several gunshots before he fell into a black abyss of unconsciousness.

CHAPTER 3

Sunday 9.00 AM - 2019

As consciousness returned the pounding in Adam's head got louder and louder. He dare not move or open his eyes until it subsided.

He began to recall what had happened on the ledge and the tragic death of Colin Gooding. He remembered that Charlie Hislop and Matt Waring had despatched the other three Taliban and arrived back at his position in time to save him from certain death. After putting a tourniquet around his thigh, they got him to a femoral clip in the APC and then back to base camp.

The mission had been a real cock-up, and Adam had never gotten to the bottom of why. Major Jones was soon transferred and not seen again.

As Adam lay in his befuddled state, it occurred to him that he knew a lot about how he had got back to base camp, but couldn't remember any of the exact details. Also, his head was still banging, but he couldn't feel any pain in his right leg.

Oh my god, he thought. He quickly felt his right leg under the duvet. *Well, at least I have still got it.*

Then his thoughts began to clear, and his eyes sprang open with the sudden realisation.

'Those bastards in the Range Rover!' he exclaimed.

He closed his eyes just as quickly due to the sudden light piercing his brain like a shard of glass. They had been open long enough to realise he was not in the camp hospital or any other hospital.

He was in his own bed, in his own bedroom, in Reading.

The pain in his head was not the result of banging it against a rock in the desert, but the effects of whatever drugs had been pumped into him.

Through the haze, he sensed someone else in the room and the smell of perfume.

'Who's there?' Adam croaked barely making himself heard.

'Oh, you are finally awake,' said the accented female voice.

Adam swallowed and said a little more clearly 'Who's that?'

He managed to open his eyes slightly. Through the slits, he could see the back of a tall slim woman with long black hair down to her waist wearing a dark blue skirt and white blouse disappearing through his bedroom door.

'Ciao darling, see you again soon,' she called as

she left.

Who the bloody hell was that? Thought Adam as he attempted to lift his head from the pillow. Only to fall back again as the inside of his head clanged about.

Giving himself a couple of minutes, he tried again managing to sit up and swing his legs out of bed. He noticed that he was naked, which wasn't unusual in itself as that was how he usually slept. But presumably someone had put him in the bed.

Staggering the few feet to his wardrobe, he grabbed his dressing gown. He put it on, looking at his alarm clock, which said 10.00am. Pulling the curtain from the window, he looked out onto a tranquil street. The only person about was Raj, the owner of the paper shop on the corner. He was delivering what must be the Sunday papers. (Raj always delivered the Sunday's papers himself.)

Adam returned to the bed and sat on the edge, cupping his head with both hands and rubbing them across his face to wake himself up. *My god,* he thought *it must be Sunday, what the hell happened to Saturday?* Hard as he tried, he could not remember a thing about the previous day. He wondered if he had been out on a bender and picked up the dark-haired girl.

It wouldn't be the first time he had brought a young lady back to his house on a Saturday night. But he would remember meeting them and would certainly have known her name. He liked a drink at the weekend, but he had never had so much that he couldn't remember the night before and definitely not the day before.

Then he remembered poor old Frank and the awful events of Friday afternoon as they came flooding back.

Anger replaced confusion as he recalled the rest of Friday afternoon's events.

He had a long cold shower, shaved and got dressed. Then went downstairs and took four Paracetamol and drank two cups of strong black coffee.

Sitting at the kitchen table cupping his coffee mug in both hands, he considered several questions. *Who had murdered Frank and why? Who was the white-haired man? Who were the men in the Range Rover? Who is Michelle? Why had he been returned to his house relatively unharmed? What happened to the 2 police officers? And who was the woman in his room?*

'A lot of bloody questions. I had better find some answers,' he said to himself, grabbing the car keys which someone had left on the kitchen table.

The car had been left unlocked, something Adam would never do. He carefully got in. Everything appeared as it should, even his mobile phone was in the cradle underneath the armrest. However, he had no intention of using it. Better to stop at the nearest shop and get a pay as you go phone.

He drove to the end of his road and stopped outside Raj's paper shop. Raj had returned from his round.

'Morning Mr Crest,' said Raj

'Hi Raj, I have an odd question for you?'

'Okay.'

'Did you deliver Saturday's paper or was it young Eric?'

'I had to do Saturday as well this weekend, Eric has gone to London with his parents.'

'Oh, Right. Did you happen to notice if my car was on the drive?'

Raj pondered for a moment 'Yes Sir it was.'

'Okay thanks, Raj. I'll pop in and pay the bill on Monday,' Adam dashed out before Raj started getting too chatty.

Next Adam drove another mile up the road and stopped to buy a pay as you go mobile phone.

Once back in the car he set up the phone and made sure that there was no caller ID.

Directory enquiries connected him to the police.

'Hello, Reading central police station.'

'Please could I speak to either PC Sharpe or PC Willis?'

'What name is it?'

'My name is James Thomas.'

There was a moment's silence, then the operator returned.

'I'll put you through to the duty officer Mr Thomas.'

'Mr Thomas, PC Miles speaking. What can I do for you?'

Adam repeated the request.

'I'll just have to check the rota, Mr Thomas.'

PC Miles disappeared for a moment then came back on the line and said 'PC Sharpe is no longer based at this station, and PC Willis is on long term sick leave.'

Damn, thought Adam although he should probably not have been surprised. Without much hope, he asked 'Can you tell me which station PC Sharpe reports to?'

'I'm afraid not Mr Thomas, is there something I can help you with?'

I Might as well give it a try, he thought.

'Possibly, it's regarding the incident at the Shell garage on Reading road last Friday afternoon. I believe there was a robbery or something?' he said.

'I'm afraid that I've been off for the last three days, so I'm not aware of any incident, but I will just check the log.'

PC Miles returned 'I don't have anything listed in the log for Friday afternoon, do you wish to report a robbery sir?'

Surprise, surprise, thought Adam 'No it's okay. I must've been mistaken, thanks for your help anyway officer, goodbye.'

This stumbling block did not phase Adam, in fact, it just confirmed to him that there were people in authority involved in whatever this was. *I'm going to need some help with this,* he thought, but *first*, he went back into the supermarket and got himself a ham and mustard sandwich and returned to the car.

Whilst enjoying the belated sandwich, he pondered, *who is Michelle?* Then he remembered, sometime early last year he'd been chewing the cud with Frank, who had mentioned that his sister Michelle would be arranging for one of her staff to look after the garage whilst he took a week off in the Summer. Adam remembered commenting humorously 'Oh, she's got staff has she.'

'Yes,' said Frank 'she married well, did our Michelle, lives in Kensington. Officially she should be addressed as Lady Gorton-Hyde. Her husband is a politician, nice fella. I've met him a few times. I let him use the old warehouse behind the garage to store his vintage cars before they go for refurbishing in Oxfordshire. I believe he's got quite a collection.'

'Crickey, I wouldn't mind a look at them,' Adam said enthusiastically.

'To be honest, I don't think they are much to look at before refurb. Apparently, they arrive in pretty poor condition, usually in crates. Either way, I don't have the key to the warehouse. He's installed his own, very expensive, computerised security system. I don't want anything to do with that,' Frank said with certainty.

'I don't blame you,' agreed Adam' best to stay away from the IT world if it's not your thing.'

The recollection of this conversation had provided him with the answer to, who Michelle was. But not what it was that 'she knew all about'. One thing was for sure he needed to revisit the Shell garage and see what he could find out. Starting the car, he set off for Reading road.

Approaching the garage slowly, without stopping, he could see that it was closed, the forecourt was in darkness, but there was some light in the shop. He decided to park in a layby further up the road and walk back.

Opening his glove box, he retrieved a flick cosh which he kept 'just in case'. He wasn't sure what it was 'just in case' of, but he felt better knowing it was there.

As he crept along the line of bushes to the forecourt, he decided to stay out of sight. Sneaking past the wall at the far side of the forecourt, he reached the back entrance door. There was a sign stating 'Closed until Further Notice' on the front door. Inside there were two, fairly chunky, Rent-a-Guard types sitting at a table playing a game of cards.

Reaching the external door leading to the office, he prepared to force it as quietly as possible. To his amazement, the door was not locked and opened when he turned the handle. *My god these two are a couple of pro's,* he thought. *They can't even manage to lock the back door, it might be easy to get a few answers out of them.*

However, he wasn't taking any chances. His fingers curled reassuringly around the cosh in his pocket.

With the element of surprise on his side, he decided on the direct approach. He walked brazenly through the back door, through the office and towards the shop shouting 'Frank, are you in?'

Entering the servery, he noticed that an efficient clean-up had taken place and not a spot of Frank's blood was evident. The two guards were sitting at the other end of the shop near to the sandwich fridge.

Startled, they both shot up from their chairs and hastened towards Adam. They were big men at over six foot and 200lbs each, so he was not going to be able to pull any punches. The first one shouted 'Oy you can't be in ere, get out.'

Adam ignored him, asking 'Where is Frank?'

'Never mind *where Frank is*, get the fuck out of here, now!'

The first guard continued to stride forcefully towards him. Adam matched his speed. A split second before they smashed into each other, Adam sidestepped to the left.

In one smooth motion, he withdrew the cosh from his pocket and activated the release. The sprung metal sleeve shot out from the handle extending 20 inches. He swung his hand up then swiftly brought it down, allowing the weighted metal end to whip across his opponent's head. The guard dropped like a stone and lay unconscious on the floor.

By now, the second guard was running towards him. Adam turned to face him and dropped to his left knee in front of him, letting go of the cosh. The guard bore down on him Adam's tightly balled fist shot upwards. He struck the guard in the solar plexus with the force of a professional fighter.

The blow's power, coupled with the guards forward momentum, caused him to lift off the ground and crash back down. The man lay disabled on the floor.

Adam stood up. Pleased with his handy work he picked up and collapsed the flick cosh then returned it to his pocket.

The name badge on second guard's chest told Adam that the man was called Jason. He dragged him across to the back of the shop and into a seat. The guard struggled to breathe. Wandering across to the useful knick-knacks shelf Adam grabbed a fistful of nylon zip ties then strapped Jason's wrists and legs to the chair. There was some groaning, but the fight had gone out of him.

He dragged the other guard, who wore the name Steve on his badge, into the back office. Carried out the same process, ensuring that Steve was also unable to move his limbs when he came round. He was also well out of sight of Jason but within earshot of any screams.

Returning to the garage shop's tools and maintenance section, he could see Frank had kept it relatively well-stocked with a variety of useful things. He chose several items from the DIY section. In the hands of someone with a creative mind, these could prove to be very persuasive.

The selection included a 3 pack of small, medium and large-sized locking grips, a metal claw hammer, a pack of 1' tacks and a hacksaw (the latter was mainly for effect.)

As Steve was still unconscious, he took the items across to Jason.

With slow, silent purpose, he laid them all out on the floor in front of him. He grabbed another chair and placed it directly opposite so that their knees were only a few inches apart when he was seated.

Adam would take no pleasure in what he was going to do after all these two were just a couple of underpaid security guards and a long way from being professionals. But he needed some information. He just hoped that they wouldn't make it too difficult for themselves.

Jason managed to drawl 'Who the fuck are you,

and what do you want?'

'Ah, that's good, you can talk,' said Adam softly, ignoring Jason's questions.

'Jason, I want you to take a look at the floor between your legs at the items that I have placed there.'

Jason's eyes moved downwards, and with a look of confusion on his face, he said 'What the hell are they for?'

Adam ran his finger across the selection of tools and picked up the small but heavy metal hammer. Rested the head of it on Jason's protruding knee cap then said 'These Jason, are to help you give me some information.'

Jason glared at Adam and shouted 'WHO THE HELL DO YOU THINK YOU ARE? I WILL KICK YOUR FUCKING HEAD IN WHEN I GET OUT OF THIS CHAIR!' He proceeded to wriggle about in an attempt to loosen his ties. All that he achieved was to further tighten them, which would soon become very painful, especially the ones around his wrists.

Without warning, Adam lifted the hammerhead, only about six inches. He brought it down sharply onto the middle of Jason's knee cap. Not enough to break it but certainly enough get his attention.

'*Ahhhgh*, you bastard!' exclaimed Jason. Adam could see Jason's hands twitching at his bindings with a sudden urge to rub his knee, which of course he couldn't.

The hammerhead moved across to the other knee and rested on the patella. He waited for the feeling of nausea to dissipate from Jason's stomach.

'Now, Jason I know that smarts, but you really need to focus on what I'm saying, or the other knee will get a much firmer tap.'

Jason, red-faced with a mixture of pain and anger, became quiet as he realised that he was powerless in the hands of this mad man.

Adam leaned forward 'I know that you and Steve are a couple of security guards just doing a job, but I do need some information from you. Your colleague is still unconscious. You should understand that whilst I don't wish to hurt you I do have some experience in this sort of thing and will do whatever it takes to get what I want,' he said with menace.

'I'm sure that you can imagine what these locking grips could do to the knuckles on your fingers when the jaws are squeezed shut. I know I don't need to explain how they work. We could start with the jaws set fairly wide, but of course, as I turn the screw at the base the gap will close, and well, I think you can work out what happens. Similarly, these one-inch tacks are relatively harmless when used at home but just think what it would feel like to have one or two hammered through the centre of your knee caps. Not a lot of effort on my part but a great deal of effect on yours. Am I getting through to you, Jason?' Adam said whilst lightly bouncing the hammer on Jason's left knee.

The colour drained from Jason's face as his mind filled with the images that Adam had put there.

'Look I don't know what you want, pal. Just ask your questions,' he said.

'Excellent,' said Adam and stopped bouncing the hammer but left it resting on the knee cap.

'Let's begin with who you work for?'

'Guard-Co,' Replied Jason.

'Okay, who owns Guard-Co?'

'A guy called Lewis Bolton.'

'Is Mr Bolton successful, is Guard-Co a big company?'

'Yeah, we do jobs all over the country.'

'Where does the work come from Jason?'

'It's mainly government contract work.'

'Mr Bolton must be well connected, who does he

deal with?'

'I dunno.'

'Oh Jason it was going so well,' said Adam and swiftly lifted the hammer about 12 inches and brought it down smartly on Jason's right knee cap.

Jason screamed in agony this time and burbled 'I don't know ..... I swear I don't know who he deals with. You'll have to ask Steve he knows more about that sort of stuff. Jesus Christ, you've broken my knee.'

Then a voice bellowed from the office 'WHAT THE HELL'S GOING ON OUT THERE?'

'Ah that's timely, it seems that you've woken your buddy up,' Adam said to Jason. 'I suspect that he may be a bit more useful anyway.'

Adam gathered up the tools and walked towards the office, leaving Jason whimpering in his chair.

He walked through to the office, and Steve said 'Who the fuck are you and what's happened to Jason?'

Ignoring the first part of the question, Adam replied 'I am afraid Jason's in a bit of a mess, and you'll need an ambulance once this is over. He just couldn't give me the right answers,' Adam said grossly exaggerating Jason's condition for effect.

He went through the same process of laying out the tools at Steve's feet and without warning gave his knee cap a smart whack with the hammer.

Steve screamed out '*Ahhhhgh* you fucker!'

Allowing a few seconds recovery time Adam said 'I hope you feel able to help now Steve?'

'We don't get paid enough for this shit. Just ask your questions, and I'll answer them if I can.'

Steve was clearly the more senior of the two, and Adam hoped a little more informed. He sat in the chair opposite him and toyed with the hammer in his hand.

'That's great news, Steve. Jason answered some of my questions, so I'll continue with you. When did you get here?'

'Friday night at around 6.00 pm,' he said sullenly.

'Who was here?'

'Mr Bolton, two coppers and some posh git in a suit.'

'By any chance does Mr Bolton have a black Range Rover?'

'Yeah.'

Adam realised that he must have been lying unconscious inside the Range Rover when Steve and Jason had arrived.

'Is Mr Bolton, a white-haired gentleman?'

'Yeah.'

Adams jaw tightened as he recalled the needle in his neck.

'Were there any other vehicles?'

'Just the black van taking the body away.'

Poor Frank thought Adam.

'Who was the guy in the suit?'

'I dunno.'

Adam raised the hammer.

Hurriedly Steve said 'I really don't know, but I heard Mr Bolton call him Larry.'

Adam rested the hammer in his hand. 'Okay, Steve. What exactly did you hear?'

'I just heard Mr Bolton say 'don't worry Larry I will take care of him' and that's all honestly.'

'Okay, Steve, now we are getting somewhere. I guess this Larry was mid-fifties dark hair and a thick moustache.'

'Yeah, that's him,' said Steve with surprise in his voice.

'What did you two do next?'

'We were told to finish the clean-up and secure the shop until further notice, but most of it had been done by the black van boys.'

I bet it had, thought Adam, who was familiar with the clean-up teams from a previous life.

'Okay, Steve, you've done well so far. Now give me the keys and the access codes for the security system in the storage buildings behind the garage,' said Adam firmly.

Steve began to panic in expectation of some more use of the hammer.

'Oh come on, mate, we haven't got anything to do with those buildings, and we were told not to go near them honest,' he said in desperation.

'Okay, okay, Steve, I believe you.'

Adam realised that he had got all that he would get from the two men and crossed the office to exit through the back door.

Steve shouted 'Hey! are you going to let us out of these chairs?'

Adam replied 'Your sitting down, aren't you? Anyway someone will be out to you when you don't check-in. Cheers guys.'

'Bastard,' muttered Steve.

Once outside, Adam went around to the back of the garage and had a look at the 3 outbuildings.

All quite large, they looked like they had once been storage barns for a local farm. Now they had new, heavy-duty roller shutter doors on the fronts.

You could store an awful lot of something in those, thought Adam. He was frustrated that he couldn't get in, but it would have to wait for another time. He needed to do some thinking and digging before he was ready to start blowing the doors off things both practically and figuratively speaking.

He made his way back to the car in the early evening darkness. He sat for a few minutes digesting the snippets of information that he had collected from the 2 guards, rubbing his right thigh, which still became quite painful when overexerted.

Whoever Larry was he must be well connected to be ordering the police about, he thought and *most likely associated with the home office.* He had discovered who his abductor was, although he didn't know why they had released him the following day. He would get to Lewis Bolton in due course.

Next, he needed to pay a visit to Michelle, or rather Lady Gorton-Hyde. Also, find out who Larry was. It occurred to him that he may make some headway by calling in a favour from his old friend Julian Lycett. He headed for home.

CHAPTER 4

2017

'Captain Crest!' said male nurse Maclean to the sleeping man.

'Captain Crest!' he repeated a little louder.

Adam awoke at the insistent tap on his shoulder. He was greeted by nurse MacLean's boxing ravaged face, a legacy from his younger days. He always used to say that they should have seen the state of all the other guys, but Adam couldn't imagine they were any worse than MacLean's.

'Oh, hi Mac I must have dropped off again, you'd think after a week of lying down that I'd be able to stay awake for more than two hours.' Adam pulled himself up in the hospital cot wincing at the extremely painful right leg.

'It was a big op, Sir, and you will need time to recover. You have a visitor, Sir, SSM Hislop is here to see you.'

'Oh, great stuff Mac, send him in will you?'

'Will do sir.'

Since the events at the Taliban compound and the sad loss of Colin Gooding, Adam learned that Charlie Hislop and Matt Waring had managed to take care of the remaining Taliban fighters. They got to Adam's position in time to take out his attacker.

Charlie Hislop breezed into the room and said 'Afternoon Sir, how are you doing?'

'I've told you before Charlie, you can drop the Sir in here.'

'Righto Adam, well, how are you doing?'

'Okay, I suppose, but it hurts like hell, and they say that I have to get out of bed tomorrow. I'm not too keen on that idea.'

'I know that you have to start using your leg or you end up even worse off.'

'You're quite right of course, anyway I'll face that challenge tomorrow. Have they shipped Colin's body back yet?'

'It went yesterday,' replied Charlie.

'I'll visit his parents and Lisa when I get back.'

'Yes,' nodded Charlie. 'I guess you won't be fit for active duty after this.'

'You're probably right Charlie, but I've still got another 2 years of my 12 to go, so who knows what I'll be doing. What's happening with you guys?'

Charlie moved his chair closer to the cot and lowered his voice to say 'It's a bit weird Adam, ever since the last mission nothing has been said. No, debrief, no feedback and the subject off-limits for discussion. Matt and I are being shipped back to Hereford tomorrow, and the OC disappeared 2 days ago. I did hear that he had a blazing row with a couple of civvies in his office, but I don't know any details. My guess is it relates to the two Arab targets.'

'I dare say you could be right Staff Sergeant, so let's just follow orders and not discuss it any further,' said Adam.

'Yes, of course, Sir.'

'I know I've already said this Charlie but I must repeat my gratitude for what you did out there. It's a certain fact that I would not be here if you hadn't managed to apply the femoral clamp and get me back. I know we'd all do the same for each other, but I'll always be in your debt.'

'Well if that means that we'll always remain, mates, that's fine by me. Now before we start getting the hankies out, I'm going to bugger off. Hopefully, I'll see you back in Hereford, and you can buy me a pint or two. You've got my number anyway, Sir.'

'Yes, Charlie, I'll see you and Matt on the other side.'

Charlie stood up crisply saluted, something that was rarely done out there, and left the room.

'Cheers, Charlie,' shouted Adam after him.

❦ ❦ ❦

Two weeks later Adam was back in England, in hospital in Hereford and doing very well on his crutches.

'You'll be moving to stage 3 physiotherapy and a single crutch from tomorrow Captain Crest,' said the nurse. Her looks were a vast improvement on Mac's broken nose and cauliflower ear. In fact, she was a very attractive blonde and looked great in a uniform.

I must be recovering, thought Adam as he put away his mischievous thoughts, at least for now anyway.

On the Wednesday of that week his OC in Hereford, Lieutenant Colonel Chambers came to see him. He dropped the bombshell that Adam had been seconded to Defence Intelligence, for the remainder of his service. Lieutenant Colonel Chambers had visited Adam on several occasions and shown a genuine concern for his condition. He was known in the ranks for being a decent boss.

'With all due respect Sir, who the hell gets seconded to DI from the SAS? I have never heard of anything like it.' Adam said with outrage.

'Yes, I understand where you're coming from Crest, and I've never come across this sort of thing before either, but to be fair, these boys are all about secrets. We wouldn't necessarily know if it had happened before. Theoretically, it can be done as DI is still part of the MoD. Regardless this order has come from on high. The reasons given relate to your combat experience and exceptional marksman's skills. Of course, your injury, preventing a return to active combat service, is a valid reason on its own. However, I would just say that I consider there is also some underlying agenda, so watch your back Crest. I've followed your career, and you are an excellent soldier but beware. You're entering the murky world of the intelligence services.'

'Thank you, Sir, I think,' replied Adam.

'Here are your orders,' said the OC handing a sealed envelope to Adam. 'It looks like you'll be on your way within the next three weeks so I'll wish you well and say cheerio.'

'All the best Sir and goodbye.'

The OC left, and a confused Adam sat down to consider his fate.

He opened the letter containing his orders and discovered that he was to report to a

Major Braden at an address at Wyton in Cambridgeshire, two weeks on Friday.

Well, thought Adam, *at least I've got another two weeks frolicking with the nurses, and I suppose some desk job in Civi Street, for the next 2 years is not the end of the world.*

❊ ❊ ❊

Adam hired a car three weeks later. Threw his kit in the boot, which was essentially all of his worldly possessions. He set the sat nav for the address provided and hit the road.

On arrival at the Cambridgeshire offices, he was surprised to find that it was a sprawling 2 storey, modern building. It could easily have been an insurance company or something similar. Sort of hiding in plain sight on what seemed to be an edge of town Business Park. The name plaque just said MINISTRY OF DEFENCE.

After parking the car, he headed for the smoked glass doors of the main entrance. He told the hard-faced middle-aged lady that he had an appointment to see Major Braden. (She looked like she would relish a few rounds with Mike Tyson.)

The receptionist tapped her computer screen without acknowledging Adam and said 'Down that corridor,' she pointed to the right. 'Turn right, second left, end of the corridor knock on the last door on the right. Here put this on,' she said abruptly and handed a visitors badge to Adam.

Adam fitted the badge to the lapel on his jacket and asked 'Don't you want to know who I am?'

'I know exactly who you are Captain Crest,' she replied without looking up from her computer screen.

'Righto,' said Adam and set off down the corridor.

He eventually reached the last door on the right as directed, without seeing another soul in the long corridors or hearing a sound from the various doors that he had passed on the way. He knocked firmly on the door.

'Come!'

Adam entered what was basically an office with nothing in it but 2 filing cabinets, a desk and comfortable looking chair in which sat Major Braden who was busy on his laptop. Adam stood to attention in front of the desk and introduced himself.

Major Braden raised his head and said 'I know who you are Captain Crest.' He gazed at Adam for a moment then his head dropped back to the laptop without speaking. After several minutes the Major finally closed the laptop and looked back up at him.

'Okay Crest, I am Major Braden, and you will report directly to me during your time with us. Is that clear?'

'Yes sir,' Adam replied under no illusions that it had better be.

'I have read your file,' he continued gesturing towards the laptop ', and I'm not entirely clear as to why you've been sent here. Apart from the obvious injury in action. However, you do possess certain skills, and I intend to make the best use of them.'

'What skills are those Sir?' Adam asked.

The Major looked a little agitated at Adams interruption and replied 'Your sharpshooting prowess Captain. We have a shortage of marksmen within our organisation.'

Adam wondered why such skills would be needed for intelligence gathering.

Leaning a little forward to emphasis his words, Major Braden continued. 'You may have experienced a more relaxed attitude to military protocols in your previous role. It is very much the opposite here. The environment and working conditions might not be as harsh, but the military procedure is followed to the letter. Understood Crest?'

'Understood Sir.'

'Your accommodation is an apartment just down the road. You can draw a vehicle from the carpool, see Florence for the details, and she will also advise you where your office is.'

Florence must be the unlikely name of my' friend' at reception, Adam thought.

'We'll start you off on some surveillance work, again Florence will give you your laptop with access codes etc., but I want you to report to the firearms range on Monday morning. Sergeant Miller will meet you with the requisite equipment. We don't want you getting rusty do we?' The major did not expect a reply and returned to his laptop.

'Dismissed Captain Crest.'

And that was that.

Adam had several questions, not least who he would be shooting at, but he felt that this wasn't the time to ask. He was probably going to have to get any further information from his new colleagues. When he found some, although probably not Florence.

For the next 6 months, Adam carried out surveillance work. He was very good at it and soon lead his own 4 man team. Much of his time was spent installing listening devices and monitoring them for hours on end.

There was precious little evidence of Major Braden's *strict procedures* when it came to warrants and permissions for this work. Not one for questioning orders Adam got on with the job. He did occasionally wonder who would be left in the hot seat if they got caught hacking someone's computer and carrying out illegal surveillance. He guessed it wouldn't be Braden.

One day an email instruction came from the Major headed <u>Terminate Target: Your Eyes Only.</u>

The target details proved to be those of two Russian males that Adam had been watching for two weeks.

Petrov and Lenko had killed two DI agents in a brutal fashion involving baseball bats and a sledgehammer. They were involved in people trafficking and prostitution. There was also good evidence that they were receiving some instruction from the Kremlin. What it was regarding had not been established, at least as far as he knew.

Adam was used to receiving target instructions but only in the field of combat. Hence, he was a little uncomfortable with this. Still, he knew one of the murdered DI agents and his family personally. These 2 morons had inflicted a great deal of pain on both men. This eased his conscience a little.

A couple of days later in the early morning, Adam knew that Petrov and Lenko were due to meet one of their *gangmasters* and collect his payment. Their 4x4 slowly cruised across the empty supermarket car park to a remote corner. Along the edge of the car park ran a raised tree-lined area. He knew that this would have to be swift and neat if he didn't want to be spotted by a member of the public.

The targets lit cigarettes and sat chatting in the car. Adam positioned himself and his sniper rifle on the grass amidst the trees. The range was 350 meters. Both men could be seen clearly through the sights. His forefinger stretched across the outside of the trigger guard.

To Adam's dismay 2, BMW's entered the car park and proceeded to stop within easy visibility of the 4x4.

He wondered whether these were Petrov and Lenko's associates if so, his support team had let him down. He curled back his trigger finger and waited without removing his eye from the sights. The risk of discovery from some passer-by increased every second he lay there.

The men in business suits got out of each of the

BMW's and exchanged greetings. Adam could see that Petrov was looking at them from the 4X4. His hand was reaching to the inside of his jacket.

One of the men opened the boot of his car, and Adam could see Petrov slide out the automatic pistol. Clearly, the two men were not their associates and were in great danger.

Shit, I will have to take the shots just to avoid a blood bath, he thought.

One of the men whipped out his laptop case from the boot and slammed it shut. 'Better not forget this,' he shouted to the other man.

'Hurry up, we are going to be late,' was the reply.

Both men got into one car and left. The 9mm automatic slid back into Petrov's shoulder holster.

Adam took the shots.

The targets were terminated with two single headshots, from L129 leaving neat holes in the centre of both foreheads. Both sets of eyes were left wide open and staring blankly through the shattered windscreen. A trickle of blood dripped down both foreheads onto the bulbous nose of Petrov and down the pox scarred cheek of Lenko.

The two had died instantly. Which was more than could be said for their victims. Killing a civilian, even bad guys like Petrov and Lenko still did not sit well with Adam. He hoped that he was not going to receive any more of these orders.

The 'cleaners' arrived quickly.

CHAPTER 5

2017

Sir Lawrence Gorton-Hyde had been sitting in the Foreign Minister's office for 15 minutes. He was becoming frustrated at being kept waiting.

Where is the bloody chinless wonder, he thought to himself.

The door opened, and the Foreign Minister breezed in followed by his Permanent Secretary.

'Morning Lawrence, sorry to keep you waiting.'

'Morning Minister. Morning George.'

'Morning Larry, shocking weather out there,' replied George.

'Umm,' grunted Gorton-Hyde. He had even less time for the permanent Secretary than he did for the Minister.

The Minister took his seat behind his desk and opened a file.

'We're coming under increasing pressure from the US to contribute to the military aide being sent to Ukraine. They have recently upgraded their supply of arms and believe that we're not pulling our weight,' began the Minister.

Gorton-Hyde's interest peaked as this was a subject close to his heart. 'Really Minister, I didn't think aide to Ukraine was of great interest to us. Bearing in mind the benefits our financial institutions currently enjoy from certain Russian's.'

'Well quite Lawrence,' replied the Minister with a raised eyebrow. 'But the PM is keen to keep the President happy. I'd like you to do a bit of digging. Liaise with our Ambassador to Ukraine and find out exactly what the Americans are supplying. Put together an advisory report with a conservative assessment of what might be a reasonable contribution from ourselves.'

Christ, the last thing I need is Sir Michael bloody Whiting, another drip, thought Gorton-Hyde. Then it occurred to him that he might be able to gain something from this situation. His private enterprise had significantly suffered after the disastrous failure of his last deal 7 months previously. He needed to rebuild his supply and regain confidence with his customer.

'I'll get straight on it Minister.'

'Great stuff Lawrence. How is your wife by the way? I heard she'd been unwell.'

'No, she's fine Sir,' he replied, thinking *what the hell's he asking about her for unless he meant her tantrum after the dinner party the other week. Stupid Bitch.*

'Oh, good. You must come to dinner soon. Sarah

and I would love to have you over.'

'Thank you, Minister, just let me know.' *The last thing I want to do is spend time with my wife, and his for that matter,* he thought. He said his goodbyes and left.

Back in his own office, he picked up the phone.

'Get me, Sir Michael Whiting.'

'Certainly Sir,' replied his secretary Alice. Although she knew he couldn't hear her as he would have already put the phone down. She made the call to the Ambassadors office and put him through.

'Michael?'

'Hello, Lawrence, to what do I owe this dubious honour?' There was no love lost between the two.

'The Minister wants a report on US Military Aid to Ukraine. Can you set up something for us with the Ukraine Ambassador? Preferably in Kyiv. Sooner rather than later.'

'I didn't think the PM was interested?'

'Just following orders.'

'OK, I'll come back with a date when I have spoken to Paliakov.'

'Thanks. Speak soon.'

Later that day, the intercom buzzed.

'What.'

'A Mr Petrovich on the phone Sir,' replied Alice.

'Put him through.'

'Alexei. This had better be urgent, you know not to use this line.'

'It is bloody urgent, and I have been calling your mobile all morning,' said the voice in a thick Russian accent.

'Oh right,' replied Gorton-Hyde opening his desk drawer to see his mobile with several missed calls on the screen. 'Ring me back on it now.'

A minute later the 'pay as you go' mobile rang.

'Yes, what's wrong?'

'I'll tell you what is wrong. My two best men have been killed this morning, by a professional. I don't need to point out that it is impossible to establish a new supply link without the men to do it. These two were close to a deal with a team in Georgia.'

'That is unfortunate Alexei. Do you know who it was?'

'It's more than unfortunate Larry. The deal is now dead in the water. No, I don't know who did it, but it was obviously someone from one of your intelligence agencies. You need to get control of your people Lawrence.'

'Alright, alright, Alexei. Calm down, all is not lost. I was about to ring you anyway regarding a new and better quality supplier. Probably at a much better price. Do you know anything about Olav Paliakov?'

Alex's voice became much friendlier 'That's more like it Larry. Yes, I've contacted Yuri who is well connected to the Ukraine Ambassador if you see what I mean.'

'Sounds good Alexei. Set up a meeting for about a month from now with yourself. I'll arrange a meeting with our Ambassador and Paliakov to coincide. Speak to your man and get whatever he has on Paliakov and send it to me.

'OK, I should have it within 7 days.'

'This might take a few months to put together, but it will be much more lucrative Alex.'

'It had better be Lawrence. Your last deal caused me a lot of embarrassment.'

Gorton-Hyde winced at the reference to Now Zad as he replaced the phone in his drawer. It served to remind him that his contacts in Saudi Arabia were still not taking his calls. *That's my next task,* he thought to himself.

By the end of the week, he had received the documents from Alexei. They were suitably revealing of Ambassador Paliakov's sexual proclivities, in full glossy colour. Some of the boys were very young, indeed. A lascivious grin appeared on Gorton-Hyde's face as he looked them over. 'What a naughty boy,' he chuckled to himself.

Six weeks later at their meeting in Kiev, Gorton-Hyde had a private discussion with Ambassador Paliakov. It turned out that he wasn't overly concerned about the potential revelations around his sex life. However, he was happy to do a deal anyway, regarding the syphoning off of a substantial arms shipment. Alex and Yuri were to make the necessary arrangements with Gorton-Hyde's man. It would take another six months to complete, but that should give him time to rekindle relations with the Saudi's.

After the official dinner that evening, he made his excuses and left to meet up with Alex and Yuri. Sir Michael was relieved to see the back of him.

Feeling pleased with himself he decided on a night of indulgence in the fleshpots of Kyiv.

The following morning he unlocked his hotel room door. After taking a look both up and down the corridor, he pushed out the two very young, scantily clad girls. Both had bruising to their face and legs. Whatever they had been paid had not been enough.

Back at his office in London, he completed his report for the Minister. The proposal was that they should not contribute to Ukraine's Military Aide as it would not serve Britain's best interests.

Perversely Gorton-Hyde did not think it right to steal from his own country but was happy to steal from the Americans.

After sending emissaries and making many calls, he eventually managed to open up a line of communication with a greedy associate of the Saudi Royal family. There followed six months of delicate negotiation, but ultimately, a deal was agreed.

At last, he thought, *the ball is rolling, I had better contact, Bolton.*

CHAPTER 6

2018

Adam continued his surveillance work, which focused on a family living near Hounslow in a pleasant leafy suburban detached house. The subject was Thomas Riley, who lived there with his wife and two young daughters. Adam and his team were installed in a second-floor flat, 300 meters down the road and instructed to carry out 24-hour surveillance reporting on all visitors to the house.

Much of the time was spent watching Melissa 6 and Laura 8, going to school, coming home and playing in the garden. They'd also become very familiar with Tom's wife Verity's work and shopping routines. Tom was away much of the week but returned at the weekends when they enjoyed a middle-class family's usual activities.

Adam had gained some vicarious pleasure from observing this idyllic family picture over the last two weeks. Something he had neither experienced nor desired, at least up to now. Partly because his occupation and lifestyle had not been conducive to raising a family but mainly because it just hadn't crossed his mind.

Apart from the usual food deliveries from

Tesco's and the occasional parcel deliveries from Amazon and others, there were no visitors to report.

The only background info on Tom Riley was that he worked for an arms manufacturer dealing mainly with government contracts and often travelled to the Middle East. His being on a watch list meant that there must be something of concern regarding his activities. Still, Adam was not privy to this information.

His heart sank, as later that day, he received another order on his laptop: <u>Terminate Target: Your Eyes Only</u>.

This time it was for Tom Riley. It was also marked '24 hour action required' which meant that it would have to be carried that weekend whilst Riley was at home with his family.

Adam stared at the screen, his mind was wrestling between his conscience and the inherent need to follow orders. This man had not threatened Adams life and as far as he knew nobody else's so how was he to justify making two little girls fatherless.

'Damn!' said Adam under his breath.

His colleague Sam removed his binoculars and looked across from the window 'What the hell's wrong Adam, you look as though you've seen a ghost?'

Unable to discuss the contents of his orders, Adam could only reply 'Oh nothing Sam just a bit of bad news, I have to leave for a couple of hours can you manage?'

'Yeah, no problem it's not exactly a hive of activity over there.'

Adam left and drove back to the office, knowing full well that Braden would be there. He always spent Friday afternoon in his office.

Entering the building, he said with a determined voice to Florence 'I need to see the Major urgently, is he with anyone Flo?'

Whilst Florence would never lose her austere façade Adam had managed to penetrate a chink of her armour and develop an almost friendly relationship.

'Captain Crest, you know that I can't discuss that sort of thing with you. However, if you were to wander down to his office when I nip to the loo that would be up to you,' said Florence turning to leave her desk.

'Thanks, Flo,' said Adam over his shoulder as he went down the corridor.

He knocked firmly on Major Braden's door and steeled himself for what he knew was going to be a difficult conversation.

'Come in Crest,' called Braden.

Of course, thought Adam *Flo might have given him some assistance in getting access to Braden, but she will also have warned the Major of his arrival.*

Adam entered, approached the Majors desk and stood to attention.

'Yes,' snapped Braden not lifting his head from his laptop.

'Sir, I have serious concerns regarding my recent orders, and I cannot carry them out,' Adam said in a determined voice. He awaited the explosion.

Braden looked up and calmly said 'Really Captain Crest. What makes you think you have that choice?'

'Sir, as a soldier, I've killed many people in the name of Queen and Country. But always in the theatre of war. Whilst I accept that I am still in Queen and country's service, I am not in a theatre of war. Essentially I'm being ordered to carry out the role of an assassin and murder a man who, as far as I know, has not threatened anyone's life.'

Braden's head slowly lifted up from the screen, and glaring eyes bored into Adams as he said 'But you haven't answered my question so I will do it for you.' His voice grew louder 'You do not have a choice. You *are* a soldier serving in the

Queen's military, and regardless of whether *you* might not think you are at war, you will carry out my orders. Is that understood?' He waited for a moment, and as there was no reply from Adam he shouted 'IS THAT UNDERSTOOD CAPTAIN CREST?'

Adam stood firmly to attention and stared Braden squarely in the eyes and said clearly 'Understood Sir.'

'Dismissed,' murmured Braden having already returned to his laptop.

Adam spun sharply on his right foot and almost stumbled as he'd forgotten how painful his leg could still be, then left the office.

After Crest had gone, Braden looked up from his laptop and stared at the closed door deep in thought. He picked up the phone and said sharply 'Flo, get me the Foreign Office I want to speak to GH ASAP.'

'Certainly, Sir,' replied Flo.

Two minutes later the phone rang, Braden quickly grabbed the receiver and put it to his ear.

'What do you want, Braden?' said the unmistakable voice from the other end.

'I want to know why I've got Captain Adam Crest with me and why we're holding him to his contract. When he should've been discharged after his combat injury.'

'I've no idea why he was sent to you. But it suits me to keep him there as he is of interest to the F.O. and we can keep an eye on him. I'm sure you'll agree he is a useful asset. I understand that you are already making good use of him.'

'That may be so,' Braden replied irritably ', but he's becoming a pain in the neck and anyway I'm sure he knows that he can get a medical discharge.'

'Well, you'd better make sure he doesn't Braden. He has upset some important people in the past, and at some point, he will be held accountable, so we need to keep him close for now,' said the caller insistently.

'As you wish. I will make sure he doesn't go anywhere,' replied Braden resignedly knowing that he would have to acquiesce to his demands. At least for now anyway.

'Be assured that it would *not* be in your interest if he did. Presumably, you still aspire to a move to Vauxhall Cross.' The phone clicked, and the conversation was over.

Braden slammed the phone back into its cradle muttering 'Whitehall Pratt. Your time will come.'

Adam marched down the corridor fuming at

Braden's attitude. It only served to make him more determined to get away from DI. He'd given consideration to gaining a premature discharge on medical grounds. However, conscience and commitment that he'd made to The Queens Military had always got the better of him. But his resolve was being tested to its limits. He was not a murderer for hire.

He considered his dilemma as he continued his brisk walk through the corridors and out of the building, casting a glare at Flo as he passed reception. This was probably a bit unfair as she was only doing her job. She didn't have to let him see Braden in the first place.

By the time he reached his car, he'd made a mental note to make it up to her next time they met.

Back at the surveillance flat, Adam gave the coded knock on the door, and Sam let him in.

'Everything okay?' said Sam

'Not really,' replied Adam entering in a sombre mood.

'Anything I can help with?'

Sam was one of the good guys, but Adam could not share his thoughts with anyone else.

'No, it's just a personal issue.'

'I didn't think we were allowed personal issues,' said Sam attempting to lighten the atmosphere.

'Yeah that's true,' said Adam returning Sam's smile. He looked through the tripod-mounted binoculars which were trained on the house along the suburban avenue.

'Anything to report?' asked Adam returning to business.

'No nothing doing, but *his lordship* should be back tonight. Do you want to do Saturday night or Sunday night this week?' asked Sam

The surveillance team would agree on who took the weekend pm 12-hour shifts dependent on their social commitments. Although Adam could not say anything to Sam, it was a bit academic on this occasion. By this time tomorrow, none of them was likely to be around.

'I'll take Saturday night it'll give you a chance to treat your latest victim er young lady to a fiery experience at the Vindaloo Palace.' Sam was a good looking young man and certainly made the most of it.

'Very funny, I will have you know that I've been seeing the same girl for 2 months now.'

'Congratulations. I'm off home for some shut-eye before tonight's shift, see you at 9.00pm tonight.'

On returning to his flat, he had a quick snack and put some of his favourite Miles Davis jazz on the

CD player then lay on his bed. During his time in combat, he had learned to clear his mind and rest effectively in short periods.

He awoke 1 hour later and allowed his thoughts to return to the imminent task. Despite his moral dilemma, he knew that he must carry out his orders. He set off to the office.

Once at the armoury he went to see Alex Miller and draw the Accuracy International marksman's rifle.

Sergeant Miller and Adam exchanged pleasantries, then he handed the weapons draw forms for Adams signature. The documents were returned, and Miller gave the 3 feet by 2 feet black case across the counter to Adam. Nothing was said, but a knowing look passed between the men. They were both aware that there was only one reason why this particular weapon would be issued.

Adam took the case and said 'Thanks Alex see you tomorrow.'

'Will do sir,' he replied.

At 8.45 pm, Adam took over from Sam at the Surveillance flat. Sam reported that Thomas Riley had returned home at 7.30 pm, and the two girls had greeted him in the driveway at the front of the house. There'd been no other visits to the house apart from Verity's return home earlier at 3.30pm.

'Thanks, Sam, see you at 9.00am tomorrow. Have a good night.'

'Do my best,' grinned Sam. 'See you in the morning.'

10 minutes after Sam had left, Adam went back down to his car, collected the black case and placed it in the corner of the room. His window of opportunity would be when Riley went for his morning run. This was his routine every Saturday and Sunday on the dot of 7.30am.

At 9.15 pm, a scooter stopped at the house, and Adam saw through the binoculars. A young white male delivered a plastic carrier bag with presumably a take away of some description. This had occurred on previous Fridays at around the same time, so he didn't consider it suspect. However, he still took photographs of the delivery man and made the necessary notes in the IPad file.

The rest of the night was peaceful and quiet as one might expect of this neighbourhood. When an important shot was coming up, he would usually dismantle and clean every component of his weapon. He felt no such inclination on this occasion.

At 6.00am he repositioned the table in front of the opened window, opened the case on the floor to reveal the deconstructed weapon with its parts all nestling in individual compartments. Even in this broken-down form, it seemed sinister. The long black barrel was securely seated in its cushioned groove which ran across the centre compartment. The shell casings were glistening with a thin coating of gun oil, and the bright gold-colour drew the eye towards the deadly ammunition.

With a practised hand he assembled the weapon including the silencer. He fitted the five Lapua Magnum .338 calibre rounds into the magazine, which he clicked into the socket under the breach. Some adjustments were made to the bipod stand supporting the barrel, and the stock stand. To achieve the correct position and angle of fire.

Looking through the telescopic sights, he made some subtle adjustments. They were set on Riley's driveway. It only remained for him to work the bolt action to fully load the weapon and flick the safety catch before firing.

Standing back, he took a perverse pleasure in looking at this darkly beautiful killing tool as if it were on display in some sort of macabre art gallery.

Putting on a pair of latex gloves, he proceeded to clean up the room. Ensuring that none of the team had left anything behind, he wiped all the furniture and door handles of fingerprints, in preparation for a speedy exit.

Taking up his position carefully behind the rifle, he leaned forward to look through the sights without disturbing the weapon. The view of the target area was clear, and he could also feel the stock firmly against his shoulder. The position was perfect. His watch said 6.30 and the sun had just cleared the horizon shining brightly onto the targets driveway. He was ready.

Staring through the binoculars, he waited for some sign of activity.

7.04 The curtains were drawn in the bay window of one of the first-floor bedrooms.

7.20 The curtains were drawn in the ground floor bay window.

Adam placed his eye on the sights and firmly but smoothly working the bolt action to chamber the round. He curled his fingers slowly around the grip keeping his forefinger stretched across the trigger guard, used his thumb to flick up the safety catch. He froze in this position. His breathing was even and shallow as he waited for the front door to open.

7.29 His body tensed slightly in anticipation.

7.30 Came and went.

7.34 o*h shit I hope he hasn't decided to have a lie-in*

for once, he thought. Adam was now wholly absorbed. His mind and body were focused on one single task, 'the shot'.

7.35 Suddenly the front door opened, and Thomas Riley emerged in white trainers, black shorts and a white T-shirt. He walked across the driveway whilst setting the required music on his iPod, strapped to his upper arm.

The thin green crosshairs of the rifle sights followed his head.

Adam's forefinger moved to cover the trigger.

Riley stopped to fit the iPod earpieces.

Without hesitation, Adam fired.

The only sound was a barely discernible thud from the silenced weapon as it sent the deadly projectile on its way.

At precisely the same moment, Mellissa came running out of the front door in her pyjamas shouting 'Daddy!' and carrying a water bottle for him. She was just in time to see her father's head explode as the bullet shattered his skull.

Riley's body dropped straight to the ground.

Adams blood ran cold. Removing his eye from the rifle sights, he saw the little girl freeze in silence. She was unable to comprehend the scene. The water bottle slipped from her fingers as she whispered *'Daddy?'* almost quizzically, then she issued a heart-wrenching scream.

Her mother and sister quickly appeared at the front door. Laura ran into the driveway but also stopped in her tracks and screamed in terror.

Verity shouted 'Oh my god!' and quickly ran to Melissa, picked her up and ran back to the house.

She shouted to Laura 'Both of you get back inside. NOW!' The girls sensing the fear in their mother's voice obeyed immediately.

Once the girls were inside, Verity ran back to her husband. She repeatedly recited 'Oh my God, Oh my God, Oh my God'.

Blood was flowing freely from Riley's body and formed a pool that spread across the driveway.

The Girls could still be heard screaming manically inside the house.

Adam finally rose and stood for a moment allowing the horror of what had just happened to wash over him. The professional kicked back in, he quickly dismantled and repacked the equipment. Taking a last look around, he could still hear the screams from the two little girls as he closed the door behind him.

That afternoon he returned the weapon to the quartermaster's stores. Once again, few words passed between himself and Alex Miller.

After a fitful night's sleep, the previous day's

events proved to be the final straw for Adam. He could not get the sound of the little girls screams out of his head. He was determined to extricate himself from Defence Intelligence or MI6 or whoever it was that he was really working for.

His instructions from Braden were that he should not copy anyone else in with his reports regarding Riley. In itself, this was against standard procedures. As usual, Adam had carried out these orders without question. This time he saved a copy on his memory stick before sending. Once emailed, the report would be automatically erased from his laptop.

He spent all of Sunday devising a plan of action starting with a visit to Lieutenant Colonel Chambers who had treated him decently during his recovery. At the very least he outranked Major Braden. At best, he could aide him in progressing his application for a medical discharge.

He'd only been seconded to Defence Intelligence. Therefore, Chambers was technically still his line officer. He knew that he wouldn't get anywhere by putting his request to Braden, who would not want to lose his 'pet' assassin.

Having driven back to Hereford, Adam knocked on Lieutenant Colonels Chambers office door.

'Come in.'

'Captain Crest,' Chambers greeted Adam. 'Take a

seat. How's the leg?'

'Much improved,' replied Adam taking a seat on the opposite side of the Lieutenant Colonel's desk. 'Although still painful on occasion, thank you, Sir.'

'Yes, not one of the fortunes of war, if indeed there is such a thing. Now, what can I do for you?'

'Sir, I think I'm right in saying that you're still my Commanding Officer, I am only on secondment to DI?'

'Yes, I wouldn't disagree with that Crest.'

'Well, I have some strong objections to the missions that I'm being ordered to carry out at DI and the insular way in which I'm reporting.' Adam continued to outline the work that he'd been doing but left out the target names. Not that he felt any allegiance to Braden. He just thought it would be interesting to see how keen Chambers might be, to know the operational details. Paranoia was getting the better of him.

Thankfully Chambers did not express any interest in the mission details. He simply said 'Notwithstanding your difficulties with DI practices, you've done more than enough in the service of your country. Your injuries in action entitle you to a medical discharge, which you can take with honour.'

'Is it as simple as that, Sir?'

'Of course, it is Crest. If you leave your contact details with my secretary I'll get your discharge papers drawn up and, as a matter of courtesy, I'll give Major Braden a call.'

Good luck with that thought Adam. 'Many thanks, Sir' he said.

'No problem, doubtless H.R. will be in touch regarding the financial bits and bobs and my secretary will give you a call to confirm dates etc. Anything else Crest?'

'No, Sir.'

'Okay, dismissed.'

'Yes, Sir.'

Adam stood to attention saluted and left the room feeling relieved. However, there was a nagging doubt as to whether it would be that easy.

About an hour later during his drive back to his flat Lieutenant Colonel Chambers rang him on his mobile 'Captain Crest I've spoken to Major Braden. It seems he is not keen on letting you go.'

'No surprise there, Sir.'

'I explained that he really didn't have a choice in the matter, but he is challenging the validity of your injury.'

'The cheeky bastard,' said Adam. 'Oh, apologies, Sir.'

'Quite alright, Crest, I couldn't agree more. However, to prevent this from getting strung out, it would be best to let the Medical Officer have a look at you, then we can get on with it.'

'Okay, Sir, when can we do it?'

'I'll get someone to organise it for 10.00am tomorrow.'

'I'll be there, Sir.'

Adam turned the car around and went back to Hereford. He booked into a Premier Inn for the night.

The following morning, he saw the Medical Officer he already knew from his military hospital time. The examination was pretty much a formality, and the MO confirmed that he was not fit for active duty.

'Right, get dressed Captain Crest, and I'll get this report off to Lieutenant Colonel Chambers this afternoon.'

'Thanks, Doc, it was good to see you again.'

'You to Captain Crest, Cheerio,' said the MO disappearing off down the hospital corridor.

A thought suddenly occurred to Adam, and he dashed after him.

'Sir! Sir!' he called.

The MO stopped and waited for Adam to catch up.

'Sorry to be a pain Doc but could this report be challenged by another department within the Military?'

'You mean DI presumably.' The MO gave him a knowing look.

Adam said nothing.

'I'm aware of your current secondment and to answer your question, in theory, yes a second opinion could be requested though that would be extremely unlikely. Some robust evidence would need to be provided to overturn my decision. I shouldn't worry about it Crest these things are usually just a matter of procedure,' said the MO dismissively as he hurried off.

Adam was left standing alone and not feeling quite as confident as the Doc.

Once again he set off back to Wyton. An hour or so into his drive, he received a call from Chambers.

'Yes, Sir.'

'Crest, the good news is that the MO confirms your condition as unfit for active duty which means that your medical discharge would be approved. However, this fellow, Major Braden is challenging our MO's findings and insists on a second opinion by one of his people. I have to say this chap Braden is becoming tiresome. I ended up essentially pulling rank and explaining that his objections were ridiculous and that we would be issuing your discharge papers without delay.'

Adam breathed a sigh of relief and said 'Thank you for your support, Sir.'

'Let's hope that's an end to it,' he said with some frustration remaining in his voice.

Adam arrived back at his flat around 6.00pm. He checked his emails then poured himself a large glass of Johnnie Walker Black and settled down to listen to some music. Eventually, he fell asleep on the settee.

The following morning he was up for 6.00am. After doing his therapeutic exercises, he drank 2 mugs of freshly ground coffee. At 8.00am his mobile phone rang, there was no caller I.D. But that wasn't unusual. Once again it was Lieutenant Colonel Chambers, and he sounded pretty pissed off.

'Crest, I don't know what you have gotten yourself involved with, and I don't wish to know. However, I seem to be spending an increasing amount of time dealing with what should be a simple procedural issue,' he said. 'Although I don't believe this situation is of your making.'

'No Sir, it is not. But I apologise for the inconvenience.' said Adam wondering what had happened now.

'I received a call from somebody at the Home Office this morning. Needless to say, we do take our instruction from the government, though not usually regarding such matters as this. It was made very clear that a second examination by the DI medical team must be permitted. You are to attend at 11.00am today for the said examination. You should be aware that the examination will involve an X-ray and an intense physical, including limit testing exercises.'

'For Christ's sake, this is getting crazy,' said Adam angrily.

'The only concession that I managed to get was to have our MO, Dr Willis, in attendance, he's on his way now. At least he'll be able to see fair play. I've also insisted that I receive a copy of the reports by the end of play today. I'll speak to you then.'

'Yes, Sir.'

'Good Luck.'

'Thank you, Sir.'

Adam threw his mobile at the settee in anger'

Right, enough is enough' he said and got dressed, went out to his car and set off at speed for the office leaving some tyre rubber on the tarmac.

He knew that Braden would be in early and unlikely to be seeing anyone before 9.00am so he would get him on his own. On his way to the office, Adam considered three questions.

Why was Braden so keen to keep hold of him? By his open admission, he didn't know why Adam he been seconded to Defence Intelligence.

What was the significance of the missions he'd carried out and why in such a clandestine manner?

Who was supporting Braden at Home Office level?

The only answer he could come up with to the first was that Braden wanted a good sniper around, but Adam knew there must be others available. He didn't have any answers for the second question, and it was probably best if he didn't know. The answer to the third question was intriguing. Braden was taking quite a risk in operating, what appeared to be, independently of the organisation, unless he received instruction from beyond the MoD.

All of this was speculation and just served to frustrate Adam even more. *Christ what happened to 'do your 12, don't get dead and get out,* he thought.

He screeched to a halt in the car park then marched briskly to the front doors and up to reception. Flo wasn't in yet, so he just called to Stan the night security chief.

'The boss wants to see me, Stan.' He turned left past reception.

Stan replied 'Okay Mr Crest. I'll sign you in.'

Christ, a lot easier to get past than Flo, he thought. Of course, Flo was military, and Stan was one of the many civilian staff working at the office. He continued his determined march through the corridors until he reached Braden's door and without knocking, he walked in.

To Adams surprise, there was another chair in the room opposite Braden's desk. It was occupied by an attractive woman, slim and in her early 30's with long black hair wearing a blue skirt and white blouse. She immediately seemed to panic and got up from her chair and brushed passed Adam almost running from the room. The smell of her perfume was familiar.

'WHAT IS THE MEANING OF THIS SOUTH?' said the outraged Major Braden.

'Don't worry, Major, I'm not interested in your private life. I have much more important things to discuss with you,' said Adam calmly, but firmly.

'Don't be bloody impertinent Crest. Now that you are here, what's your problem? Make it quick as I have a meeting in 10 minutes.'

'My *problem* is your interference and attempted blocking of my medical discharge and this ridiculous secondary medical examination. Which I have no doubt will show the opposite result to the Army MO's.'

Braden sat back in his chair and looked at Adam with a slight smirk on his face.

'I think you'll find that the insistence on a secondary assessment is coming from beyond this building. I have to say that I couldn't care less whether you go or stay. I admit that you have served a useful purpose, but you're by no means indispensable. I've no idea why there is such interest in keeping you around. Still, you need to take grievances up with Lieutenant Colonel Chambers. The best of luck to you and him with that,' Braden ended sarcastically.

'It's not as simple as that Braden.' All deference had gone from Adam's address. 'As your sarcasm suggests, I'll be passed from pillar to post chasing this through the MoD and possibly the Home Office. I don't understand why you're making this difficult, and I don't care. I just want out, and you are going to make it happen.

The smirk disappeared from Braden's lips.

'This conversation is becoming tiresome Crest. I think it's time you left my office.'

'I won't be leaving this office until you've removed your request for a second opinion on my medical condition and signed off my exit papers,' said Adam in a calm and determined tone.

'I will do no such thing,' said Braden, but his voice lacked conviction. He was starting to wonder what was giving Crest so much confidence.

'You will recall our initial meeting. The one where you made it clear that military procedure must be strictly adhered to at all times. This would include mission reports. Naturally, a copy of which should go to the mission administrators. As you're aware, certain reports have been sent to yourself only. On your specific orders.'

Feigning disinterest, Braden had returned his attention to his laptop. Still, Adam could see a flicker of recognition on his face as his words struck home.

'It occurs to me that my team and I have been carrying out unauthorised surveillance. I've carried out 3 assassinations which are more akin to MI6 operations than Defence Intelligence. All of which have been subject to singular reporting and I suspect illegal.'

Braden raised his head and leant back in his chair.

Adam continued 'If I were to take this upstairs, it would doubtless bring a ton of shit down on us all. Not that it is of any great concern to me as I was "just following orders". Any legal action would be on your head. If my guess is right, you've got career ambitions beyond this office which would certainly be dashed.' Adam refrained from mentioning that he had retained a copy of the last report.

Braden was silent and continued to sit back in his chair but swivelled it away from Adam towards the office window. He gave this, mostly speculative statement, some thought. Although he wasn't too worried about the veiled threats, he was a little concerned at the mention of MI6. More importantly, it was quite clear that Crest was no longer of any use. The question was how to let him go but keep him on a leash to satisfy his 'associates' at the Foreign Office.

Coming to a decision, he swung back his chair to face Adam. He said in an even tone.

'Captain Crest. This outburst and personal attack on a senior officer could easily be considered gross insubordination and should end in a dishonourable discharge. Of this, you can be assured.'

Adam breathed in ready to release another tirade. But before he could start, Braden raised a forefinger from his desk to stop him. He continued, 'However it is now abundantly clear that you'd be of no further operational use to this department. It's in both our interests that you receive your early discharge. I am sure I'm right in assuming that an exemplary officer such as yourself, at any rate until today, would prefer a medical discharge as opposed to a dishonourable discharge. Would that be correct, Captain?'

Wondering what he was up to but feeling things were going in the right direction Adam replied 'Of course.' He could not have lived with a dishonourable discharge.

'I thought so,' he said smugly.

'I'll remove all opposition to your medical discharge with immediate effect, and you'll be released from your contract with the MoD within two weeks. However, there will be one condition.'

'Oh, yes!' Adam replied cautiously.

'You've recently been involved in a highly complex mission that will take a year or more to be completed. Therefore, I will require you to remain on immediate recall to this department for two years. You will remain contactable via a dedicated mobile phone which must be kept serviceable and on your person at all times. You will be required to sign an agreement which will form part of a side letter to your discharge papers.'

Adam stood in silence, considering what he had just been told.

'Well Captain Crest, are we in agreement?'

'It seems that I have little choice. Yes, Sir, we are in agreement.'

'You're right, you don't. I'll cancel the secondary medical examination and advise Lieutenant Colonel Chambers immediately.'

'You, Captain Crest, are very definitely dismissed.'

Adam turned and left the office, omitting the salute.

A few minutes after Adam had closed the door. Braden picked up the phone.

'Flo, get me G.H. at the FO ASAP.'

Later that day Chambers rang Adam to confirm his discharge papers would be with him by the end of the week. They had to be signed and returned by the following Wednesday. Including the side letter which he did not make any reference to. He just said 'I warned you that you were entering a murky world with these boys Adam, but it seems you have just about escaped although I wouldn't count any chickens. Don't hesitate in contacting me for references etc., in the future. All the best.'

'I can't thank you enough for all of your help, Sir. All the best.'

An inauspicious end to my military career, he thought.

CHAPTER 7

Monday 9.00 AM - 2019

Julian crossed Marsham Street on a wet Monday morning, his umbrella providing shelter from the driving rain. He peaked from underneath the edge to see how close he was to the front of the Home Office building. Entering through the glass doors, he collapsed and shook the rainwater from his brolly then brushed his long black raincoat to remove any additional moisture. Checking that his black Italian leather shoes were not too wet, he proceeded briskly across the entrance hall towards the lifts. He paused briefly to complement Alison at the reception desk on her new hairstyle.

'Thank you, Mr Lycett,' she said 'It's nice that someone's noticed.'

'I have an eye for detail, Alison, you know that,' said Julian cheerfully continuing across the wide hallway.

He stepped from the lift on the sixth floor. He entered the first office he came to, through the double doors and continued along the natural corridor created by six work cubicles on either side. All were occupied by busy administrative assistants.

'Morning all,' he threw into the air.

'Morning, Sir,' came the chorus.

Stopping at the next door, he fished out his security card from the small pocket of his waistcoat and presented it to the sensor. Some had said that waistcoats were out, Julian disagreed.

The carpet underfoot suddenly became lush and deep with warm red colouring. The corridor had the muted ambience of a library suggesting that this may well be one of the 'corridors of power'. The Home Secretary's office was at the end of the corridor; however, Julian's was first on the left with Sir Williams's office two doors down on the right.

He swiped the security card, entered his office, hung up his raincoat and umbrella, and then put his attaché case on his desk. Turning to the wall mirror, he checked that his thick black hair was still well parted and in position. He adjusted the knot on his bright green chartreuse silk tie which showed prominently against his crisp white shirt and black suit. He was ready for the day.

Julian opened his case and removed the laptop. Sifting through the many emails that had arrived during the night and early this morning, he prioritised them for replies then began the task.

Just after 9.00am the phone buzzed on his desk 'Yes Jenny?'

'A, Mr Crest is on the phone for you.'

'Oh thanks, Jenny,' replied a delighted Julian, 'please put him through.'

'Hi Jules, how the devil are you?' said Adam.

'Very well, Adam but more importantly, how are you we haven't spoken for ages. How is your nasty injury?'

'It's fine now just the odd twinge every now and then, nothing that I can't handle.'

'You always were my brave little soldier.' Came the typically Julian reply.

'Yeah I know Jules, hey I thought you were supposed to play it straight at the office.'

Julian sighed 'Yes, quite right, you never know who's listening nowadays.'

'Julian, I could do to have a chat with you, I need some advice. When are you free?'

'That sounds a bit serious,' said a more business-like Julian.

'No, not really. I just seem to have gotten mixed up with something that's all.'

'Okay does it need to be lunchtime or can it wait until tonight at my flat?'

'Better make it lunchtime, but we'll need some time and privacy.'

'Sounds like my kind of meeting, I can't wait. See you at 1.00pm at the DoubleTree Hilton it's just down the road from here. Meet you in the lobby.'

'Will do, cheers for now,' replied Adam.

Julian pondered for a moment, he was looking forward to seeing his old friend but did wonder what he could have gotten involved in that could require his help.

Julian Lycett was the same age as Adam Crest, and they had grown up living next door to each other on a middle-class housing estate in Reading. They couldn't have been more different as individuals, Julian of slight build and sensitive nature and Adam a muscular tough boy, yet they were close friends. Neither boy had any siblings so would often join each other's families on summer holidays.

They went to the same junior and secondary schools. There were many occasions where Adam had protected Julian from the school bullies. They found him an irresistible and easy target due to his slight frame and delicate nature. However, they soon discovered that Adam was not to be tangled with. If they made the mistake of jumping Julian when Adam wasn't around, they soon experienced a bloody nosed revenge attack. Julian was the nearest thing he had to a brother, and he treated him as such.

It was also true that Julian, who was very bright, had saved Adam's bacon on many occasions with homework and school project commitments. Adam preferred to play football, cricket or rugby in the evenings and on the weekends. Ever loyal, Julian was also there to cheer him on at the crucial matches.

By the time that the boys had reached 15 years of age, it had become apparent that they would be taking different directions on the romantic front. Although neither of them was aggressive in chasing relationships, it was clear that Julian was gay. Although Adam struggled to comprehend why Julian should be attracted to boys rather than girls, it didn't affect the core of their friendship. In fact, Adam had been supportive when Julian had come out to his parents a year or so later. Whilst his mother was fine, his father didn't speak to him for over 2 months. Adam showed true friendship during this period.

After 'A' levels Adam went off to Reading University, and Julian left for Cambridge University to study Politics and Economics. A first-class honours degree would eventually lead him to the Civil Service and ultimately to his current position at the Home Office as Personal Private Secretary to Sir William Guthrie the Permanent

Secretary.

During his climb up the greasy pole, Julian had learned that although the civil service flew the diversity flag the day to day reality was different. 'No camping' during office hours.

This was a rule that Julian happened to agree with as he took his work very seriously. Apart from those that knew him well, most people would be surprised to find out that he was gay. Once they did, the impeccable dress sense, excellent manners and the sometimes brighter than usual ties seemed to fit better. He did, however, make up for his cultural restrictions in private where he enjoyed a healthy love life and an exuberant, colourful lifestyle at his flat in Belgravia.

Adam took a completely different direction after university, joining the army, which proved to be a lifestyle he was perfectly suited to. Despite their separate paths, the 2 of them remained in regular contact and firm friends.

✻ ✻ ✻

Just before 10.00 am, Julian's intercom's buzzer sounded, and Sir William's name flashed up on the screen. 'Morning, Sir,' he said.

'Morning Julian, can you come across?' said Sir William in a dismissive tone.

The old fossil sounds in a great mood', Julian thought to himself, wondering what could be wrong.

He got up from his desk, checked his appearance in the wall mirror on the way past and hurried across the corridor to Sir Williams's door and knocked. There was an audible click as Sir William pressed the button under his desk, releasing the security lock. Julian entered the office.

In contrast to the rest of the building, it was old fashioned with some extremely valuable oil paintings on the wall and the large carved oak desk at the end of the room. There was still an odour of stale cigar smoke emanating from the carpets. Sir William refused to allow them to be cleaned mainly, Julian suspected, because the smell masked the fact that he was still having a crafty cigar early in the mornings and late at night when the staff weren't about.

Sitting behind the desk was the 'old fossil' himself in his vast leather chair which was more akin to a throne than a piece of office furniture. He gestured to the wing-backed studded leather chair opposite the desk without looking up from the document in his hand. Julian took the seat, and eventually, Sir William looked up.

'Bloody Hell Lycett,' he exclaimed, 'you could've warned me about the tie.'

'Sorry Sir, yes it is one of my more eye-catching shades,' said Julian shifting uncomfortably in his chair.

'Eye-catching. More like blinding if you ask me.'

'Quite Sir, I will avoid this one in future,' Julian said apologetically.

'See that you do,' replied Sir William sounding more like an ageing Brigadier than a civil servant.

'Now then, there is a bit of a fracas at the Foreign Office. Something to do with a chap that was murdered in a petrol station last week in Reading. A couple of local PC's attended but were superseded by two senior people. One of whom presented a Foreign Office ID. The two officers were subsequently removed from the case by the local Chief Superintendent. One of these officers suddenly went off on long term sick leave, and the other was transferred to a station in Middlesex. The one that has been transferred, er ... PC Sharpe.' He said, referring to his notes, 'is creating a real stink and objecting to his enforced transfer to a station miles from his home. He's shouting about employment rights and tribunals etc. More importantly, he has written to the Foreign Office alleging that there is some inproprietary regarding the handling of the murder investigation. It also seems that the murdered man is related by marriage to a senior chap at the FO. All sounds a bit queer to me if you'll pardon the expression,' said Sir William raising his eyebrows at Julian.

Julian stifled a smirk and did not respond but waited for Sir William to continue.

'Needless to say, they are looking for us to assist in quietening this police officer down before things get out of hand. Can you go and see Ben Gifford and get the details. I would imagine some sort of financial settlement should close the issue. Better let me know the result, and I'll pass it on to the FO.'

'Do you think that something is going on, Sir?'

'Not sure at this stage, as I said it all seems a bit quee... odd to me,' said Sir William correcting his words. 'Not sure why CTC is involved, but I know one thing for certain, if there's a drama, you will dig it out!'

'Yes Sir,' said Julian well aware that this wasn't meant as a compliment Sir William had always considered him a bit of a gossip. Julian preferred to call it healthy curiosity.

Julian returned to his office and pressed the button on the intercom 'Jenny, please can you get DCI Gifford on the phone?'

'Will do,' replied the ever efficient PA.

Two minutes later, the phone buzzed.

'Hi Ben, are you well?'

'Can't stop laughing.' Replied Ben with equal measures of sarcasm and humour.

'Yes, I know the feeling. I know it's not really your department, but the old man has asked me to speak to you regarding a PC Sharpe. He's causing a bit of a fuss concerning a murder last week. Are you free this morning? I can get across in about half an hour.'

'Yes, no problem Julian. I've heard about this, it's all a bit weird. But I'll tell you when I see you.'

'Okay, Ben, see you soon.'

Ben was Special Branch (Counter Terrorism Command as it is now known) and one good guy. In his 50's and looking forward to retirement, he was happy to speak plainly. He had no time for the political games that were played nowadays. They'd helped each other out on many occasions, bending a few rules on the way.

Julian arrived at Ben's office at 11.00 am and declined the offer of coffee which he knew would be instant, in a paper cup and disgusting.

'I don't blame you said Ben. Time was I could drag out a bottle of single malt from the desk drawer, but sadly those days are gone. Anyway, let's get down to business.'

'Probably just as well Ben I've a lunch meeting at 1.00 am.'

'The essentials of the story are that a garage owner on the Reading Road was, allegedly, murdered in his shop last Friday. A customer reported the body's discovery, and two uniforms attended, PC's Sharpe and Willis. Fifteen minutes later, two blokes from the Foreign Office turned up. The PCs were instructed by their Chief Inspector to hand over the customer, who was also their only suspect. PC Sharpe seems to think that the chap doing the talking showed him a Foreign Office ID card. To date, we have not managed to contact the Chief Inspector, who also instructed them to leave the securing of the scene to the Foreign Office team. Once the mortuary van arrived, they left. Clearly out of their depth, Sharpe and Willis just did as they were instructed by a senior officer. They went back to the station and completed their reports and handed them in that evening. The following day Sharpe was transferred to Middlesex, and Willis sent in a sick note. He has not been contactable since.'

Julian opened his mouth to ask questions, but Ben held up his hand before he could say anything.

'Before you begin the questions you'd better hear part 2. Yesterday PC Sharpe, apparently a bit of a militant type, rang our HR department to complain about his short notice transfer. He threatened union action which could likely end up at an employment tribunal. He also said that he would put in writing an official complaint to the Foreign Office and the Commissioner of police regarding the Chief Inspector's unorthodox behaviour and the Foreign Office employee at the scene. I rang the FO to see if anything had arrived and warned them that something may be on its way, which I guess prompted the call to yourselves.'

Once again, Julian, now bursting, opened his mouth to speak. Once again, Ben held up his hand to stop him.

'Hang on, this gets even odder,' he said. 'At this moment in time, there is no record of a murder at the petrol station on Friday night not even a call to the emergency services. We're now unable to contact PC Sharpe as he and his wife have taken a last-minute holiday for two weeks in Thailand, would you believe? PC Willis, a single young man, isn't at his flat or at his parent's house. There's no record of SOCO attending and no sign of Sharpe or Willis's reports at the Reading station. In fact, if Sharpe had not rung HR and relayed these events, which fortunately were recorded, there would be no evidence of the incident at all.'

Julian leaned back in his chair and took a moment to consider all of the information Ben had just imparted not really sure what to make of it. He asked 'Do we know who the supposed victim is?'

'Well, all I can say for certain is that the garage owner is a chap called Frank Patterson, and he's also gone missing. However, his sister is Michelle Gorton–Hyde. Her husband is high up at the Foreign Office. Also, he's *Sir* Lawrence, and she is *Lady* Michelle.'

'Okay, do we know who the customer/suspect is?'

'No idea at this stage,' said Ben. 'In fact, the only thing I can say for certain is that something happened at that garage very recently. I only know that because I sent our Crime Scene guys down there and they tell me that the entire servery area has been replaced including the floor surface. They also had a spray around with Luminol and picked up some small but widespread blood spatters on the skirting boards under the desk behind the counter. The shop itself was spotless and tidy. Make what you will of all that.'

Both men now sat back in their chairs and pondered what had been said, for several minutes.

Julian spoke first. 'This stinks of some sort of a cover-up. By whom and to what end, I have no idea, but I am inclined to share Sharpe's concerns.'

'Agreed but apart from some random CSI evidence we have nothing to go on!'

'True, nevertheless you must carry out an investigation with what you have and hope that you can track down Sharpe or Willis. In the meantime, I'll speak to Charles Renton and see what I can shake loose at the Foreign Office end. I would also suggest that we both need to take care until we know exactly who is involved. Perhaps we should keep things between ourselves until we know what this is about.'

'Agreed. Do you think this might be that important?'

'I don't know, but it appears that someone, well connected to the police authorities and maybe to a government office, might be involved in a murder. Someone has gone to a great deal of trouble to make the evidence disappear. Whoever is responsible is unlikely to welcome any interference in their plans,' said Julian. 'I suggest we proceed with care.'

'Yes, I guess so,' said Ben thoughtfully.

'Okeedokee.' Julian said, suddenly returning to

his lighter self and making Ben jump. 'I have a lunch meeting to look forward to with an old friend, so I must bid you farewell for now.' He firmly shook hands with Ben and looked him squarely in the eyes, saying, 'Keep in Touch.'

'Will do,' replied Ben. He was left under no illusions that this was an instruction rather than a request. He watched Julian's tall slim raincoated figure glide out of his office.

CHAPTER 8

Monday 10.00 AM - 2019

Adam replaced the receiver thoughtfully after speaking to Julian. He looked forward to seeing his old friend even though not really sure how much help he might be. If nothing else he would have an enjoyable lunch.

His next task was to locate whatever contact details he could for Michelle Gorton-Hyde, via the internet. The question was, should he speak to her now or wait to catch her in person at Frank's funeral, assuming that there was one. He decided to call straight away as he needed to know what he was involved with.

Adam dialled the landline number that he had picked up on a website. *Presumably, they had ex-directory numbers for private use,* he thought as the phone continued to ring.

'Good Morning this the Gorton-Hyde residence,' said a well-spoken female voice.

'Good Morning, my name is Adam Crest could I speak to Lady Michelle Gorton-Hyde please?'

'Might I say what it concerning Mr Crest and I will see if her Ladyship is available?'

'I am a friend of her brother Frank.' *I should have*

said was, he thought.

'Please hold, Mr Crest.'

The next voice on the line was a more mature female, 'Hello Mr Crest this is Michelle Gorton-Hyde I understand that you are a friend of my brothers.'

She didn't use the past tense either, thought Adam.

'More of a customer based friendship really but we had gotten to know each other quite well over the last year, and please call me Adam.'

'Well, *Mr Crest*, my brother is not here at the moment. Being a customer, you will be aware that the garage is closed during his holiday to the Maldives.' She said matter of factly.

Adam was taken aback at this as he was just about to offer his condolences to the grieving sister. *Does she not know of Frank's death? Is she part of some sort of cover-up? Or maybe she just doesn't want to discuss it with a stranger,* he thought. He decided to go along with the story.

'Oh, of course, I knew the Maldives trip was imminent, but I didn't realise it was so soon.'

'Yes, quite, Mr Crest,' she replied with uncertainty in her voice.

She's not very good at this, he thought then decided to go out on a limb.

'It's a bit of a nuisance really as he must've forgotten our meeting with the financial advisor this afternoon. I'm an accountant you see Lady Gorton-Hyde, and I've been helping Frank with some business development proposals at the garage and the outbuildings at the rear.' He added just to see what the reaction might be.

'Really Mr Crest,' she paused, 'perhaps I could be of assistance in Frank's absence as I have always taken a close interest in the business. Where is the meeting and at what time?' she said, still sounding unsure of herself.

Bingo thought Adam.

'That's most kind of you, Lady Gorton-Hyde, I'm sure that would be very helpful. We'll be meeting in the coffee lounge at the Radisson Blu on Cromwell road at four o'clock.'

'Er, four o'clock,' she said.

Adam was scared that he might lose her and said quickly 'we can make a little earlier or later if that suits you?'

'No, no that will be fine, Mr Crest,' she said, recovering her composure. 'I presume that you will have all the necessary proposal documents.'

'I will, Lady Gorton-Hyde. See you at four o'clock, then. Goodbye for now.'

Adam ended the call, thinking *that will be an*

interesting meeting. He then found a picture of her on a celebrity website and was pleasantly surprised.

His next task was to find out more regarding Lewis Bolton and Guard-Co. Once again, this was not difficult as Guard-Co had a website that boasted a highly professional and elite international security service. *Not sure that Steve and Jason fitted that description* he thought, smiling to himself. Guard-Co had offices in Manchester and Birmingham with a head office based in Slough. *I guess I'd better pay a visit to Slough,* he thought, *but first I'd better check in with my employers with an update on my 'condition' and a chat with Harry Oldman.*

Adam pressed Comm-Sec head office on his mobile.

'Hi Margaret, its Adam Crest could you put me through to Harry please?'

'Ohh Hi Adam, how are you?' she replied with delight. Margaret liked men with a hard shell and soft centre. Adam was aware that she fancied him, but in her early 20's she was a bit too young for him. However, it proved useful whenever he needed to bypass admin procedures.

'Struggling on Mags, just a bit of stick from the old war wound, as they say, looks like I'll be out of action for a few days,' he poured it on a bit.

'I look forward to you getting back soon, look after yourself,' she almost whispered then the call was transferred.

'Hi, Adam, how ya doin?' Said Harry in a friendly voice. Harry was ex-military and had seen some action himself so got on well with Adam even though he was his boss.

'Harry, sorry about this but I damaged the leg during training at the weekend, and the quack says I must stay off it for a couple of weeks and have some physio.'

'No problem mate, it's fairly quiet at the moment anyway.'

'I really appreciate that it shouldn't be more than 10 days, I reckon. Hey, Harry, have you heard of a security firm called Guard-Co?'

'Yeah sure, they're a pretty big set up, more into manpower and personal security than us. Not as systems focused as we are. The top man there is Lewis Bolton, a bit of an evil bastard by all accounts. Some of the stuff they do abroad can be a bit suspect if you know what I mean. I believe he originally set the company up with his brother as Bolton Brothers Security. Still, he was killed out in the Middle East a couple of years ago. They seem to get a fair bit of work from the government. I'm not sure whether its SIS outsourcing or direct contract stuff but I am sure there'll be a few brown envelopes exchanging hands. Not really our thing. Why? You're not jumping ship are you?' He said with some concern.

'Good God no, they're doing some work at a friend of mines business, I just said I'd check them out that's all.'

'Oh right, well the only complaints I have heard are at a local level and mainly about the quality of their operators, the real suspect stuff comes in higher up.'

'Okay, thanks for that, Harry. I'll give you an update on Monday regarding my return if that's alright.'

'Yeah no problem Adam, I'll be sure to let Margaret know,' he said with a mischievous chuckle.

Adam looked at his watch and decided he would take a look at Guard-Co's head office on his way into London to meet Julian. He grabbed a quick shower then dressed in his best suit and tie. He knew that he couldn't compete with Julian, but at least he would be acceptably attired for lunch at the Hilton. Guard-Co address entered into the Sat Nav he set off.

An hour later he stopped in the farthest corner of the large car park at the front of a modern four-storey office building. There was a large sign, above the glass double doors announcing 'GUARD-CO International Security.' There were no other signs, so Adam presumed that it all belonged to Guard-Co. He got out of the car and wandered around the outside of the building. He took note of the external walls, windows and especially the fire escape at the rear. It was a pretty standard office building.

Back in his car Adam considered what he might need for a return visit later that night. He set off for London to meet Julian.

※ ※ ※

Adam walked into the Hilton Lobby and immediately saw Julian standing at the reception, looking more like a celebrity than a civil servant. Of course, he was flirting with the young man behind the desk. He heard Adams footsteps clicking across the faux marble floor, turned and with some flamboyant arm-waving rushed across to greet him. He threw his arms around him. Adam reciprocated in a much less effusive fashion. He was not one for the man hugging, Julian was his one exception also he wasn't given much choice.

'Oh, darling boy, it seems like forever since I've seen you and how is that terrible wound?' He said, eventually pulling away from Adam.

'Bloody hell Julian it's just as well nobody knows me here.'

'You know you love it, dear boy and anyway everybody does it nowadays, the French started it.'

'Yes but not with your enthusiasm,' said Adam disentangling himself from Julian's arms.

'Adam aren't you pleased to see me?' said Julian feigning emotional rejection.

'You know I am,' said Adam' now let's go through to the restaurant I want to talk to you.'

'Okeedokee,' said Julian mischievously linking arms with him.

Adam shook him off, and they went to their table in the far corner of the restaurant.

'I asked Didier for this table so that we would have a little privacy.'

'Good idea, thanks, Julian.'

Didier took their orders, the prawn Marie Rose and rare sirloin steak for Adam and the Quinoas salad followed by Lemon Sole Veronique for Julian with a bottle of Lalomba Rose between them.

'Your diet doesn't get any more refined Adam,' observed Julian.

'I know what I like and like what I know.'

'You are in a serious mood, something is clearly troubling you is it work a woman or money?'

'None of the above I am afraid Julian.'

'Ahh then it is serious,' said Julian, all signs of frivolity gone from his voice. 'You had better start from the beginning.'

So Adam did, from his arrival at the petrol station to his visit to Guard-Co this morning, not missing a single detail. There was only one person in the world that he completely trusted and that was Julian Lycett.

Apart from the occasional clarification, Julian did not interrupt until the end. His face didn't show the knowledge he had already gained from his earlier conversation with Ben Gifford. Still, he felt the blood draining from his face as Adam progressed through the story.

They had finished their main courses and both having declined desserts were on the coffee. Julian began to speak, and it was Adams turn to feel the chill down his spine.

'Adam, you'll find this difficult to believe. I had a meeting this morning with a close colleague of mine at Scotland Yard regarding exactly what you've just told me,' said Julian with a sombre expression.

'How is that possible?' Said Adam with incredulity.

'Sir William Guthrie, my boss, received a call from the Foreign Office this morning ....' Julian then relayed to Adam the content of his conversation with Sir William and Ben Gifford. When he had finished, he let the content sink in then said 'Putting both sets of information together what conclusions can we draw from this Adam?'

Adam sat back in his chair, feeling a little baffled. Eventually, he leaned forward then began slowly and quietly 'I believe that all of this revolves around the outhouses' contents behind the garage. Agreed?'

'Agreed,' said Julian.

'We can say that the interested parties are Lewis Bolton and Sir Lawrence Gorton-Hyde as they were both there on Friday night. Sir Lawrence is openly using the outbuildings as storage supposedly for vintage cars. However, we cannot say why until we know what the real contents are. Agreed?'

'Agreed,' Julian confirmed listening intently.

'We can assume that Bolton murdered Frank, not least because I saw someone fitting his description, leaving the building and nobody else was around. Agreed?'

'I can agree, that is a reasonable assumption.'

'Okay, we can also assume that Michelle Gorton-Hyde is involved, either innocently or otherwise because of Frank's last words. Plus, she agreed to meet me on the bogus premise that I invented during our telephone conversation. Agreed?'

'Once again, I can agree with the assumption, but we need clarity, and please stop saying 'agreed' like that Adam.'

'Sorry,' said Adam 'I am just trying to get things straight in my mind.'

'Of course,' said Julian. 'But beyond that, all we have is a lot of questions. We shouldn't lose sight of the fact that, as far as the bad guys are concerned you're a dangerous loose end. This begs the question, why are you still in one piece, and how long will that last?'

'An excellent point, Julian' observed Adam thoughtfully. 'I guess they don't feel threatened by me going to the police. Which is even more of a worry.'

'I have a theory about that,' replied Julian

'Ahhhh, I thought you might,' Adam said wryly knowing it wouldn't be long before Julian's quizzical mind would come up with something.

'You know me too well,' he acknowledged. 'Frank obviously found out something that he shouldn't. I think the original intention was to murder him and mess the shop up to make it look like a robbery gone nasty. Once the fuss had died down, they could return to remove the 'illicit' goods. Unfortunately, for all concerned, you drove onto the forecourt before the job could be finished and spotted the culprit. Our murderer then reported this to his boss, and they returned to take care of you. Okay so far?

'Carry on.'

'The boss man, let's call him Larry, is someone of bearing. He takes care of the police and other authorities and assists the white-haired man, let's call him Bolton, to abduct your good self. This means their plans have had to change, and they can no longer leave the process to take its course around a 'burglary'. You and Frank will have to disappear. The cleaners arrive and remove poor Frank's body and sort out the mess in the shop. Bolton installs a couple of his security team. Then you're taken elsewhere to be dispatched. No doubt yours and Frank's bodies would never be seen again. Word would be spread of Frank's sudden and probably extended holiday. Naturally, the garage would temporarily close for business. This would leave the protagonists to return and remove whatever is in the storage barns. The mystery is why were you released?'

'Exactly,' agreed Adam emphatically.

'Well, I have a theory on that too.'

'I thought you might.'

Julian grinned then continued 'I think we have to assume that 'friend' Larry is well connected. When he went through your pockets, he discovered your real identity and made some enquiries, which must have taken about 24 hours. Once he realised that you were fairly recent ex-military intelligence, bumping you off might to risky. So they drugged you up to the eyeballs and decided to dump you back at your house. Of course, as previously mentioned. We should not forget that apart from the two boys in blue who have already been taken care of, you are the only witness to their wrongdoings. You must be in danger and no doubt under observation. What do you think?' Julian finished triumphantly.

'Well, it's certainly a theory.' Adam was kicking himself a bit. He should have realised they'd discovered his real identity. How else could he have woken up in his own bed at his home address? 'But why kill poor old Frank in the first place?'

'I can only guess that curiosity regarding the outhouses had got the better of him and he'd somehow discovered the contents, which he also revealed to someone else. Most likely, his sister, going by his final words.'

'Hopefully, I'll be able to confirm that after our meeting later this afternoon.'

'That's true, Adam, but you need to be careful. We don't know the extent of her involvement yet, although her willingness to meet bodes well. Just remember that her husband is a powerful man and clearly comfortable with murder. You're going to have to get them before they get you.'

'Yes, I'll have to play it by ear with Michelle,' Adam replied thoughtfully. 'Look Jules I'm grateful for all of the information and help today, but I don't expect you to get any more involved in this affair.'

'Dear Adam,' Julian replied confidently 'I appreciate the sentiment, but I wouldn't dream of leaving you to sort this out on your own. Besides some of the fish that you're after, swim in my pond and I'm much better equipped to deal with them than you.'

'I guess you're right about that,' agreed Adam 'but you must promise me that you'll back off the moment you feel that your life or your job are under threat.'

'You must remember that we are no longer fourteen-year-old school boys and I can look after myself. However, you have my word Adam,' replied Julian with sincerity and patted the back of Adam's hand on the table.

Adam was secretly relieved, he would have struggled to get inside government departments.

'What about Sir William?' asked Adam.

'At this stage, I don't intend to tell him anything but, to continue the analogy, if my disturbing the pond waters courses excessive ripples I may have to. He might even be useful from an influential point of view. Our biggest asset at the moment is the fact that the enemy doesn't know of our relationship and shared knowledge. However, time is not on our side. Gorton-Hyde and Bolton will undoubtedly be aware that Sharpe's bleating and complaining have let the cat out of the bag,' Julian said, raising his eyebrows.

'I'm sure you are right. My next task is to meet with Lady Gorton-Hyde then pay a nighttime visit to the offices of Guard-Co. We also have to find a way of getting into the garage outhouses, before the contents have been shipped out. See if Ben Gifford can help with that then maybe we can avoid having to break in?'

'I'm still deciding how to make the best use of Ben. He only has a small part of the picture and doesn't need to know any more at this stage. His investigations around trying to source Sharpe and Willis and digging around the garage for more forensic evidence will prove a useful irritant to the enemy. It may prevent them from revisiting the outhouses for now. At best, it might draw someone out of the shadows to try and call him off. At the very least I can use Ben, to gain a warrant to get inside the outhouses as part of his investigation at the garage. I'll ring you as soon as I have access.'

'Sounds like a plan,' said Adam. 'We'll have to keep our comms very tight, but you can't use your mobile, it may already be compromised. You take this one, it's a 'pay as you go' that I have just bought, I'll buy another as soon we leave here and text you the number.'

Typically Julian would have made a humorous James Bond reference but recognised that this was a serious matter and replied 'Okay Adam, will do.'

'Right, we'd best get going I'll pay the bill,' said Adam.

'Okeedokee,' Julian said brightly. 'But I'll get the bill or rather the department will. Although I've enjoyed your excellent company, this has most definitely been a business lunch.'

'Speak later,' said Adam as they left through the hotel's front doors and shook hands before heading in opposite directions.

Both failed to notice the woman with the long dark hair sitting in the window of the coffee shop opposite with the back of her mobile phone pointing towards them.

CHAPTER 9

Monday 2.00 PM - 2019

Adam set off to the Radisson Blu, stopping to purchase another 'Pay As You Go' phone and text the number to Julian. He also called at a shopping area and purchased:

A battery-operated drill.

A small Tozo drone.

Several small reels of electricians tape, in various colours.

A reel of Duct tape.

Some thin wire.

A reel of fishing line.

A wire cored washing line.

30 feet of nylon rope.

2 feet of steel pipe.

A thick bathroom towel.

A headband LED light.

A small LED torch.

A thin metal strip.

An auxiliary power car charger, for the drone

and drill.

He also bought a backpack to put it all in. *That should be everything I need for tonight,* he thought as he got back into his car.

Once he had put the batteries for the equipment on to charge, he headed for his meeting with Lady Gorton-Hyde. After a discussion with Julian, he had decided to be extra cautious.

Arriving twenty minutes early, he left an envelope at the reception desk. Ordered a coffee in the lounge and took a seat at a table in the corner, allowing him good visibility of the entrance.

He waited.

At 3.50 pm, he could see that a taxi pulled up through lounge windows at the hotel's front. A woman got out and headed for the entrance. The woman then proceeded to the coffee lounge and entered looking a little nervously around the room. She was undoubtedly a 'lady' and attracted the eye of most of the men as she walked around the room.

Clearly looking for someone she eventually decided to sit at a table and wait. Picking up a drinks menu from the table, she began to read through it, trying to blend into her surroundings.

Moments later, one of the receptionists entered the room and made his way across and said 'Excuse me, Lady Gorton-Hyde?'

'Yes,' she said, looking up with some surprise in her bright blue eyes.

'A gentleman left this for you at the reception desk earlier madam.'

'Thank you,' she said, taking the white envelope.

She ran her forefinger along the inside of the envelope, took out the white sheet of paper and read:

Lady Gorton-Hyde, please accept my apologies, but our meeting venue had to change at the last minute. However, we are just along the road at the V&A Museum in the Garden Rooms Café if you don't mind the short walk.

Adam Crest.

She replaced the letter and thought for a moment, made her decision, got up and left the Coffee Lounge. Turning left out of the main entrance, she walked up Cromwell road towards the V&A.

Adam followed pleased that so far all was well. He had noted that she had arrived in a cab, not spoken or gestured to anyone and so far, didn't seem to have a tail. She also looked suitably nervous, as if she were unaccustomed to subterfuge.

Apart from frisking her for listening devices, he couldn't do much more.

As Lady Gorton-Hyde entered the Garden Rooms Café Adam quickly caught her up and touching her elbow.

'Lady Gorton-Hyde?'

Somewhat startled, she turned and replied 'Yes.'

'I'm Adam Crest, please accept my apologies for the short notice venue change,' he said proffering a hand towards an empty table in the corner of the room.

'It's not a problem Mr Crest it was only a short walk,' she replied whilst taking a seat at the table. Her self-confidence had quickly returned.

'We'd better order a couple of coffees before anything else,' said Adam.

'Should we wait for your Financial Advisor to arrive first?'

'Er, well Lady Gorton-Hyde,' Adam began but was interrupted.

'That's alright, Mr Crest. I realise that there will not be a financial advisor meeting us. After our telephone conversation, I recall Frank mentioning you becoming friends, and I know you're not an accountant,' she said with a smile that quickly disappeared.

She continued 'I'm very worried about my brother Mr Crest, and I'm hoping that you can help me regarding his whereabouts. So to begin with, please tell me why you rang me this morning and why we are meeting today?'

Whilst she seemed sincere, Adam needed to know a lot more before revealing too much information.

'I guess you're here to find out what has happened to your brother and I'm here to find out what you know about the contents of the petrol station outhouses. My question to you is why do you think something has happened to Frank?'

Her confidence visibly dissolved as she took a sip from the china coffee cup.

'Mr Crest,' she paused. Then carried on decisively 'I am married to a very powerful man. You may be aware, he works for the British government. He also has many 'other' business interests. Some disclosed and some undisclosed. Over the 15 years of our marriage, I have occasionally become aware of some of the details. I've also seen the particularly ugly way that he protects those undisclosed interests. On several occasions ....' she hesitated for a moment clearly uncomfortable discussing her private life with a complete stranger.

Feeling there was little choice she continued

'Suffice to say, this knowledge has led to a life under constant threat of violence. Worse, if private information were to be disclosed either advertently or inadvertently.'

Adams could see the pain in her eyes. *She's either an excellent actor or here for the right reasons,* he thought. But he still had to be sure and said 'I'm sorry to hear that, but what do you think this might have to do with Frank?'

'A couple of years ago Frank told me that he'd agreed with Larry, my husband, that he could store some of his vintage cars in the outhouses behind the garage. In return, Larry would upgrade the buildings internally and fit security alarms etc. In itself, this was innocent enough, but I know Larry and nothing he does is entirely innocent. All I could say to Frank was keep an eye on him. Unfortunately, Frank always sees the good in people.'

'True,' Adam agreed and allowed her to continue.

'Well, a couple of weeks ago Frank rang me in a bit of a panic. He said he must see me urgently, so I went to his house in Reading. He told me that the previous night after the delivery guys had unloaded and stored the latest couple of Larry's crates in the outbuildings. They'd forgotten to set the alarm and left the side door unlocked. Frank was locking up that night, he noticed that the door was ajar and went inside. He knew nothing about the alarm system or how to set it but thought if he could find a key or padlock in there at least, he could secure the door.'

Adam was leaning forward now in expectation of finally finding out his worst fears.

'Once inside Frank flicked the light on and discovered that the three apparently rickety old buildings had been completely refurbished with sheet steel, wall cladding. They had been knocked through into one large storage area the size of an aircraft hangar holding several of the 'vintage car' sized crates. Frank had always wanted to have a look at some of these cars. Unfortunately, his curiosity got the better of him. He used a crowbar to prize off the front of one of the large crates. Once open, he discovered no vintage cars but dozens of metal cases in various sizes. He opened one of those and found it full of automatic rifles. He opened another to discover it full of shells for rocket launchers. The writing and names on all of these weapons was quite clearly a mixture of English and Russian. Frank could be a naïve man, but he wasn't a fool and soon worked out that this must be a storage area for some sort of illegal arms. He said that he nailed the crate back up, found a key hanging on the wall near the door, locked the place up and left.'

Adam's heart sank as not only had his worst fears been realised, but he knew that Frank's actions had led to his own death.

'Bloody hell, Lady Gorton-Hyde .....' Adam began, but she waved her hand at him.

'Please call me Michelle, I think we are past the formalities.'

'Of course, Michelle. You realise that they will know he's been in there not least because the alarm wasn't set and they'll have sweated out of those delivery boys the facts about the door being left unlocked.'

'Yes, Adam, that's my fear, but there's more,' said Michelle starting to feel some relief as she unburdened herself to this friendly stranger.

'Frank would visit my house every Saturday morning without fail, Larry was always out playing golf or 'whatever', and we'd have a coffee and a chat. Frank didn't show up this Saturday and didn't ring either, and he's not answering his phone. I have to consider that the two things might be related. Also, Larry told me that he'd heard a rumour that Frank had taken a holiday to the Maldives. Frank wouldn't have done that without telling me and, in any case, Larry would not bother to comment on something so mundane.' Now with a tremble in her voice. 'I fear for Frank's safety. He's not equipped to deal with someone like Larry. Adam, what am I to do?'

Now, what do I do? Thought Adam. He couldn't tell Michelle what had happened to Frank as she would very likely say something to Gorton-Hyde. It was of paramount importance that he did not know that anyone was onto him. Yet he really felt for this poor woman. He convinced himself that she would be in more danger if she knew the truth.

He said softly 'Michelle, Franks a good guy and I think you're a good person, so I'm going to help you, but you're going to have to trust me. I know I'm a stranger to you, but I can assure you that I have a vested interest in getting to the bottom of this, not least for my own personal safety. I can't tell you much, but I do have a military intelligence background. I also have some contacts in the government who will help me to investigate.'

'Oh god you're not part of this are you?'

'No, no, Michelle. I'm exactly what I said I am. A customer of the garage and a friend of Frank's. Its pure bad luck that I've become embroiled in whatever this is. Unfortunately, I can't say any more than that, and I cannot stress enough, the need to keep all of this between us. I'm sure you can imagine the potential consequences should your husband and his cronies find out about our conversation,' he said. He took care not to mention that her husband already knew what Frank had discovered.

Having regained her composure and once again become Lady Gorton-Hyde, she said 'I quite understand Adam. Living with my husband has meant a life of subterfuge in one form, or another so don't worry about me causing any problems. Now, what do you want me to do to help?'

Adam found her endearing, and he felt a little guilty that he'd not told her about Frank's death. He had to consider that Gorton-Hyde would think it odd that she had so readily accepted his story about Frank taking a short-notice holiday and may become suspicious.

'Absolutely nothing for now just carry on as normal until I get in touch.' Adam thought for a moment then continued 'or possibly a chap called Julian might call you.'

'What if I need to get in touch, in an emergency?' she asked.

'Take this mobile number but please don't use it unless you have to.'

'Thank you, Adam,' she said with affection and kissed his cheek.

They left the V&A and went their separate ways.

That wasn't what I had expected, he thought as he wandered back to the car park. She had certainly removed any suspicions about her involvement. He was also quite taken by her.

He got back to his car and set off for Slough. On the way there it suddenly occurred to him that Julian's tame policeman would be getting a warrant together. If they hadn't already then, they would shortly be storming the outhouses. Now that he knew what was in there, the stakes were a lot higher. They needed to stand back and wait for Gorton-Hyde and Bolton to return for the goods then catch them red-handed. If not they would just deny all knowledge.

Oh crap! he thought as he pressed the dial icon on his phone.

CHAPTER 10

Monday 2.30 PM - 2019

After leaving Adam outside of the Hilton, Julian went back to the Home Office. He checked in with Jenny to see if Sir William was in. He entered his own office intending to make some calls before reporting to his boss.

His first call was to Charlie Renton, his counterpart at the F.O. Who worked for Sir Arthur Hill.

'Hello Charles, how are you?'

'Good afternoon Julian, I'm thriving as always and your good self?'

'Excellent form thanks,' Julian replied in an almost competitive manner.

'Charles, I could do to pick your brains regarding an issue that's cropped up if that's okay?'

'Of course, as long as it's not a sensitive issue.'

Charles had always been a bit pompous and considered that the F.O. was a step above the H.O. Despite that, they had still got on, helping each other out on many occasions. Sometimes bending the rules, although neither of them would ever admit it.

'I don't think it is at the moment. It's essentially

a Home Office H.R. concern that might stray onto Foreign Office territory regarding a disgruntled Police Constable.'

'How does this concern the F.O.?'

'Do you ever come across someone called Gorton-Hyde?' Said Julian plunging straight in.

'Sir Lawrence Gorton-Hyde?'

Julian could almost feel Charles stiffen at the other end of the phone.

'Yes, that's the fellow,' said Julian. 'Do you have much to do with him?'

'You didn't answer my original question, Julian, what is this to do with the F.O.?' Charles said now becoming a little defensive.

'I'm not really sure. It's just that this chap Gorton-Hyde has been mentioned in dispatches, as it were, regarding a police officer's complaint.'

'Look, Julian, Gorton-Hyde is not a man to cross. He has his fingers in many pies from SIS operations to membership of the Joint Intelligence Committee to foreign trade policy committees and much more in between. Several of my colleagues have suffered his wrath simply for questioning his involvement. One or two have even been known to make a sudden departure from the Foreign Office.'

'Sounds like a bit of a tyrant. Who does he answer to?'

'His title is Special Advisor to the Minister, but he doesn't seem to report to anyone, I can only presume that the minister knows what he's up to.'

'Sounds like a bit of a mystery man, but he must have a dogsbody?'

'Well yes, I suppose that would be Ralph Naylor, but he's hardly ever in the office or even the country. From the little I have seen of him, he seems to be more of a thug than a Foreign Office representative. I wouldn't want to cross him either,' said Charles a little fearfully.

Sensing his discomfort regarding this topic of conversation, Julian said 'Alright Charles, you have been most helpful. The only other thing was, have you come across a Lewis Bolton or his security company Guard-Co.'

'Yes, of course, they handle all sorts for us from secure package transfers to personal protection. Lewis Bolton seems to be very well connected. I'm surprised that you don't use them at the Home Office.'

'Good point Charles. I haven't come across them. I suppose there must be a reason. I must check on that. Well, thanks very much for the info Charles I owe you a Latte.'

'Reading between the lines Julian, you seem to be getting involved with matters well beyond a simple H.R. issue and potentially with some difficult people. I would watch your step maybe kick it upstairs to Sir William, and he can speak to Sir Arthur.'

This was Charles way of saying that he didn't want anything further to do with this which was a little spineless in Julian's opinion, but not surprising.

'Oh, I'm sure it will not come to anything. Ta ta for now Charles.' He said cheerfully.

I wonder if he will take the bait and look into Guard-Co, he thought to himself.

Next Julian rang the Home Office head of security to speak to someone he should have already consulted.

'Hi Ray, its Julian Lycett.'

The head of security was a typically no-nonsense type. Whilst he found Julian to be a bit 'dramatic' he was likeable and always direct.

'Afternoon Julian. What can I do for you?'

'Who do we use for outsourced security, Ray?'

'Tech-Sec,' was the short reply.

'Do you know of Guard-Co?'

'Of course, why do you ask?' Mellors was now showing interest.

'What's your opinion of Lewis Bolton, if you have one?'

'I certainly do. However, it might be something best discussed in person.'

It sounded like Ray had some dirt to dish, so Julian replied keenly 'No problem Ray. Are you free for a cup of coffee now?'

'Yes, see you in 10 minutes.'

10 minutes later, Julian sat in Ray's office coffee in one hand and a thick dossier in the other. Ray had done some considerable homework on Lewis Bolton, which may have been due diligence before hiring Tech-Sec. But Julian felt there was more to his interest.

The dossier showed that there had been several incidents of poor performance by Guard-Co not least the escape of suspected terrorists whilst in their custody. Lewis Bolton had connections in Britain with some known Russian villains. His brother was suspected of involvement with the illegal arms trade until he died in Afghanistan two years ago. Despite all of this, Guard-Co was retained on a lucrative contract by the Foreign Office.

Julian put the dossier down. 'What do you think

is going on here, Ray?' he said seriously.

'I don't think anything is necessarily 'going on' Julian. Not all departments are as meticulous as mine when it comes to vetting. It wouldn't be the first time that the F.O. had not carried out their due diligence before awarding contracts. However, I would certainly not use this company. What is your interest, Julian?'

'In my opinion, Lewis Bolton is in league with someone at the F.O., and they are trading in illegal goods of some description.'

'That's a pretty serious allegation, Julian. Why haven't you taken it upstairs?'

'Two reasons, 1. I don't have enough evidence, and 2. I don't know how far upstairs I need to go before I'd be dealing with the right people. However, I will get to the bottom of this.'

'Okay, what have you got so far?'

'Two names at the F.O.' Julian paused 'Ralph Naylor and Sir Lawrence Gorton-Hyde.'

'Interesting,' replied Mellors raising an eyebrow. 'Look, Julian, I may be of some help on this one. Can I ask that you keep me in the loop regarding your progress?'

'That would be great, Ray. It would be best if we only make contact via my PAYG phone and your secure contact number.'

'Of course. A prudent precaution.'

They swapped numbers, and Julian sensed that the meeting was at an end.

'Ciao for now,' said Julian a little mischievously to the austere security man.

'Umm' grunted Mellors.

Julian returned to his office, feeling quite pleased with himself. *Adam should be quite chuffed with my progress. Right stage 3,* he thought.

He punched Ben Gifford's number on his mobile 'Hi Ben, how's it going?'

'Not great I am afraid, I'm getting nowhere on the two uniform guys.'

'No surprise there,' thought Julian.

'The CSI guys haven't come up with anything more, and we still don't know who our mystery customer was or where Frank Patterson's body has gone. I can't say for definite, but I feel like we're being blocked by the local boys, you know, simple things like duty rosters, call logging and reports still missing. I'm even struggling to get hold of the Chief Inspector, he still hasn't returned my calls.'

'What's his name?' asked Julian

'Reynolds, Martin Reynolds,' answered Ben.

Another name for Ray thought Julian.

'In fact, the only thing we have got to work on is the outhouses, I am just waiting for the warrant.'

'Well, at least that is something when do you think you'll get it?'

'Within the next couple of hours. I'll let you know when we are going in.'

'Thanks, Ben. I do have something else for you to look into from my end. My probing has whittled out a company called Guard-Co owned by a chap called Lewis Bolton. I'm led to believe they have a substantial contract with the F.O. It's possible he also does some secured transport work to, maybe from these outhouses.' It was an educated guess about the secure transport, but it wouldn't do any harm to have someone else looking into Guard-Co.

'I've come across Mr Bolton in the past and not in a good way, so it'll be a pleasure to renew our acquaintance. I'll let you know as soon as the search warrant is through.'

'Cheers, Ben.'

Okay now for Sir William, thought Julian, got up from his desk, checked his appearance in the wall mirror and smiled. *Green chartreuse twice in one day there will be scowling.* He left his office smiling.

He knocked on Sir Williams's door, awaited the click. As predicted, there was a scowl at the returning vision of Julian's tie but no comment this time. 'Sit,' he commanded.

Julian sat in the wing-backed chair, and Sir William moved his laptop away from the centre of his desk. He leaned forward onto the green leather centre pane.

'Well Lycett have you got an update on the strange affair of the winging policeman?' he said almost flippantly.

'Not really, Sir, just more mystery. The two uniformed officers have disappeared completely, to date there has not been a letter received at the F.O. and so far no dead body.'

'Jolly good, no issues then let's move on.' Julian guessed that by 'move on' he meant that he could finish for the day and get off to his club.

'Not quite, Sir.'

Sir William scowled again.

'A CSI team have picked up evidence of blood spatters to the skirting board in the garage shop. There are also new servery fittings. The locked outhouses to the rear of the garage need to be entered and investigated. The search warrant is on its way.'

That was all Julian was prepared to reveal about

the story as he still didn't know how far up the ladder this went. At the end of the day, someone from the Home Office must be keeping the local police under control. He didn't really think it was Sir William but who knows who he might speak to regarding the matter.

'Alright give me an update tomorrow,' said Sir William rising from his chair.

Time to go thought Julian.

'Will do Sir,' he said as he left the office.

Julian returned to his office and looked at his watch. *Adam should be finishing his meeting any time now,* he thought. He was looking forward to updating him on the day's activities.

Just after 5.00pm, his phone rang.

'Julian!' shouted Adam over the road noise in his car.

'Adam, you will not believe the day ....'

Adam interrupted. 'Stop talking Julian! Has Ben Gifford entered the outhouses yet?'

Realising the urgency in Adam's voice, he answered immediately 'I spoke to him half an hour ago. He was still waiting for the warrant, what's wrong?'

'End this call and ring him immediately. Tell him under no circumstances must he enter the outhouses, in fact, pull the CSI team out of there completely then ring me straight back and I'll explain.' Adam ended the call before Julian could answer. He prayed that it wasn't too late.

Five minutes passed then ten, after fifteen minutes the phone rang 'Mission accomplished Adam, now what's going on?'

'Well done Julian you're a star,' Adam said with noticeable relief.

'Well I know that, but it doesn't do any harm to hear it,' said Julian appreciatively. 'Ben took a bit of convincing, he'd only just received the warrant. CSI has vacated the site and just left two uniforms as security.'

'Better make it four men. Two won't be enough and might end up disappearing like Sharpe and Willis.'

'Okay, Adam, I'll tell him. Do you want to tell me what's going on?' said Julian now becoming impatient.

Adam outlined the full content of his meeting with Michelle. Following that Julian updated Adam on the events of his day.

'We appear to be making progress,' said Julian.

'You could say that, but I'm not too keen on the illegal arms part.'

'It sounds like Gorton-Hyde is doing the finance

bit and Bolton the transport.'

'Yes, the question is, where are they going and who is paying for them? Let's hope I can glean some more info at Bolton's office tonight.'

'On the plus side,' said Julian' we have effective control of millions of pounds worth of illegal weapons which they need to get hold of and moved out. Also, Guard-Co will be getting some unwanted attention, now that Ray Mellors and Ben Gifford are involved. It's quite likely that Charles Renton from the F.O. might rattle a few cages as well.'

'Yeah on that subject Julian, it's great that you've set the hounds on Guard-Co, but you might as well paint a target on your back. It won't take them long to work out who's initiated all of this attention. Now we're both in danger with no one to run to, until we are certain of who we can trust. So you need to get back to your flat, pack a bag of practical clothes and I mean practical clothes. You won't need anything for the opera if you know what I mean. Understand Julian?' said Adam firmly.

'Yes I get it, Adam,' he said tersely. 'I suppose it's going to be Travelodge's and Premier Inns for a few nights.'

'Got it in one.'

'What about Lady Michelle? It sounds like she is

also in some considerable danger and literally in the lion's den. It also sounds to me like you may have taken more than a liking to the lady.' Julian said mischievously.

'Never mind that, Julian.' Replied Adam although he was correct of course she had gotten under his skin a little.

'You're right, though. She is in danger, but I think Gorton-Hyde will be preoccupied trying to get the weapons out of the country. At the same time, he'll be fending off the various inquiries into his pal's company without drawing attention to his own connections to Guard-Co. With luck, he's going to be far too busy to deal with Michelle until after he has sorted that lot out. Hopefully, we'll see to it that he never does.'

'Agreed Adam. What's our next move?'

'That depends on who, in the various agencies that you've set upon Guard-Co, you can trust most to deliver?'

'Without a doubt, Ray Mellor's head of Home Office security,' Julian replied with certainty.

'That's interesting, not Ben Gifford then?'

'No Ben is a good guy but he's a copper at the end of the day and thinks two-dimensionally. He's process-driven. Ray thinks outside the box and is both committed and tenacious.'

'Okay,' said Adam impressed with Julian's judgement. 'In answer to your original question. Your next move is to contact Ray for an update on Guard-Co's reading area activities, whilst I visit their head office. You could also contact Ben Gifford and plan to remove the police officers on guard at the garage tomorrow afternoon. We can be certain that Bolton's men will be watching so we should expect them to move the containers tomorrow evening once the police have left. It's of the utmost importance that we don't lose sight of the goods as they will eventually lead us to the end-users.' He neglected to mention to Julian, his vengeful intentions towards Lewis Bolton regarding Frank's death. Also, payback for his own abduction.

'I'll speak to Ray and Ben when we have finished.'

'Ben needs to accept that his team have to take a back seat on this and must not blow our surveillance. Would he be able to raise some suitable manpower at short notice if needed?'

'Ben will be fine we have a good relationship, as for manpower that might be a bit more difficult 'off book' as it were but as I said Ray thinks outside the box.'

'Get yourself booked into a cheap hotel somewhere near Reading and I'll give you a call late tonight.'

'Will do.' Julian replied.

'There was only the-*Sir*-missing' thought Adam. Julian was responding well to the challenge. He just hoped that he would hold up when things got more physical. Adam chose his next words carefully. 'Julian, things are going to get a lot more actual than theoretical soon, and there may well be physical dangers that we cannot foresee. This is much more my sort of game than yours, and I would never hold it against you if you preferred to take a back seat.'

'My dear boy, I'm not a fool, I understand the risks, and I wouldn't miss it for the world although I have to say that I won't be much use in a punch up. But then you are twice as good at it as most men so we should be alright.'

'Well said,' Adam replied. 'I'll ring you later.'

CHAPTER 11

Monday 11.15 PM - 2019

Arriving at the Guard-Co head office, Adam parked around the corner on the main street not wanting to be picked up by the car park's cameras. Before parking, he had followed the roads around the building and noted that two hefty sized night guards were standing in the well-lit foyer, behind the large glass doors at the front. He couldn't see any other person, and the rest of the building was in darkness. Most importantly, nobody was behind the reception desk, which was where the CCTV monitor would be.

Reaching into the back of the car for his backpack, he took out the cheap mini drone. He also took out his black polo neck jumper, balaclava and leather gloves and put them on. After setting up the drone and linking it to his phone, he replaced the kit in his backpack. He rolled the steel piping up in the bath towel and taped it up to avoid unravelling and placed it in his pack. He slung it over his shoulder.

Exiting the car, he headed for cover behind the perimeter foliage. There was a thinning of bushes halfway across the rear of the building in shaded darkness despite the general spread of the halogen lighting to the business park. Pushing through, he flattened himself against the wall of the newly built brick building.

Although reasonably sure that nobody was checking the monitors, it still made sense to avoid detection. The CCTV cameras were positioned on each corner so their weakest spot would be halfway between. He stood with his back to the wall. He looked directly up to see that from the 6th down to the 1st floor, the fire escape stairs zig-zagged along the wall descending to a final landing on the 1st floor, twenty feet above him. There was an extendable ladder for the last section. He guessed that there would be some form of a release mechanism for its use in an emergency allowing the fleeing staff to reach the ground safely.

With some fishing line attached to the Tozo drone's body, he launched it upwards towards the lowest landing, feeding the line out as it travelled. He was experienced in using similar equipment, so fairly adept at flying the drone. He sent it over the metal bannister at the front then passing it back through the gap in the supporting ironwork underneath. He brought the drone back down to earth with the line following behind.

Once unfastened, he pulled the line until he could see the nylon rope, attached to the other end, begin to travel upwards towards the balcony. The rope was tied around the middle of the wrapped steel bar that was soon raised to the fire escape bannister. Adam tugged a little to get it over the top, it fell with a muffled thud to the metal floor and lodged firmly across the ironwork of the balustrade.

Although conscious that one of the guards might appear at any time, he continued to work calmly and quickly. Pulling the rope taught, it became apparent that the bar was well-positioned and would take his weight.

After packing away the drone and slinging the pack across his shoulder, he climbed the rope up to the landing, grabbed the ironwork and hauled himself over the bannister. He didn't know how diligent the night guards might be, but he had to expect a perimeter check at the very least, so he pulled up the rope and stored it in a corner. Next, he climbed the fire escape stairs up to the second-floor landing. Although there was some pain from his right leg, he was quite pleased with his fitness condition.

A blue wooden fire door faced him. Removing his backpack, he took out a thin metal strip about a credit card's size with a one-inch lip at the end towards him. He tore off a strip of Duct tape and held it in the other hand. Slotting the metal strip in between the top of the door and frame, slid the strip along from right to left until he felt the edge of the alarm sensor, which he knew would be near to the top left of the door. Sliding the strip between the sensors, he applied the tape to the raised edge on his side. Thereby securing it to the top of the door frame keeping the strip in position and the alarm bypassed.

He removed the handheld drill from the backpack, fitted with an eight-millimetre wood drill bit. He checked below the landing to see if anyone was about. He drilled two holes with the aid of headband LED, one just above the handle mechanism and one vertically in line just below. Feeding the thin wire which had the fishing line entwined around it, through the top hole he then turned it to release the line once it was far enough in. The line would dangle over the fire door opening lever on the inside.

The wire removed he bent the end into a small hook to pass through the lower hole. When he was sure that it had gone far enough, he slowly began to draw it back and as the hook reappeared so did the other end of the line caught in it. He removed it and started to pull. The line was attached to some strong nylon washing line that passed in through the top hole. As he pulled, it eventually emerged from the lower hole having travelled over the push lever on the other side.

With a firm grip to the top and bottom of the

line he carefully pulled the 2 ends until he could feel it was tight against the opener on the inside. He checked to see if either of the guards were about before firmly yanking both hands back. This depressed the lever on the inside, and the door sprang open.

Equipment packed away he tore off two pieces of the blue electrician's tape and covered the holes on the outside of the door, which was a pretty good colour match to the door's paint job. He entered the hallway inside.

Quietly closing the door behind him. He noted that the inside of the door was painted red, he selected the appropriate coloured tape and covered the holes. Of course, this would not pass close inspection but would hopefully avoid attention in the short term. He proceeded down the corridor, looking for the Administration office.

There were no signs of any internal CCTV cameras or movement sensors, much to his surprise and relief. He crept along the carpeted passageway in the near darkness until he came to a door on the left, marked H.R. and Administration. The door was not locked and opened easily. Adam guessed that the door at the other end of the corridor leading to the elevator and stairs would be locked preventing access to the landing from the other end.

He entered stood with his back to the door. Due to the light streaming through the plate glass windows from the sodium bulbs outside, he could see that the office had filing cabinets along three walls. Several work stations were positioned in the middle of the room. In the far left corner of the room was a door which he guessed lead to the manager or supervisor's office. This was the most likely place for him to find valuable information, so he switched off his LED and moved around the sides of the room.

Skirting the edges, he took care to remain in the shadows. Using his handheld torch, he checked the labels on the cabinets as he passed them, discovering that those on the left wall were all personnel files in alphabetical order. *Presumably, the files on the other sides are invoices,* he thought. Reaching the office door, which was not locked, he entered and continued using his handheld torch to look around.

The office seemed quite plush for an Admin Manager. There was a deeply cushioned leather swivel armchair behind a sizeable modern desk. A thick carpet underfoot. There was also an espresso machine in the corner. At the other end of the room behind the desk and swivel chair were two good quality filing cabinets.

He went over to the two cabinets. One was marked 'National Clients' and the other 'International Clients'. He was just about to open the cabinet marked 'National Clients' when he heard a door slamming which he could only assume was the door to the main corridor at the top of the stairs.

Scurrying out of the office, crouching below window level, he ran to one of the admin cubicles at the opposite side of the room. He ducked down behind the screening. Keeping his breathing even and quiet, he heard the voices of 2 people talking. The door to the room opened. They did not turn the main lights on but walked across to the office that he had just left.

Although he dare not lift his head above the cubicle partition, Adam overheard a man's somewhat surly voice saying.

'Regardless of what Larry might think I have the transport arrangements in hand and as long as he holds up his end with the air transport the goods will be in Afghanistan within 48 hours. I'll see to the handover to the client personally.'

A female voice replied 'I think that we both know why there are concerns Mr Bolton, not least the fact that the 'goods' as you put it, are currently not even in your possession.'

Adam detected a Brummy accent as Bolton replied 'Don't you worry your pretty head about that Ayesha babs it's all under control. Those containers will soon be recovered from the storage sheds and on the road to Norfolk. They'll arrive by 8.00 am tomorrow morning. I've also arranged for the permanent removal of the four plods on guard duty tonight.'

Shit thought Adam *he's taken matters into his own hands. I need to get hold of Julian quickly and have those officers removed before they get hurt.*

He considered leaping out and exacting his revenge on Bolton, but now was not the time. He was hoping to gather more information from their conversation. He also wanted to find out who Ayesha was and what her connection was to 'Larry'.

Once inside the office, they turned on the lights and continued their conversation with the door left ajar. Adam sneaked back across the room and installed himself in the admin cubicle closest to the office door to eavesdrop.

From his new position, he could see into the office through the open door. As expected, there was Bolton's spiked white hair atop a real bruiser of a man. Ayesha stood with her back to him, and all he could see was that she had very long straight black hair dropping nearly to her backside and was dressed smartly.

Their conversation continued as Ayesha said in a stern voice.

'Mr Bolton, let's hope you do have things under control. Because if you screw this up not only will you lose millions in government contracts. You will also incur the wrath of some unforgiving and extremely ruthless people in the middle east.'

'Now then, now then Ayesha,' said Bolton' let's not get overheated. Please, call me Lewis and lets you and I have a drink. I know my Admin Exec keeps a bottle in his desk.'

In a cool voice, Ayesha replied.

'Mr Bolton I am certainly not 'overheated', and I do not want a drink. We came down here to see your plans and itinerary for the safe delivery of the crates to their destination, so please let's get on with it.'

'Please yourself,' said Bolton realising that he wasn't going to get anywhere. 'You don't mind if I have one?'

'As you wish.'

Bolton found the bottle in the desk drawer and poured himself a large one then wandered over to the filing cabinet marked International Clients and withdrew a file from the top drawer. He threw the file onto the desk triumphantly and said 'There you go that's the entire plan showing the route, transport methods, timings and rendezvous personnel along the route. Take a seat and have a gander.'

'Thank you, Mr Bolton, I will.'

Bloody hell I could do with a look at that, thought Adam who was now getting a bit stiff from his cramped position.

After flicking through the dozen or so pages in the file, Ayesha said 'Well, assuming this all goes to plan we should all enjoy a healthy payday. However, you have omitted to explain what you're going to do about the loose ends?'

Adam could see-through door that Bolton's expression had grown dark.

'I guess you're referring to Crest, well you don't have to worry I'm keeping a close eye on him albeit from a distance. As requested.' His voice became sinister 'I have a personal issue to settle with Crest once this is over. It was a happy coincidence, him being at that garage last Friday. That's to say happy for me, definitely not for him. The only reason we let him go was because of his temporary value to Larry.'

What the hell was Bolton talking about? thought Adam. *What value and what personal issue was he referring to? I'll have to give thought to that later.*

In a lighter but still threatening voice, Bolton continued 'I'm also aware of his gay friend Lycett who is apparently high up in the Home Office. He's trying to stir things up for me at the Foreign Office end. However, I'm sure that Larry will limit any damage in that area, at least I hope he will because it would be in *his* best interests not hang me out to dry. After all, I know where all the skeletons are. More specifically, I know the names of all involved and who's making the real money in this deal.' He glared at Ayesha for a moment then winked as if to release the tension.

Unperturbed Ayesha said.

'Very well Mr Bolton I will report back that you appear to be on top of things and we can expect a successful conclusion to our endeavours.'

'You certainly can babs. Now I'll have to say goodbye as I have a jam-packed night ahead. I'm sure you understand.'

'Of course Mr Bolton, I will be in touch. I can find my own way out,' she said as she stood up to leave.

'It's OK I'm leaving to so I'll come with you,' said Bolton clearly keen to see her off the premises.

Adam hunkered down behind the screen as they both left. Once he heard the door slam at the end of the corridor, he dashed into the office and opened the drawer of the filing cabinet. He grabbed the top file. Without taking the time to read the contents, he took pictures of all twelve pages on his phone then replaced it. Now under time pressure, he needed to get back to Reading, but first, he had to contact Julian, the bad guys were already on their way to the garage.

Apart from a couple of pieces of tape on the fire door, he exited the building without leaving a trace. He repositioned the steel bar on the outside of the fire escape so that when he reached the ground and released the rope, it merely fell silently to his waiting arms.

Back in the car, he took a hurried opportunity to flick through the pictures of the file on his phone. The arms cargo would be travelling from the storerooms behind the garage in Reading to an abandoned ex RAF airfield in deepest Norfolk to meet up with a Super Hercules transport aircraft. This was doubtless arranged by Gorton-Hyde. *He must have someone assisting him in the military, even an influential fixer in the F.O. can't simply call up a Hercules aircraft,* thought Adam.

Norfolk was peppered with ex RAF airfields, he needed more time to examine the file properly. But at the moment, his priority was to get to the garage before things started to disappear.

Once underway, he rang Julian.

CHAPTER 12

Monday 7.00 PM - 2019

As soon as his phone conversation with Adam had finished, Julian headed back to his flat. He kept a close eye on his rearview mirror just in case he had an 'admirer'. Once home, he spent a short but, what he considered an essential amount of time selecting his clothes for the coming day's exertions. He couldn't take his expensive jeans or trainers so his scruffs would have to do.

Half an hour later he was on his way, his Pay as You Go phone was in his shirt pocket in case Adam rang.

By the time Julian had settled into his humble lodgings at the Premier Inn and eaten what passed for an evening meal at the Beefeater next door, it was 10.30. He made himself a coffee and put on the television then sat down and waited for Adam to check-in.

At 1.00am the phone vibrated and beeped in Julian's shirt pocket several times before he awoke. He sat up with a start and quickly fumbled for the phone in his pocket 'Hi Adam, sorry I dozed off.'

'No problem Julian, it's probably just as well because we are in for a long night.'

Adam quickly brought Julian up to date with his discoveries at the Guard-Co offices including Bolton's mysterious reference to settling a personal score with himself. He also described Gorton-Hyde's girl, Ayesha, such as it was, but it didn't ring any bells with Julian.

'It sounds like there might be a lot more information in those files. We'll need to get to them when time permits. I guess the priority must be keeping an eye on the goods. I'll ring Ben and warn him about the potential risk to his men, on guard duty at the garage. I'll ask him to keep them around until I get there I'm only fifteen minutes away. I'll ring you back.' said Julian.

'Okay, watch your back. Speak later.'

Julian rang Ben next. 'Hi, Ben.'

'Julian?' replied a groggy voice.

'Sorry to wake you Ben but things seem to be moving along a bit, and you need to pull your men out before they get their heads knocked about or worse.'

'No need to worry Julian. I used four local officers, they got a call earlier this evening from their Inspector telling them to pull out.'

'Oh crap Ben,' replied a panic-stricken Julian whilst pulling on his black leather bomber jacket and grabbing his car keys. 'Why the hell didn't you call me?'

'I assumed the order had come from your end.' Ben replied defensively.

'Well it didn't, if it had I would have let you know,' said Julian finding it hard to hide his frustration. 'This has obviously come from dodgy Chief Inspector Reynolds.'

'Right, so what do you need me to do?' said Ben apologetically.

Julian felt a little guilty for his shortness with Ben' Nothing, for now, Ben, I'll get over there before Bolton's crew. Be in touch later.'

Julian dashed out of the hotel to his car, and once underway he put a call into Ray Mellors.

'Mr Lycett, I presume. What can you want at this ungodly hour?' said a grumpy voice.

'Yes, apologies for the hour Ray but there have been some developments regarding the matter we discussed.'

'I am aware of that, Julian. What can I help you with?'

'I need you to look into a Chief Inspector Martin Reynolds.'

'He's already on my radar, but I suspect he may be a small fish. Dare I ask what you are up to at this time of night?'

'My suspicions were correct, and I'm now on the trail of an illegal arms cache if I get there in time.'

'Now listen to me Julian,' said Ray in sombre tones 'you're getting involved in some high-risk fieldwork which you're not trained to deal with nor have the aptitude for. Tell me where the arms are headed, and I'll arrange for my team to stop them.'

Julian thought for a moment then replied 'I appreciate your concern Ray, but speed is of the essence right now. They're likely to be on the move imminently, and I don't want to let my colleague down. He's only an hour or so away.'

'I presume you mean Mr Crest. Whilst he does have the necessary skills and training, please have the good sense not to put yourself at risk until you meet up. In the meantime, I will raise a support team.'

'Thanks, Ray I'll update you later when I have movement details for the cargo.'

'As you wish Julian.' The phone went dead.

He seemed well informed, thought Julian, *but I suppose that's his job.*

❋ ❋ ❋

In the study of a large detached house in Hampshire lit only by the desk lamp. Ray Mellors put down the phone then unlocked the drawer in his desk. He took out the 'burner' phone and selected a number to call.

The voice at the other end said 'Yes.'

'Lycett is proving to be quite tenacious, although I'm not sure that he knows exactly where the package is headed,' stated Mellors.

'Yes, surprising for his type,' sneered the voice at the other end. 'Where is Crest?'

'He won't be joining him for another hour.'

'I'll deal with Lycett, but we need to keep Crest in the field for now.'

'What about the Chief Inspector?'

'Pay him off but make sure you have the photographs of the cash handover for future reference.'

Mellors replaced the phone in the desk drawer and locked it.

✣ ✣ ✣

At the other end of the call at a town-house in

Kensington, a slim female figure slinked away from the half-open door of her husband's bedroom, to the comparative safety of her own having overheard the conversation. She sat on the edge of the bed, desperate to make a phone call but frightened that her husband might overhear. She was startled as her husband threw open her bedroom door his tall physique filling the gap.

'What on earth are you doing wandering around the landing at this time of night my dear? You'll catch your death one of these days,' he said with a hint of menace in his voice. 'I'm going away for a few days. You and I will have a chat when I get back.'

Still recovering from his sudden entrance, the women managed to say defiantly 'A chat about what?'

'I think you know my dear,' he replied. 'In the meantime, there will be someone along to keep you company.'

He slammed the door and went down the stairs grabbing his overnight bag on the way and thought to himself *the time is fast approaching for me to deal with that problem.*

Once she heard the front door close, she composed herself and thought *I know I said that I would only use the number in an emergency, well I guess this is it.* She took the phone from her nightstand drawer and made the call.

※ ※ ※

Julian's next call was to Adam, who was less than happy to hear his news regarding the police guard.

'Bloody hell Julian, we don't want to lose sight of those containers. We still don't have an exact destination, Norfolk's a big county.'

'I know, if they haven't already gone when I get there I'll make sure that I follow them if they leave before you arrive,' said Julian trying to reassure his friend.

'Yeah, I know you will Julian,' replied Adam amicably 'but I would rather you didn't. It's far too risky, just wait until I get there.'

'I'll let you know what I find when I get there, I'm only five minutes away now.'

It was 1.30 am by the time Julian reached the garage, and as he approached, it was clear that there was a lot of activity at the site. Three huge flatbed trucks were parked on the garage forecourt. Two of them were already loaded up with three large containers, each big enough to hold a couple of family cars.

One thing is for sure, Julian thought, *they don't*

contain vintage cars.

He drove past and parked near the roadside hedge, further up on the left almost exactly where Adam had stopped a few nights previously. Closing the car door quietly, he climbed over the gate. In the field and he ran down the inside of the hedge to the edge of the forecourt. He peered through the hedgerow.

The forecourt looked very industrious with the florescent lights shining down onto the big trucks. Eastern European voices were coming from the men who were busy securing the cargo, the last of which had just been loaded. They fitted large dirty green tarpaulins over the containers to ensure anonymity, not that anyone could tell what was inside.

He frowned when he noticed a workforce member bend over to tie off a securing line, revealing an automatic pistol stuffed down his waistband at the rear. It was reasonable to assume that they would all be armed.

Now, what do I do, thought Julian realising that these guys were just about ready to leave? He looked around to see who was in charge. He knew that Bolton wouldn't be there as he had only left the Guard-Co office just before Adam. A few seconds later, his question was answered. A man wearing a dark tan leather jacket appeared around the corner of one of the trucks and started shouting at the other men. They were ordered to get into the lorry cabins, 3 to each vehicle. It was a bit hard to tell at a distance, but he appeared to have a long scar down his left cheek. *Probably not a duelling scar,* Julian thought.

Considering his options, he came to the conclusion that he didn't have any. His only choice was to follow the convoy to its destination. His next thought was whether to call Adam first, but he knew what he would tell him to wait until he got there. That wasn't really an option as Adam must still be half an hour away by which time they would have lost track of the trucks. There are several routes across to the East coast.

Deciding not to allow Adam to stop him, he scurried along the edge of the field back to his car intending to follow the convoy. He would call Adam when he was well on the way.

The three low-loaders turned left out of the garage forecourt one behind the other, as the road was empty they remained in convoy. Julian saw them approach in his wing mirror and ducked down as they drove passed. He waited until they were just out of sight then pulled out slowly, concentrating on catching up but keeping enough distance to avoid arousing suspicion.

He was feeling quite pleased with himself, but he was so focused on looking forward that he didn't notice the black BMW slink out of the forecourt behind him. The scar-faced driver's lips forming a dark sneer as he remained a cautious distance back.

After about twenty minutes of driving it became apparent that the wagons were keeping to the 'A' roads and not taking the motorway route. On a relatively open section of the road, the last truck suddenly indicated left, and Julian quickly slowed down, wondering what the problem was. He soon realised why as the dim lights of a truck stop café appeared. The wagons turned in and pulled up on the rough terrain of the lorry park.

Julian followed but stayed as far back as possible. He stopped right on the edge of the parking area with the car's passenger side almost covered with branches from the wild hedgerow.

Getting out of the car to see what was going on, he decided it was time to update Adam. His call came back with the busy signal. *Damn,* thought Julian, *who can he be talking to at this time of night?*

Suddenly he heard the crunch of boot on gravel behind him. Before he could turn around, there was a 'THWACK' and an incredibly sharp pain to the back of his head as the cosh struck his skull, knocking him unconscious. His phone dropped to the floor and bounced under the car. The man with the scar caught Julian under his armpits as he collapsed, he whistled across to the driver getting out of the last truck.

'Hey Stefan, give me a hand to get him into the container and hurry up,' he said, not wishing to attract any attention from the cafe.

Stefan immediately ran over and grabbed Julian's legs. There wasn't much weight to him, so it didn't take long to transport him across to the back of the trailer. By this time one of the other men had gotten out of the cabin, pulled the tarpaulin from the rear of the container and opened the bolted door to reveal piles of coffin-sized metal crates. There was enough space between the crates and the door for them to dump Julian on the floor. A trail of blood began to trickle from the back of his head onto the metal surface.

'Tie him up!' ordered Scarface.

Stefan produced several nylon zip-lock cables and wrapped two around Julian's wrists behind his back and two around his bare ankles. He pulled them so tight that they bit threw the skin, drawing blood from the sock-less ankles. They would be painful when Julian woke up if he woke up.

Scarface returned to Julian's car and checked the inside for his phone. He couldn't find it, so he went back to his BMW. The men returned to the cab, and they were all back on the road within minutes.

* * *

Adam had been driving for nearly half an hour since speaking to Julian. He was growing impatient waiting for his return call. He was just about to ring him back when a call came through 'Julian?' he said.

'No, sorry, Adam, its Michelle.'

'Michelle!' said Adam with surprise 'no, don't be sorry I was just expecting a call from Julian, that's all.' He suddenly remembered Michelle had said that she would only use this number in an emergency. 'Are you okay, Michelle? Has something happened?'

'Yes I'm okay, but I've just overheard Lawrence talking to someone on the phone. He mentioned dealing with Julian and something about keeping you in the field, whatever that means. I thought you should know.'

'It means Julian is in the shit if I don't get to Reading soon. Did he say anything else, Michelle?'

'Not really no .... but...' She hesitated.

'What Michelle?'

'After the phone call, he burst into my room, and I'm sure he knew I'd overheard him. He said that we would be having a chat when he returned from his trip.' She hesitated 'I'm afraid Adam. I think I may be becoming too much of a liability.'

'Don't worry Michelle. I think we need to get you out of there. Do you have any friends or family that you can trust?'

'The only family I had was Frank. Any friends, would-be wives and girlfriends of Lawrence's colleagues. I doubt that they would be trustworthy.'

'Okay, well your safe for the moment, let me make this call to Julian then I'll come back with a plan to get you out of there.'

'Adam, I know we've only just met, but I really don't know where to turn.'

She was not the type to burst into tears, but Adam could tell that she was terrified.

'Yeah, I know we only met once Michelle, but I enjoyed it, given the topic of conversation. In any case, there is no way that I'd leave you in the clutches of Gorton-Hyde so don't worry, just keep the phone nearby, and I'll call back soon.' Adam's dislike for this man had moved up another notch.

'Thank you so much, Adam.'

As soon as the phone clicked off, he pressed Julian's number, and the call went straight to answerphone. He didn't leave a message but rang again two minutes later once again it went to answerphone. *Who the hell is he on the phone to?* Adam thought *unless he isn't on the phone!*

Once on the Reading road, Adam headed for the garage, and ten minutes later, he pulled onto the forecourt. The place was in total darkness and not a soul about. *Either I'm just in time or far too late,* he thought and took the torch from his backpack before cautiously getting out of his car.

He approached the shop door, which was locked. Shone the torch through the windows, but there was no one about. It looked like someone had helped themselves to some of the food and drinks shelves, but beyond that, everything seemed undisturbed.

Next, he went down the side of the building and carefully looked around the corner of the rear wall, his heart sank as he observed the wide-open doors of the storage barns. He was too late.

Running across the yard into the barn, he confirmed what he already knew. The light from his torch reflected off the warehouse's steel-clad walls, showing a completely empty building. Even the small office in the corner was bereft of any paperwork or information.

He returned to his car with thoughts of what could have happened to Julian running through his mind. *I should never have let him get involved, Christ if he has decided to follow the cargo they'll most certainly have spotted him.*

Once sitting back in his car, Adam ceased the recriminations and the mind of the professional returned. He formed a plan of action. He needed to make contact with Ben and find out why the police guard had been removed prematurely. Then contact Ray Mellors and arrange some backup. Julian seemed to trust the guy.

Julian was still not answering his mobile, so he had to assume that he was incapacitated somehow. Of course, it could be something as simple as a flat battery or poor signal. Either way, he needed to ascertain his whereabouts ASAP.

Then there was Michelle who was also in potential danger, he had to get her to safety.

Also, Gorton-Hyde and Bolton were undoubtedly keeping tabs on him. He hadn't detected a tail so far, which made him even more uncomfortable. He put this thought aside to focus on the matters at hand.

Fortunately Julian had sent him both Ben and Ray Mellors numbers, so he dialled Ben's. It was now 3.00am, but eventually, he answered.

'Hello,' came the gruff voice.

'Ben Gifford, this is Adam Crest Julian's pal. I'm

really sorry to ring at this time, but I need some info urgently.'

'Oh, yes Julian has mentioned you. How can I help.' he said much more alert.

'What happened to the police guard at the garage? Are you aware that the storage barns are empty and do you have any idea of Julian's whereabouts?' said Adam getting straight to the point.

'As I explained to Julian, the guards were local officers who were ordered to leave by their own Inspector without my knowledge. As Julian has not rung me back, I'm not aware of the storage barns being emptied. Apart from Julian telling me that he was on his way to the garage a couple of hours ago, I've no idea of his whereabouts. All of which is not much help Mr Crest, however, I would suggest that Julian might be in some trouble. Later this morning I'll find out where the order to remove the guard originated and also track down what must be a large shipment travelling from Reading.'

'Okay, Ben, thanks for your help. I appreciate that you don't really know me but can I ask that we still keep any info between ourselves. You might look in the Norfolk direction for 2 or 3 low loaders carrying shipping containers. More importantly, can your tech people trace the whereabouts of Julian's phone?'

'I don't have a problem with that Mr Crest although this is all a bit unorthodox. Please keep me updated, especially regarding Julian's whereabouts.'

'Will do,' said Adam.

Before calling Ray Mellors, he brought up the pictures of Bolton's file on his phone. He took the time to read through the details hoping that he might get a clue to the cargoes and Julian's destination.

❊ ❊ ❊

At the house in Kensington, Michelle sat on her bed, waiting for Adam's call and trying to think of a way to help him with her rescue. She didn't have immediate access to a car but could call a cab to take her to any destination that might help. She should also pack some sort of bag and put on some practical clothes.

She was mulling over these thoughts when the front doorbell rang. *Who can that be at this time of night?* She thought to herself half, hoping that Adam had managed to sort something out this quickly.

She tied her dressing gown and was halfway

down the long staircase when Jane, the housekeeper, emerged from the servant's overnight quarters. Pulling on her own dressing gown she walked across the marble-floored hall.

Michelle shouted to her 'It's alright Jane, I'll get it. I've an idea who it might be.'

'If you're sure madam,' Jane gratefully replied and turned back towards her quarters.

Michelle opened the front door, and 2 large men in black uniforms with 'Guard-Co' stitched across the left lapel filled the entrance. Both of them with unshaven and unsmiling faces.

'Lady Gorton-Hyde?' One of them questioned.

The disappointment showed on her face 'Yes, who are you?' she replied with a short tone.

'Sir Lawrence Gorton-Hyde has requested some additional security at the house Madam. It seems he's involved in some high profile work at the moment and would feel safer if we were here,' said one of the men flashing an ID card. He stepped across the threshold and pushed passed Michelle into the entrance hall. She was not given a chance to object. As he passed by her, she noticed the butt of an automatic pistol protruding from a black leather shoulder holster. His colleague followed without saying a word and closed the door behind him.

Michelle felt threatened but with measured indigence said 'I was not informed of this and you are certainly not from the Foreign Office.'

'Yeah, it's all a bit last minute. We're with Guard-Co. We've a contract to provide this sort of security for Foreign Office personnel,' said the same man as he helped himself to a good look around. Opening various doors from the hall.

'Is this the way to the rear entrance?' he said, pointing to the direction that Jane had come from earlier.

'Yes, but before you do anything else, I need to contact my husband and confirm this arrangement.'

The man gestured his colleague to go through the door and take a position at the rear entrance.

'Not much point your Ladyship he won't be contactable until later today. Best go back to bed and get your beauty sleep,' he said with patronising finality.

Michelle knew when to back off, and two large armed men were more than she could handle. It was clear that she was effectively a prisoner in her own home. Dejected, she climbed the stairs to return to the relative safety of her bedroom. There was only one thing that she could do, she had to call Adam.

* * *

Having spent a good twenty minutes going through the files on his phone, Adam knew that the goods' destination was a disused airfield near Fakenham. He checked on the internet and discovered it was an ex RAF base for Lancaster Bombers during the Second World War but was still used as a general airfield today. The rendezvous and transfer time was to be 8.30am.

He checked his watch, and it was just coming up to 4.00am. He should easily make it in time and hoped that Julian was either being held captive or at the very least he would find out where he was, if not with the trucks. The phone rang, and thankfully it was Ben.

'Hello Mr Crest,' came the almost animated voice. 'We've located Julian's phone. It's at a truck stop just passed Henley-on-Thames about 20 minutes from where you are, if you put your foot down. It's not active, but at least we know where it is.'

'That's fantastic, Ben, many thanks, I'm on my way.'

'Give me a call when you get there.'

Adam clicked off as he didn't want to make any promises and didn't really want to involve Ben any further. He would need some less constrained and better-trained assistance to deal with these guys, ideally from one of the Security Services. He would get to Julian's phone before ringing Ray Mellors by then he'd know what he needed him to do. He gunned the Audi down the Reading road heading for Henley-on-Thames.

He was turning off into the truck stop car park barely 15 minutes after leaving the Garage, making record time on the empty roads. The car park was empty except for a couple of wagons, a light still shone in the cafe.

Driving slowly around the edge, there in the shadows, he saw Julian's car. He got out cautiously and approached it from the rear and tried the driver side door which opened. Poking his head inside, he found it to be empty. *Too much to hope for I suppose,* he thought to himself. He checked everywhere for the phone but could not see it so closed the door and looked around the outside of the vehicle.

When he'd completed the circle and come back around to the front, the spotlights from the cafe behind him illuminated the ground, he noticed a trickle of dried blood on the gravel near the driver's door. Bending down to inspect it, he saw the mobile phone lying underneath the car behind the front wheel.

'Oh shit,' he said to himself.

There was no doubt that he had been captured. He put the phone in his pocket and returned to his car. He needed to get to Norfolk sharpish. He would make a call to Mellors on the way to arrange for back up.

Adam pulled out of the truck stop car park and put his foot down, he was just about to press the call button for Ray Mellors when the phone rang.

'Hello,' he said.

'Adam thank god, I'm so sorry to call you again, but things seem to have taken a turn for the worse here.' Michelle's voice sounded shaky as she was obviously trying to conceal her distress.

She told him about the arrival of the two supposed security guards. He agreed that she was indeed being kept prisoner until her husband returned, *or perhaps she was to be 'removed' whilst he was away*. Adam did not mention his last thought to Michelle.

'Where are the two men now?' he asked.

'They're downstairs, one at the front door and one at the back.'

'Can they see each other?'

'No, but they're in contact via radio.'

'Okay,' Adam went quiet thinking for a moment, he knew that he really needed to get her out straight away. Still, at the same time, he needed to get to Fakenham for Julian and of course to catch Bolton and Gorton-Hyde.

'Adam …. are you still there?' her thin voice said.

'Yes, just thinking of the best course of action,' he paused for a moment. He didn't want to do this over the phone, but she needed to understand the situation's gravity. 'Michelle, I have to tell you something that will be painful for you to hear. I wanted to tell you the other day but couldn't.'

'Oh God, something has happened to Frank. What is it, Adam?'

'I'm afraid he's dead, Michelle. I found him on Friday. He was stabbed.'

There was a quiet sobbing coming from the other end of the phone. Adam waited until Michelle was able to speak. Eventually, a tearful voice said 'I suppose I knew that something dreadful must have happened to him after our conversation. I just didn't want to think the worst. He was all I had Adam.'

'I didn't want to tell you like this, but you needed to know how much danger you're in.'

Michelle's voice grew in strength as she rallied

'Of course, I understand. There will be time for grief later.'

Impressed by her courage, he came to a decision. He couldn't be in both places at the same time, and it was a fact that Michelle was in clear and present danger. Whereas Julian had been captured and would likely be taken to the rendezvous. If they were going to kill him, he would have found his body in his car instead of an empty vehicle. There was also a strong possibility that he may have some value to them, after all, he was an important member of the Civil Service. He could be more use alive than dead.

Adam decided that he would go back to London and get Michelle. In the meantime, he would ask Mellors to arrange for his team to take care of things at the airfield. Depending on how things went in London Adam might still be able to get there in time to rescue Julian and deal with Bolton.

'Michelle, you're in Phillimore Gardens, I believe.'

'Yes, 32.'

'Give me some idea of the external layout.'

'It's a five-story detached house with a porched front entrance, a balcony to the first floor front windows, walled rear garden with a large first-floor veranda overlooking a patioed area.'

'That's very helpful, I guess you can see what I'm planning. How high is the garden wall, whereabouts is the rear guard positioned?'

'He seems to wander around a lot. He's been right up to the top of the house and checked every room then returned to the patio. He lit a cigarette, and that is where he is at the moment standing under the veranda. If you could climb over the side passage gate, walk down the passageway and look up to your right, you would see the veranda balcony.'

'That sounds promising.' said Adam as he joined the M25. 'How high is the balcony?'

'About twenty-five feet.'

'Are there any vehicles parked in front of the house?'

'Only the van belonging to these two security guys.'

'Good, as it happens I have just the right kit with me.' He glanced at the backpack on the rear seat. 'I need you to get yourself dressed in some practical clothes, jeans and polo neck jumper or similar, in black if possible. Something to cover your blond hair. Very pretty but not great for sneaking about at night. You'll also need some sort of shoulder bag or rucksack with whatever additional things you might need for a few days away.'

'No problem, I'm ahead of you on that one, I've dug out my old hiking gear.'

'Sounds great,' said Adam a little surprised at the hiking gear. 'I'll call you ten minutes before I arrive. Position yourself on the veranda, and I'll get a rope up to you via my toy drone. You'll have to tie it off and climb down. Are you okay with all of that?'

'Yes, no problem. But I can't guarantee where the guard is going to be.'

'Leave that to me. I'll ring you later, good luck.'

'And to you. Adam thanks again for your help.'

'Don't thank me just yet, see you soon.' He ended the call.

Quite a gutsy lady, he thought then pressed the call button for Ray Mellors.

The call was answered promptly considering the time 'Hello, who's calling?'

'Is that Ray Mellors? My name is Adam Crest, a colleague of Julian Lycett's.'

'Ah, Mr Crest I was rather expecting a call from Julian. How can I help you at this ungodly hour?'

'Julian believes that you're the only person he can trust.'

'A very astute man Mr Lycett,' he said wryly.

'Things have escalated, and we need some support.'

'Carry on.'

Oh well in for a penny, thought Adam and proceeded to bring him up to date with the night's events omitting the part regarding Michelle. He also kept back the information that he had gleaned from Bolton's file regarding the delivery of the goods to Afghanistan. Partly because they would not reach Afghanistan and partly a gut instinct that told him to keep it to himself.

He ended by explaining that he needed his help with Bolton's people at the airfield and although he was on his way there, it might touch and go for him to get there on time.

'Well Adam, if I might use your first name, you have indeed gotten yourselves into difficulties. I did warn Julian of this.'

'Call me what you like Ray.' *A bit pompous this bloke,* he thought. 'Just let me know if you can help.'

'After my last conversation with Julian, I had anticipated something of this nature, and I can get a twelve-man team out there in two hours.'

'That's right on the button Ray.' said Adam pleased with the efficient response.

'I'll put the wheels in motion. What is your ETA?'

'I guess around 8.00am depending on traffic.' He replied, not wanting to go into the details of his other task.

'Whenever you do arrive please report to Captain Tasker.'

'Will do and many thanks, Ray.'

'Not at all. It seems you and Julian have dug up a bit of an anthill, there will be ramifications after this action.' The call ended.

A Strange guy thought Adam. At least he knew that the necessary action was being taken and he could focus on getting Michelle out of danger.

✲ ✲ ✲

Back at the house in Hampshire. Ray Mellors once more unlocked his desk drawer and withdrew the mobile phone. He pressed the call key.

'Yes'

'Crest called.'

'How much does he know?'

'Everything regarding the shipment from this side. But no reference to delivery on the other side.'

'What about Lycett?'

'Still detained, Crest is asking for assistance in a rescue.'

'Damn! Have you reassured him of your support?'

'Yes.'

'You know what to do.'

The call ended, and Mellors replaced the phone in his drawer.

CHAPTER 13

Tuesday 4.00 AM - 2019

Adam turned on to Kensington High Street and called Michelle.

'Adam, are you nearby yet?' she sounded a little nervous.

'Yes just on the High Street, are you alright?'

'Yes, these to thugs keep wandering around the house, and I reckon it's only a matter of time before one of them decides to pay me a visit. The bedroom door is locked, but that won't stop them for long.'

'I'll be there in five minutes. When you hear the front doorbell ring, leave your room, head for the veranda. Wait at the left-hand side of the balcony. You'll see a small drone fly up to you, grab the thin line attached to it. Pull it up until it becomes a thick rope. Tie that off to the balustrade, wait until I've tested that the knot is strong enough then climb down. Understood?'

'Understood.' She confirmed.

Turning onto Phillimore Gardens, there was a long line of white-fronted detached townhouses. He parked six houses before number 32.

Grabbing the backpack, he got out of the car,

opened the boot and took out the 2 plastic bottles he had purchased at a motorway station. It was still dark, save for the street lighting. There were enough shadows for Adam to sneak down to number 32 undetected. He glanced at the dark passage that ran down the left-hand side of the house. The metal gate at the entrance was about five feet high. He could manage that easily enough.

As he approached number 32, he could see the newish looking black Ford or minivan parked outside the house. Ducking down behind it, he crawled around to the driver side door, he could not be seen from the house. Taking out one of the plastic bottles of BBQ fuel, he poured the contents over the top of the front tyre and over the edge of the bonnet. Some of it seeped into the engine bay. He then did the same with the rear wheel and the boot.

Taking a box of matches out, he lit a bunch of four. Moving away from the back of the car, he threw the lighted matches at the pool of fuel. It ignited with a whoosh and quickly travelled to the front wheel.

Nipping back down the pavement a few yards, he turned and walked back towards the house as if to be a passer-by. Entering the porch of number 32, he rang the doorbell several times.

The door flew open, and an angry Guard-Co operative said 'What's your problem, pal?'

As innocently as possible, Adam replied 'Is that your black van?'

'Yeah, what's it to you?'

'Well, it seems to be on fire.'

The flames were now starting to become visible from the vehicle's passenger side as they licked across the bonnet and boot.

'What the fuck!' exclaimed the guard and immediately grabbed at the two-way radio in his pocket. 'Carl, Carl get yourself out the front now. The bloody vans on fire,' he shouted into the radio.

He ran up and down the pavement in a panic with not a clue what to do. The bright yellow flames continued to take hold of what was no doubt a company vehicle and his responsibility. As guard number two came bursting out of the front door, Adam took the opportunity to disappear down the passage and quickly climbed over the metal gate. He ran to the end, hoping that Michelle had managed to get to the veranda.

'Hey Michelle, are you there?' he said in a shouted whisper.

'Yes, Adam. What on earth's going on outside?'

'Don't worry about it, I'll explain later,' he said whilst connecting the fishing line to the drone.

He launched the drone.

'Can you see it yet, Michelle?'

'Yes, it's coming up now. I can see the line as well.'

'Right grab it.' commanded Adam.

Michelle tugged at the line, and it came away from the drone, which then descended back to Adam. She pulled as previously instructed until the thicker rope appeared which she duly tied to the iron railings. 'Okay, try that,' she said.

Adam pulled hard at the other end and lifted his own weight off the ground. 'That's fine,' he said 'drop your rucksack to me then climb down.'

'Here goes,' came back the nervous reply as she dropped the rucksack which Adam caught easily. Michelle climbed over the edge of the balcony keeping a tight grip on the rope and allowing her body to dangle from it over the balcony side. She twisted her ankles around the line and lowered herself slowly and efficiently to the ground.

Ready to catch her if necessary, Adam glanced back down the passageway just in case the guards had got their act together and decided to look for the mystery visitor. However, there was no real danger as he could still hear the panicked voices shouting something about buckets and water.

As soon as Michelle was within reach, Adam grabbed her around the waist and lowered her to the ground. 'Well done you,' he said 'you look like you've done that before,' as she let go of the rope and placed her arms around his shoulders.

'Thank you so much, Adam,' she replied a little out of breath.

They stood like that for a brief moment looking into each other's eyes. Michelle's were still red from her earlier tears. Suddenly Adam felt awkward and said 'Right we had better make a quick getaway.'

'Yes, of course,' replied Michelle sounding equally awkward.

Adam packed the gear away, and Michelle put on her rucksack over the black polo neck jumper.

They reached the gate and Adam cupped his hands. Stepping into them, she climbed over the top with ease. He followed her over then put his hand on her shoulder, holding her back. 'Just let me check first,' he said.

Poking his head around the corner of the house, he could see the guards busy with a plastic bucket each but not achieving a great deal. 'That's not going to end well,' he said. He could see that the fire had taken a stronghold at the car's rear where the fuel tank was situated. He waited until they had both disappeared back into the house for more water a then said 'Okay, now turn right and run down to the silver Audi.'

Both of them dashed out of the passage, reached the car together and jumped in. They removed their packs and Adam started the car. He turned it around and headed back up Phillimore Gardens at speed. Michelle turned to look out of the rear window and could see the flaming vehicle and the two guards feebly hurling buckets of water at it.

'There are fire extinguishers in the kitchen.' she said with some concern.

'Well they will either work that out or they won't. Whatever happens, they'll have a lot of explaining to do to Mr Bolton.'

They both burst out laughing, and Adam could see Michelle's cheeks were flushed with the excitement of it all.

'God it feels good to be free,' she said with relief.

'Let's hope we can do the same for Julian,' said Adam soberly.

'You mentioned him the other day. Is he a friend of yours?'

'Yes, he is. Thanks to me, he is mixed up in this mess as well and currently being held captive.'

'Oh my god Adam, you should have said something. I could've waited.'

'No need to concern yourself, Michelle. I made a calculated decision, and in my view, you were in greater immediate danger than Julian. I believe your husband to be a ruthless man. You have nothing to feel guilty about. However, we do need to get to Julian as quickly as we can.' With that, Adam put his foot down and headed for the M25.

'I think you're probably right Adam. Things were coming to a head with Lawrence and considering what happened to Frank,' she said resignedly. She bucked up and said 'Let's go and get Julian. Where are we going and how long will it take to get there?'

'We must get to an airfield near Fakenham in Norfolk before 8.30am. That's where Julian is being held captive. It'll be a bit of a push for two and a half hours. However, I've a solid back up plan in place in the form of an MI5 task force who will get there before us. They'll rescue Julian and hopefully bring this whole affair to an end. It'll only remain for us to make sure that your husband is firmly implicated and arrested. He may not be the actual murderer, but he's definitely the man responsible. Then you'll be safe.'

'Will that bastard Bolton be there?' Said Michelle, with hatred in her voice, the vicious murder of her brother still painfully raw.

'I certainly hope so,' he replied quietly. Adam still planned on getting a face to face with that man.

They were both quiet for a few minutes sitting in the semi-darkness of the car.

'He was a nice fellow, Frank,' said Adam breaking the silence. 'I used to see him at the garage most Friday afternoons and shoot the breeze for half an hour. We'd have a couple of pints most Sunday lunchtimes at the local pub. He never had a bad word to say about anyone, and you got the feeling that he'd do anything for anyone. He even spoke well of Lawrence. I guess that changed when he made his discovery in the outhouse. Were you always close?'

'Yes,' she said, clearing her throat to remove the emotion from her voice 'he pretty much brought me up from the age of 15, he was 10 years older than me. My parents had me quite late in life, and my mother died of cancer when I was 13, then my dad died from a heart attack when I was 15.'

'I am so sorry, Michelle.'

'That's kind Adam but its 25 years ago now. I was fortunate to have a brother like Frank, he essentially became a father figure. We were left well provided for with a large 5 bedroom detached house on the outskirts of Reading. There were ample finances, my father had been a professor at Reading University and left things very well organised.'

'Crikey, I went to Reading Uni. I got my degree in Physics, what was your dad's subject?'

'Economics,' she replied. 'I don't suppose you will have come across each other.'

'No, I spent most of my time on the sports field anyway. Did you go to Uni?'

'Yes, I went to Reading Girls School, then on to Oxford to study English Lit and History. Frank made sure that my education was not neglected, but he also ensured that I had a happy and healthy home life. We used to do everything together, he was a keen shooter and won a gold a Bisley. I was his spotter.

Adam thought briefly of Colin Gooding who had been his spotter.

'I also spent many weekends at the Reading gun club shooting handguns, in fact, I was quite a good shot. The Browning automatic was my favourite.

'I didn't have you down as a firearms expert,' said Adam clearly impressed.

'Oh, definitely not an expert I just enjoyed it. After graduating Frank and I went hiking around Cambodia, Vietnam and Thailand for six months to broaden my horizons and his I suppose. We got into some pretty hairy situations out there, but it was the best six months of my life.' She said a little sadness creeping back into her voice. 'When we came back, I eventually got a job in the city with Lloyds and ended up at the Foreign Office after several years. At the age of 29, I became Lawrence Gorton-Hyde's trophy wife. His first wife had died the year before in a car accident. By this time, Frank had decided to use the land on Reading Road that father had left. He built the petrol station and shop to provide himself with a living, now that I was settled in life.'

'You must miss him.'

'I do. He was not just a brother he was a father and a close friend as well. I hope his murderer is made to pay.'

'He will Michelle, he will,' Adam vowed.

Michelle seemed very comfortable talking to him about her private life, so he encouraged her to continue 'What was life like as Lady Gorton-Hyde?'

'Lawrence was is in his 50's, so it wasn't stimulating. It was quite glamorous and enjoyable for the first couple of years, you know cocktail and dinner parties. He had no interest in children or family. As time passed, it soon became apparent that he wasn't all that interested in me either. Especially as there were plenty of interested 'twenty-something' women around for him to play with. I was in my mid 30's by then. His circle of friends took a turn for the worst and more and more suspect looking men, accompanied by what was obviously their mistresses, attending the dinner parties. In particular, one of them was always leering at me and making distasteful references to the tightness of my dress or other creepy comments about my appearance. He was Lawrence's right-hand man doing lots of lucrative deals in Ukraine and the Far East from what I could gather. He could, therefore do no wrong. I remember now, his name was Tom Riley.'

The car suddenly swerved as Adam momentarily seemed to lose control with the image of a rifle sight cross-hair on the head of Tom Riley flashing into his brain.

'Are you okay?'

'Fine... fine I thought I saw a Deer in the road.'

'It wasn't was it?' she said with concern.

'No, no. Carry on.'

'Well one night, during a dinner party at our house. I told Lawrence that enough was enough with this guy, left the party and went upstairs to my room. He simply dismissed me with the wave of a drunken hand. As we had long since agreed on separate bedrooms, this was the only place that I felt comfortable. I had gotten undressed and was just walking across the room to the bathroom in my underwear when Lawrence's protégé burst through the bedroom door. Drunkenly, he staggered across the room towards me, suggesting that we have some fun. He was a big man, and I knew that I wouldn't get away from him or around him. Lawrence wouldn't be coming to my aide, so I welcomed him with open arms. The leer on his face became even wider, and he put his arms around me. I can still remember the feel of his sweaty palms, grabbing my buttocks and his whisky soaked breath on my cheek. I drew my right leg back as far as possible, brought my knee up and slammed it hard into his crotch. He let out a scream and dropped to his knees. I grabbed a clump of his hair in my left hand and pulled his head back then I launched my knee and struck him sharply under his chin. This knocked him backwards across the floor. I bent down close to his face, whispered into his ear that he should get out of the house and never come back or I would kill him. He quickly crawled out of the bedroom, and I never saw him again. I don't know what excuse he gave Lawrence for not attending any future parties.'

'My Knee was bruised for over two weeks after

that,' she complained, all the aggression having left her voice.

Adam turned his head to look at Michelle feigning a look of fear and said 'my god remind me never to get on the wrong side of you!'

Michelle laughed 'I'm sure that could never happen,' she said, touching his arm affectionately.

'Anyway I heard that he died not too long after that, a plane crash I believe, couldn't have happened to a nicer bloke,' she said sarcastically. 'Still, I did feel sorry for his wife and two daughters.'

Adam stared thoughtfully ahead and simply muttered 'Yeah.'

They were quiet again for a while until Michelle broke the silence.

'Sorry for prattling on Adam, it must be a release of stress.'

'Not at all, it was good to hear about your life.'

'Okay well what about you, let's hear a bit about your life?'

'Not much to tell really I grew up in Reading living next door to Julian's family, our respective parents got on so we become good friends. We both went to the local comprehensive and were more like brothers than just friends. We looked out for each other, which mostly meant me protecting him from bullies and him protecting me from detention. After school, he went off to Cambridge, and I went to Reading. We still knocked about together between terms until I joined the Army and Julian joined the Civil Service.'

'What about girlfriends?' Said Michelle mischievously.

'They didn't really enter into things, for different reasons, Julian is gay, and I was just a late developer,' he said matter of factly.

'Oh, right. I presume that you did develop eventually?' she said with a little more mischief.

'Yes, of course.' he said defensively. 'Just nothing serious that's all.'

'Only teasing Adam.'

'It's not easy to have a long term relationship in the forces plus I ended up in the SAS which is not a good basis for marriage etc.'

'Did you really. That must have been a fascinating life.'

'I don't know about fascinating, but it was certainly satisfying until I got wounded that is.'

'Really. What happened?'

'A Taliban terrorist decided to cut my leg to bits and severed my femoral artery. My guys saved my life and got me back to the base hospital. Afterwards, I was transferred out to military intelligence until I was eventually discharged. I joined Comm-Sec about eighteen months ago and became the UK advisor to their large Commercial clients. I look after their security systems and of course, sell them the necessary kit and services. I was living a quiet life until last Friday. Since then, things seem to have gone from bad to worse. Apart from meeting you, that is.' He looked at her with a grin.

'What a creep,' she said, returning the grin.

'True,' he agreed. 'Anyway, now that we know each other's life stories, we had better focus on getting to Fakenham asap. At the moment the sat nav is telling us that we'll only just make it.'

They sat quietly for a while in the early morning light. Michelle glanced across at Adam, making a mental assessment of her knight in shining armour. He seems a nice man, even unshaven he still has the clean-cut appearance of a military type. He also looks as though he has kept himself in good condition, she mused.

At 8.00am they left the main road and took the cross country route for the airfield. The Norfolk land was flat for as far as the eye could see which meant that they could be easily visible to a vigilant enemy. He parked the car on a grassy verge next to a field on the airfield's perimeter.

Taking out a pair of binoculars from his glove box he got out of the car. Resting his arms on the roof, he scanned the horizon. Less than half a mile down the road he could see the gated entrance to the airfield which had a Landover strategically parked across it. 2 men were standing nearby smoking and chatting.

Moving the glasses further right and about 100 yards along there were another 2 men. He looked back at the gate then traversed left to find another 2 men. None of the guards appeared to be armed. However, he was one hundred per cent sure that they would all be carrying a concealed weapon. I need to get closer to the airfield, he thought and looked further around to the right until he spotted a clump of trees at the farthest edge of the field. Mellor's team must be located somewhere in that area, he thought. He needed to locate Tasker and find out the plan of action.

Back in the car, he said to Michelle 'I'll have to go on foot across this field to the perimeter and see what's happening and locate Tasker. Keep your head down until I get back.'

'I will do no such thing.' Objected Michelle.

'What do you mean? You can't come with me, there's likely be to be some shooting, and I don't want you getting hurt.'

'Well I appreciate your concern Adam, but I am more than capable of looking after myself.' she said now becoming a little heated.

'How do you know? You haven't done this before?' said Adam becoming frustrated.

'Look, I don't want to fall out over this, but I am coming.'

Adam realised that he would not win this argument, so he opened the glove box and reached in for his Commando knife. After clipping it to his belt, he said 'Okay, we haven't got time to discuss this. Put your woollen hat on and gloves, if you have them and stick to me like glue.'

Michelle grinned to herself in satisfaction and did as she was instructed.

The ground underfoot was mud and manure, which was soggy after the recent rain. Keeping their heads down, they crossed the field to the copse where they settled, confident that they were unobserved. Adam had been impressed by Michelle's speed and agility in getting across the field. She'd done as requested and stuck to his side. He lifted the field glasses and was able to see across the perimeter fence into the airfield. There it was.

Sitting at the end of the old runway was the colossal presence of the Hercules transport plane.

He couldn't believe that they'd managed to get hold of it, never mind land it here. There was a lot of activity with several men guiding the flatbed trucks onto the sloped loading ramp which were then winched into the plane's cargo bay.

They were about to load the last truck when a tall man in a tan coloured leather jacket came out of the Airfield cafe. He was carrying what appeared to be pre-packed sandwiches and a couple of water bottles.

Adam heard him shout to the other men' Hold it! We don't want him to die from starvation on the way across.' He laughed, and the others joined in as they opened the metal door at the back of the container. The man in the leather jacket went inside then soon re-emerged without the food and drink. 'Okay get on with it, or we'll be late getting going,' he shouted.

'Bloody hell!' said Adam' those bastards must be talking about Julian.' His anger rising at the thought of his friend trapped in the container and most certainly injured in some way.

In an attempt to calm him, Michelle said 'I guess they must be, but let's focus on the positive. He's alive, or they wouldn't be feeding him, and they are feeding him, so the intention must be to keep him alive.'

'Yes your right Michelle,' he said a little calmer.

'But we've got to get him out of there, they'll be taking off soon.'

The next thing he saw was the arrival of two cars. He recognised both. One was a black Range Rover and the other a black Mercedes. The unmistakable white-haired head of Bolton appeared from the Range Rover, and a tall slimmer man emerged from the Mercedes. Adam quickly passed the binoculars to Michelle and asked 'Is that your husband?'

She took the glasses and put them to her eyes 'My God! Yes, it is.' she confirmed feeling a chill down her spine.

Adam took some pictures on his phone.

The Hercules' colossal propeller engines had started, so they couldn't hear what was being shouted above the sound of the thundering motors. Both men went into the cargo hold presumably to check the merchandise and came out after a few minutes. Bolton gesticulated to the man wearing the leather jacket, then at his Range Rover which the man then got into. He drove the car up the ramp and into the hold.

'I don't believe it. He's only taking his bloody car with him,' said Adam in astonishment.

Bolton and Gorton-Hyde had a chat and shook hands then Gorton-Hyde went back to his car, and it sped off the airfield. Bolton boarded the passenger section of the plane as the cargo hatch was starting to close.

Once again, Adam made sure that he got some photos of the two men shaking hands.

'Christ where the hell is Tasker and his men, I appreciate he wants to catch them red-handed, but he's leaving it until the last minute. We are going to miss them if he's not careful.'

Adam scanned the Airfield perimeter with field glasses from right to left but couldn't see a soul. Michelle joined in shading her eyes and straining to see anyone apart from the Guard-Co personnel. They both looked back to the airfield from their hiding place, the cargo door was now closed.

Adam swiftly scanned the perimeter again, but there was no movement in the surrounding fields, just the Guard-Co men.

'Where the hell are they?'

The engine noise from the Hercules more than doubled as the revs built up.

His heart now thumping in his chest, Adam continued surveillance, he was desperate to see some sign of the task force making their move.

The Hercules was starting to trundle down the runway, and Adam could only look on. It reached take-off speed, lifted off from the tarmac and climbed into the air, it banked left and flew off into the distance.

Adam slowly removed the glasses. Michelle could see the look of shock and disbelief on his face, slowly turn to one of anger.

The realisation came to him that there was no task force. 'What the bloody hell is going on?' he said 'I need to get hold of Ray Mellor's double-quick.'

Michelle turned sharply from viewing the sky where the plane had been and said 'Do you mean Ray Mellors from the Home Office?'

'Yes. Why, do you know him?' said Adam selecting his number on the phone.

'Oh no Adam!' she said with dismay.

'What's the matter?'

'Ray Mellors is one of Lawrence's cronies. He's been to several of the dinner parties over the last couple of years, and I have often overheard Lawrence on the phone to him. They sounded as thick as thieves. I'm so sorry, Adam.'

Adam pressed the dial button anyway but was not surprised when there was no reply. It didn't even go to answerphone. 'The bastard!' he said exasperation in his voice. 'He will pay for this.'

Michelle looked at a furious Adam and kept quiet sensing that now was not the time for discussion. She simply said quietly 'let's get back to the car.'

He did not reply just set off back across the field with grim determination.

By the time they got back to the car, he had decided on a plan of action. They got in and set off back to the A11.

Once ready to talk, Adam said 'Okay, this is the plan.'

Michelle sat up, attentively in her seat.

'The only person that I have left to trust in all of this is Ben Gifford, he's a senior police officer in Special Branch and a pal of Julian's,' he explained to Michelle to which she nodded not wishing to interrupt his flow.

'I'm going to call him shortly and fill him in with the entire story. I'll send him the pictures incriminating Gorton-Hyde and Bolton. Then he can organise the arrest warrants. I'll also ask him to get hold of NATS, I can't believe that there isn't some sort of flight plan lodged with them. However secretive the flight might be. Even the RAF must let NATS know when they're in commercial airspace,' he stated.

'Once we know where the Hercules is landing, that's where we'll be going. However, I'm going to need some help as there's a strong likelihood that we'll end up in Afghanistan.'

Michelle was aware that Adam was just using her as a sounding board, but that was fine, so she kept on nodding in agreement.

He continued 'I guess Harry at Comm -Sec can help with the air transport. I'll need to get hold of Charlie and Matt to see if they are up for it. One of Charlie's merc pals will help out with some kit and an additional seven personnel with a bit of luck. How does that sound?' He said to himself, really.

Michelle replied 'Sounds great to me bearing in mind that I haven't a clue who or what you're talking about.'

Adam looked blankly at her then laughed 'Sorry I was thinking aloud, but will you help me organise things on this side?'

'Yes, of course. I've nothing else to do but go back to an empty house in Reading, sort out a divorce and start a new life. But that can definitely wait.' Besides, she thought to herself I will be coming with you. She knew that there was no way Adam would want to take her, but she would deal with that issue later.

Adam called Ben Gifford first and gave him the full story he also sent him the pics from his phone. Ben confirmed that he would get on the case immediately and put together a warrant for Bolton. Still, he was going to need more evidence before going after Gorton- Hyde. He would also get hold of NATS and come back with a destination for the Hercules, its tail number was on the pics that Adam had sent.

Next Adam called Charlie Hislop whom he hadn't seen since their chat in a camp hospital in Afghanistan.

'Hi, Charlie?'

'Yes. Is that you, Sir?'

'I've told you about the Sir thing, Charlie. How are you?'

'Fit as a fiddle thanks, Adam. More importantly, how are you?'

'A hell of a lot better than I was thanks, Charlie. I'm looking for a favour.'

'Just name it.'

Michelle, who was listening to the conversation on the car speaker, was impressed by the apparent respect this man had for Adam.

'I want you and Matt to help out with an extraction, in Afghanistan, obviously a private job. A pal of mine has been abducted, but it's all a bit complicated, and I can't trust the legitimate channels to get him out. We'll meet some organised resistance, but a dozen of us should handle it.'

'Sounds like fun, Capt... er Adam.' he said, forgetting himself again.

'Do you think Matt will be interested?'

'Yeah, he's spent most of his time on quality control at the local pub since we got out.'

Adam laughed, and Michelle stifled a laugh in case he heard her.

'I should let you know that there is a lady in the car that can hear every word just in case your language gets any fruitier.'

'Poor woman, what's she done to deserve that,' joked Charlie.

'Someone has to keep him under control Charlie,' said Michelle joining in the banter.

'You must be a formidable lady. I look forward to meeting you.'

'Me to Charlie.'

Adam cut in 'that's enough of the mutual admiration you two. Charlie this is a short turnaround I'm looking to be off first thing tomorrow morning. Michelle's brother Frank was murdered by the same team that has my pal, Julian. They put an Arab ceremonial knife in his chest. They're already on their way over there.'

'Christ, Adam. I'm sorry to hear that, Michelle.'

'I also need you to contact one of your merc friends. Jack Taylor might be best, he'll do anything for cash. We'll need some kit and 7 additional personnel.'

'Will do Adam, yeah Jacks still out there. Do you have a budget yet, and where are we meeting?'

'I'll have to come back to you on both, once my secretary here has organised a hotel for tonight, but it will most probably be near Stanstead.'

Michelle immediately started Googling hotels in the Stanstead area for four rooms for that night.

'I'll text you with Matt's confirmation. Cheers for now.'

Adams next call was to Harry at Comm-Sec. After his usual flirtation with Margaret, which Michelle enjoyed overhearing much to Adams embarrassment, he got through.

'Hi, Harry.'

'Adam, are you recovering okay?'

'Well about that Harry, I haven't really given you the full story, but I'm going to now.' he said apologetically.

'Okay Adam, shoot, I'm all ears.'

Adam proceeded to relay the pertinent bits of the story to Harry. When he'd finished, it was quiet for a moment at the other end of the phone.

'Crickey Adam, you've gotten mixed up in a real mess by the sounds of it and your friend is definitely not in a good place. Bolton isn't a man to cross especially as he has already got Julian out of the country. I guess you are calling me for some assistance so what can I do?'

'You're a good man Harry. My intention is to get Julian out and at the same time do as much damage as possible to Bolton's operation. Some of my old team are helping with personnel and kit, but we need to get out there within the next 24 hours. My questions are. Do you still use the private charter jet out of Stanstead to visit foreign clients? Also, and I know this is a big ask Harry, could you set up a flight to Afghanistan for some time tomorrow?'

'Blimey, you don't want much. I'll have to have a word with the boss man, but I guess I can set something up. We're overdue for a courtesy visit to one of our clients in Saudi. We could stop to refuel on the way if you see what I mean. But Afghanistan is a big place you'll need to give me a stop-off destination.'

'That's great, Harry, I'll come back to you with our destination shortly. I'm just waiting to hear from someone with the details.'

'Okay, how many seats do you need?'

'Three please.'

Adam suddenly exclaimed 'Ouch' as Michelle nipped his thigh and vigorously pointed at herself. He shook his head equally vigorously.

'You got someone else in the car, Adam?'

'Yes, Harry. Frank Patterson's sister, Michelle.' Harry had joined Adam and Frank for the occasional beer in the past.

'Hello Harry, I will need a seat as well,' Michelle said aloud.

'No you won't,' insisted Adam 'I am not taking you to a war zone.'

'Yes I will,' she said equally insistent.

Harry butted in 'It sounds like you've got your hands full there Adam, just confirm the passenger list and destination later today.'

'Will do, speak later, Harry.'

Adam turned to Michelle and raising his voice said 'What the hell Michelle? You have no idea what you are suggesting. This is not a tourist trip. There are no rules out there just a lot of crazy people with guns and bombs. Bolton will not just handover Julian to us we'll have to take him which means armed conflict. I don't need the extra worry of keeping you safe.'

Michelle turned slowly to face him her cheeks now flushed red with anger and said slowly with equal volume 'I am not a fool Adam. I'm well aware that this needs to be a military operation and I've no experience in such things. However, I am my own person, and I want to see that my brother's murderer gets what is coming to him. I'm also partly responsible for Julian's current position. We both know that he wouldn't be in the hold of that plane if you hadn't come to my rescue. Despite needing to be rescued, I'm not some feeble damsel in distress. I'm much more capable than you think and also a bloody good spotter, which I guess you will need.'

Outburst ended, she turned her head away and stared straight ahead at the windscreen and became quiet.

Her passionate display gave Adam pause for thought. After sitting in silence for five minutes, he said quietly 'I'm sorry for raising my voice, Michelle. I appreciate your reasons for wanting to do this, but your life would definitely be in danger. However, as you say, it is your own life, and you're right, I may well need a spotter. If you were to come along, it could only be with the agreement of Charlie and Matt. It wouldn't be fair of me to expect them to accept responsibility for a non-pro in the team without consultation and agreement. I'll book four seats on the flight, and we can discuss the matter with the lads tonight.'

'Thank you, Adam, that means a lot to me,' she replied in a conciliatory tone. 'I'm sorry for being such a diva. It really isn't like me. But I do feel strongly about this.'

'Yes, I got that,' he replied. 'Hey, have we just had our first row?' he said jovially.

'I guess we have,' she replied, laughing. 'We should probably kiss and make up.'

Adam blushed 'No time for that sort of thing.'

She leant across and kissed him on his cheek and said 'that'll have to do for now.'

He continued to blush and focused on the road ahead. Suddenly the phone rang. *Saved by the bell*, he thought. It was Ben calling.

'Adam, I've got the destination for the Hercules they are landing at Darwaz private airport in Afghanistan, ETA 4.00pm today.'

'That's great thanks, Ben. How are things going with Gorton-Hyde?'

'He's booked on a flight to Paris tomorrow evening. Needless to say, we'll be right behind him.'

'Yes, my guess would be that he's meeting to collect payment for the supplies once delivery has been confirmed. As they are going to Southern

Afghanistan, we have to assume that the weapons are destined for the Taliban. I would love to know who is paying for them. I guess Gorton-Hyde will have bought them from the Russians for next to nothing. They'll be only too keen to see further disruption in the area so his profit margin will no doubt be substantial.'

'I'm sure you're right, but this is all getting a bit above my pay grade, Adam, eventually I'm going to have to notify the Foreign Minister.'

'I completely understand Ben but can you please just wait another 48 hours so that we can extract Julian. Hopefully, you can catch Gorton-Hyde with his hand in the till? We just don't know who else he has on his payroll at the FO.'

'Okay 48 hours it is, but I will need to bring MI5 in for the operation in Paris. If we pull this off, I'll be a hero, on the other hand, if we don't I'll probably lose my pension.'

'Don't worry, this is not our first rodeo. Just keep me up to speed with developments if you would and of course let me know as soon as the trap is sprung. That way we can ensure that the same thing happens at the dirty end before they realise. Best contact me by secure email with any updates. I don't know where I might be and who with'.

'Will do,' the call ended.

Adam immediately called Harry with the necessary details.

'The nearest we can land is Qala Nau International at Kandahar on a refuel basis, leaving Stanstead at 6.00am tomorrow, landing at 11.00am,' said Harry.

'That's fine Harry leave the Kandahar end to me. We'll meet you at Stanstead in the morning. It will be four seats unless anything changes tonight.'

'I thought it might be,' said Harry wryly.

Michelle hid her grin from Adam and concentrated on her smartphone, making the room bookings at the Premier Inn at Stanstead.

'Four rooms booked for tonight at the Stanstead Premier Adam.'

'Great stuff.'

Suddenly Adam's phone buzzed with an incoming text.

'Please could you read that out whilst I'm driving? It will be Charlie.'

Michelle took the phone and read from the screen:

'A'

'Spoken to JT and he confirmed 6 assets available tomorrow AM so 1 short. I have provided provisional kit requirements pending available budget. Kit, transport and assets coming in at £250k at the moment. MW confirmed. Please confirm the budget ASAP.'

'C'

'Good news and bad news there, it seems. Kit and men are available, albeit one short but about £150K over my budget. Bugger.'

Michelle pondered for a moment 'I know this might not sit well with you, but I'd like to contribute to this venture financially.'

'It wouldn't be my first choice, but as I can't get hold of Julian for assistance, my options are minimal.' He glanced across at her. 'What's your proposal?'

'I have over £1.5 million sitting in my bank account which, by the way, Lawrence cannot access. It's available to you. Its money that I have saved over the last thirteen years. From the, ridiculously large allowance Lawrence provided. It was to ensure that I was always 'presentable' and suitably 'bejewelled', when *on show* with him. I didn't receive any adverse comments regarding my appearance and certainly did not find it necessary to spend such large amounts.'

'Good for you.'

'If you only need £150K that's fine, but you're welcome to whatever you need. As I mentioned before, this mission is important to me. My guess is that the better the tools, the more likely a successful outcome.'

Adam glanced across at her and said 'You're right of course on all counts and I've no choice but to accept your offer. Thank you, Michelle.'

'Should I confirm the budget to Charlie?'

'Yes please, just say £250K budget confirmed and ensure that the L115 is included plus sighting scope, meet 5.00pm tonight at Stanstead Premier.'

Michelle sent the text, and a thumbs-up emoji came back immediately.

As everything now seemed to be in place, they both sat quietly for the rest of the journey each contemplating what the coming 24 hours might bring. Adam wondered what Julian's condition might be. Michelle considered where her brother's body was, and if she would get to bury him with dignity at some point.

They arrived at the Stanstead Premier Inn in a sombre mood at 4.30pm.

After ordering a coffee at the bar, they sat near the window and waited for Charlie and Matt to arrive.

On the dot of 5.00pm, Adam said 'Here they are, just parking over there,' he pointed out of the window.

Michelle suddenly felt a little excitement in her stomach as if she were meeting some old friends. Which she thought was a bit odd as she had never met these two gruff-looking ex-soldiers before. She hoped that they would become friends.

They went into the lobby to meet them. The men shook hands and clapped each other on the shoulders exchanging playful banter. Adam introduced Michelle 'This is Lady Michelle Gorton-Hyde.'

'That's a bit formal, Adam,' she said 'Just Michelle is fine thanks. Charlie and Matt, isn't it?'

Both men were surprised to see the attractive women with Adam.

'Yes Mam er Michelle I mean,' said Charlie as he shook her hand.

Matt also shook hands.

They checked into the hotel, fortunate to get four rooms next to each other.

'We'll meet in my room in 30 minutes for a briefing,' said Adam.

'Will do Sir,' said Matt.

'For god sake drop the 'Sir', Matt.'

'Old habits, Adam.'

'Charlie, we'll need the list of kit and a rendezvous plan for Kandahar Airport.'

'Will do Adam, I'll contact Jack.'

They went to their respective rooms, Adam and Michelle were both desperate for showers after the previous night's events.

Half an hour later, they all gathered in Adams room. Sitting on beds and chairs with Michelle now looking a little less like a commando having changed into a blouse and applied a little makeup. She had also brought a book of lined A4 paper and a pen to take some notes. Charlie passed the kit list to Adam which contained everything from uniforms for the three men, sidearms, automatic rifles, grenades, C4 explosives and claymore mines. Also a full comms pack and of course Adam's L115 and sighting scope.

Adam looked over the list and handed it to Michelle then cleared his throat 'Thanks Charlie this looks fine, but before we go any further, we need to discuss something. As you can see, we have Michelle with us, and she is helping with the mission set up. I am proposing that she become part of the team and come with us on the mission.'

Both men looked at Adam with surprise and avoided eye contact with Michelle.

Adam continued 'I know that this is not protocol, but this is not exactly a military operation, so the choice is ours. Michelle does have some firearms experience and is an excellent spotter. I think I am right in saying that she has gained some rough terrain experience from time spent in Cambodia and Vietnam.' He looked at Michelle for confirmation.

'Yes, it was over 20 years ago, but I learnt to take care of myself whilst out there with my brother, Frank.'

Charlie had already told Matt about Frank's demise.

'However, she doesn't have any military or combat experience and is at best a capable civilian. Therefore Michelle will only be accompanying us if you two agree.'

Adam gave Michelle a reassuring wink as Charlie and Matt looked at each other.

Matt was the first to speak and said 'It's fine by me.'

After a moments pondering Charlie said with some resignation in his voice 'Well, if you are happy about this Adam then I guess I am.'

'Thank you both,' said Michelle 'I will make sure that you don't regret your decision.' She focused her words on Charlie as it was clear that he was not entirely committed to the idea.

'I didn't mention this before to avoid influencing your decision, but Michelle has also contributed £150K to the mission budget with the offer of more if needed.'

'Okay, now that's out of the way, let's get some sort of operational plan together. If you could take care of the notes please Michelle. Charlie, can you liaise with Michelle over the budget management and payment transfers? Matt, would you see to the transport and the briefing for the six guys joining us at the other end?'

They nodded their agreement.

Adam continued 'Charlie, can you give us the initial brief?'

'Yes, Adam. Our ETA at Qala Nau is 11:00 hours tomorrow on a refuel basis, so we will have to disembark swiftly. Jacks men will meet us there, they'll have greased the necessary palms to afford us a back door exit from the airport. Once outside they'll transport us to their nearest camp where Michelle and I'll check off the uniform and equipment inventory. Matt will check over the transport and fuel. We'll then change into our working gear, check our individual weapons and ammunition. When all is present and correct the final payment to Jack will be made. I will make the necessary internet transfer along with Michelle, I guess. Whilst this is being completed, Matt will carry out the mission briefing with the merc team. Once all of this is completed, we'll be ready to move out. Over to you, Adam.'

'Very good Charlie.' Adam nodded to him, pleased to hear that he was readily involving Michelle. Although, under no illusion that he was not happy with the arrangement.

'This is where it gets tricky as Intel is sparse. All we know is that Bolton's team is landing in Southern Afghanistan. Which is a pretty big place. There are plenty of secluded spots for arms transfers to be carried out in the Helmand Province, and the place is crawling with Taliban. On the plus side, we're looking for a pretty big cargo load, common sense says that we should head west towards their landing destination. I know we've been out of it for nearly two years, but if possible we should pick up with any local contacts that are still around for information. I'll speak to Jack in the hope that he might be able to tell us something. Once we locate the transfer venue, our first objective is to extract Julian then destroy the weapons cargo. However, we have to coordinate this carefully with a joint operation in Europe. The mission is fluid due to the lack of Intel, and so is the exit strategy. At the moment we will plan to head for Camp Shorabak. Camp Bastion as was,' he said for Michelle's benefit. 'Any questions?' Adam said in a tone that expected none.

Michelle looked up from her notes at the stone-like faces of the three men. After hearing the contents of Adams military-style briefing, she felt nervous for the first time since suggesting that she join them.

Both men shook their heads.

'I have one,' said Michelle.

All three men turned to her with raised eyebrows.

'When do we deal with Lewis Bolton?'

'At an opportune moment,' said Adam' and if one doesn't arise, we will make one,' he said grimly.

She nodded slowly.

'I suggest we all go and have a wash and brush up then we will go and get some steak and chips at the restaurant next door before an early night,' he said in lighter tones 'see you in the bar in twenty minutes. The first round is on me.'

They got up and returned to their respective rooms.

Later that evening they all enjoyed some food

and wine though not to excess. Adam noticed that Charlie was somewhat subdued. He would have to find a way to ease his resentment of Michelle's involvement in the mission.

They were all back in their beds by 10.00pm.

Adam's head gratefully hit the pillow for the first time in thirty-six hours. He lay there in the darkness mulling over the crazy sequence of events of the last few days that had brought him to a return to Afghanistan, essentially as an unpaid mercenary.

As his mind was beginning to drift off to sleep, he heard a slight click of his bedroom door then felt a movement under the duvet. He thought he must be dreaming as he felt Michelle's soft, warm flesh against his naked skin. Her perfumed arms and legs wrapped around his body. He turned and drew her towards him, feeling her naked breasts against his chest. He kissed her tenderly on the lips. They made love without saying a word. Slowly and passionately. It was as if they had known each other many times before, without strangers' awkwardness and with the consideration of true lovers. Then they fell asleep in each other's arms.

Adam awoke at 3.00am and lay there looking at her, carefully brushing the blond hair away from her beautiful face, which expressed the innocence of sleep. He had never been a promiscuous man, and the few relationships he'd experienced were long term and generally ended by the female party. He was wary of starting a new one, but last night had felt so natural that he hoped for more. Eventually, she stirred and opened her eyes immediately murmuring and cuddling up closer to him with her head on his chest.

'Mmmm that was nice,' she said.

'Yes, it was,' he replied softly 'I hope it wasn't a singular performance?'

'Certainly not,' she replied 'we have another half hour before we need to get up.'

They made love again with a little more vigour this time before Michelle kissed him, got out of the bed and slid on her dressing gown.

'I'd better get back to my room in case the guys are about, probably best to keep this to ourselves until the mission is over.'

'I'm pleased to hear that you're planning on more of 'this',' he smiled at her.

'I most certainly am Captain Crest,' she grinned back at him.

'Hey! How did you get in here last night?' he said with mock objection.

'I pinched your spare key-card when we were in the briefing yesterday. See, I'm not without skills.' she laughed as she left the room.

CHAPTER 14

Tuesday 8.00 AM - 2019

The first sensation that Julian felt was a dull ache inside his head and soreness to the back of his skull just above his collar line. There was a constant clattering going on all around him. As far as he could tell in the pitch darkness, he was in some sort of metal container which was, in turn, being pitched up and down and side to side. He tried to lift his head, but the sharpness of the pain to the back of his skull was unbearable. He lowered it back to the cold metal floor.

Whilst jostling around, he attempted to bring his arms from behind him only to discover a new sort of pain where the nylon ties had cut into his wrists. He also became aware of the lack of feeling in his feet which were also secured by over-tightened nylon ties. They had been placed around his bare ankles. The hard plastic had already cut through the skin, which was bleeding freely.

He tried to clear his head, amidst the cacophony and the pain. Gradually his memory returned to him. With it, the realisation that he must have been captured by Bolton's men and thrown into the back of one of the weapons containers. As this reality came to him, the truck hit a pothole or something similar, causing Julian's battered head to bounce hard on the metal floor. He was unconscious once again.

His next awareness was of being slapped across the face and the sound of an unfriendly voice shouting at him 'Wake up you Pratt!!'

A shaft of daylight streamed through the half-open metal door blinding Julian even through squinting eyes. He immediately put his right hand up to protect his face from further assaults and in doing so found that his hands were no longer bound.

'You're awake, about bloody time. There's some food and water on the floor next to you. Best eat up as we don't want you popping off halfway there, do we?' said the voice, laden with sarcasm.

Julian's hazy thoughts fought their way through the banging pain in his head, and he croaked 'Where am I? Please can you release my ankles, I can't feel my feet?'

'Tough shit,' sneered the man in the leather jacket.

The big metal door slammed shut, and Julian heard the bolt being slid back into place. Once again, he was in complete darkness. He quickly fumbled around on the floor next to him, not wishing to lose the food and water, which he clutched to his chest.

He ate the sandwich and drank half of the water. He felt a little better after that but the aches and pains all over his body, from the constant bashing it had received during the journey so far, soon returned. 'I must be covered in bruises,' he said into the pitch darkness. Leaning forward, he reached the end of his legs to loosen the ties around his ankles. A searing pain ran through his calves, he winced. The straps had cut into the flesh. He could feel the sticky dampness on the material of his jeans which he guessed was blood. Tentatively he moved his hands up to his shins and could feel the swelling on both legs above the ties, yet he could feel nothing of his feet.

My god they must've cut off the blood supply to my feet, he thought fearfully. He knew that he would not be able to stand, let alone walk even if he got the chance.

Shuffling back, he leant against the metal of the container. Sitting in the blackness, his thoughts became clearer, and he pushed away the fears that were creeping into his brain. He had worked out that he had been jumped by one of Bolton's men and thrown into one of the containers. This meant that he was probably on his way to the trade-off venue wherever that may be. Presumably, he was being held as some sort of security against the success of the weapons deal.

This gave him some comfort as he was less likely to be killed if he had some value which also explained the food and water. There was further consolation in the thought that Adam would not leave him to die. I'm sure he's already on the way to save the day, he thought, that's assuming he can find me.

'Oh shit,' he said out loud as he suddenly remembered that they were heading for an airfield. As if to confirm his fears, there came a sudden deafened sound as the engines started on the Hercules transport plane. He felt the motion as it began to roll forward gathering speed on its journey down the runway.

After several moments, the engine revs surged. The container walls began to vibrate as the giant plane suddenly lurched upwards. Julian was unprepared for this, and his body was flung about like a rag doll. Crashing against the metal wall at the back, he managed to provide some protection to his head now that his hands were free. Still, he cried out in pain as his bleeding ankles smashed against the hard surface.

As the plane levelled off, he could not see in the darkness, and he fell back to the floor with a bang, his face struck the corrugated steel. He moved his hand up to his nose and mouth where he could feel the flowing blood, he could also taste the sticky liquid's saltiness in his mouth.

Oh god, I hope my teeth aren't broken, he thought to himself.

His best bet was to lie still as the plane had settled into a level flight path and just hope that there wasn't any turbulence. Easing off his trainers, he managed to relieve some of the pressure on his swelling bare feet. Unfortunately, he had lost track of the water bottle and had no chance of finding it in the darkness so was likely to become thirsty in the next few hours. He lay still and began to feel a little sorry for himself.

After some considerable time, he guessed at about five hours. He noticed that the container's temperature was increasing and the numbing cold was disappearing. He'd worked out by now that they were most likely heading for Afghanistan or possibly Syria.

He was becoming fearful. He knew that the Arab males were not known for their care and understanding towards Europeans. Particularly where gay men were concerned.

The engines changed tone as the plane slowed down for decent and there was a whirring noise from the undercarriage motors as the wheels started to come down. Suddenly there was the sound of metal grinding on itself, and the plane juddered as one of the wheels tried without success to exit the body of the aircraft. A loud crack followed as if something had snapped.

Julian, who wasn't the most mechanically minded, worked out that at least one set of undercarriage had not descended. In the darkness and unable to stand up, he couldn't do much to brace himself. He did his best to curl up into a foetal position. He closed his eyes and hoped for the best as the plane continued to drop from the skies.

There was an almost eerie stillness as the engines were cut back. A few seconds later a thud as the right-hand side underage wheel hit the runway followed by an almighty crash when the left-wing hit the ground.

Inside the container, Julian was launched from the floor and hit the ceiling hard then plummeted back to the floor headfirst, which once again rendered him unconscious. The plane spun on its fractured wing eventually coming to a grinding halt amidst the clouds of dust and sand.

The next thing Julian knew he was back to being jostled about presumably travelling on the flatbed truck again. The container had now become a sweatbox as the Arab sun baked down on it. He feebly stuck out his hands like a blind man patting at the floor in the vain hope of finding the half-empty water bottle but to no avail.

After several hours of road travel, they finally came to a stop. Julian could hear a lot of shouting outside of the container, a mixture of guttural sounding Arabic and some English voices. Suddenly he heard the steel bolt being slid across. The door was flung open, and the bright lights of several torches pierced his eyes. He immediately screwed them shut to keep out the light.

The man in the leather jacket, Bolton and a couple of local Arabs looked down at the pathetic form. Dishevelled, covered in blood and sweat. His face was pale and drawn. His nose and mouth bloody and bruised, lips dry and cracked. He was on his knees, his hands held up in front of his eyes to protect from the torchlight.

The men stood for a moment looking at him then, almost simultaneously, they all burst out laughing. Julian curled up into his foetal position once again fearing a kicking.

'What a fucking state, he looks like he's done ten rounds with Mike Tyson,' observed leather jacket in between guffaws.

The 2 Arabs replied with something in excitable Pashto.

Bolton brought the laughter to a close with a raised hand and said loudly 'Right, you've had a laugh now get him out and clean him up.' He grabbed leather jacket by the shoulder and continued emphatically 'get him tidied up, fed and watered and don't forget we need him alive. Well at least until Thursday morning. DO YOU GET ME BRAD?'

Brad stopped laughing and replied sheepishly 'Yes, boss, I'll sort it.'

'Stick him in one of the rooms upstairs in the house,' said Bolton pointing to the single-story white building set in the remote desert area, surrounded by a 3-meter high wall.

'I'm going to contact our friends at Now Zad and let them know that we have arrived at Tall Kala. I'll leave you to deal with this Brad,' Bolton glared at Brad as he did not have much faith in his abilities. He went off to make his call.

Once Bolton had disappeared into the blackness of the desert night, Brad started to shout at the 2 Afghanis. He was aware that even with their limited understanding of the English language, they would've worked out that Bolton had demeaned him in front of them. 'You heard what he said, get him out and take him into the house, Yalla …. Yalla … Imshi,' Brad said gesticulating at Julian.

The 2 men climbed inside the container and took Julian's arms. They dragged him out and threw him off the back of the truck onto the desert floor. He cried out as his battered body hit the hard sandy surface.

'For Christ sake, be careful we need him in one peace,' shouted Brad. He knew that they wouldn't understand half of what he had said, but they'd got the drift. The 2 men once again grabbed one of Julian's arms each but this time a little less roughly and dragged him slowly towards the building face down.

Whilst they seemed to be taking some care, it was little consolation to Julian. His blood covered legs and feet were still bound by the nylon ties and battered against stony ground. Once away from the trucks, they moved through the darkness, which gave his eyes time to recover. When he managed to raise his head, he could see they were heading towards some opened doubled gates at the building's front. Illuminated by one external spotlight. His head dropped again as he was dragged across the courtyard and into the building.

They passed through the living area in the house, he could see that it was furnished with several low couches and an old wooden table in the middle of the room. There were automatic weapons scattered all over the floor. A wooden staircase ascended from this room to the first floor sleeping quarters.

Five or six fellow Afghans sat around two of them on mobile phones. The others shouted comments to the men dragging Julian across the room, referencing their sorry-looking burden. They returned comments at an equally high volume.

Brad interrupted the banter 'Alright, alright, let's get him upstairs, Yalla, Imshi,' he once again shouted and pointed at the stairs. The two men proceeded to drag Julian up with his feet banging on the hard wooden steps. He let out a gasp of pain at each one until they reached the top.

Looking up, he saw that they were on a corridor running right and left with several doors off it. They turned left and took him to the last room, and opened the door, dragged him across the ill-fitting floorboards. He was dumped unceremoniously in the corner of the empty room.

'Get a bucket of water and some clothes, then clean him up,' commanded Brad. The two men looked at him blankly, so Brad repeated himself, adding some hand gestures to make himself understood. He left the room having lost patience with the 2 Afghans.

One of the men fetched a metal bucket filled with water and some stained rags that passed for towels. They both stood in sinister silence over Julian. As far as they were concerned, all white men were Americans, and all Americans deserved to die slowly. Now that they were no longer under Brad's watchful eye, they felt at liberty to express themselves. One of them looked down at the blood-soaked jeans and kicked Julian's tethered ankles causing him to cry out. His nicotine coated teeth were revealed as he grinned.

The other swung his booted foot into Julian's stomach then picked up the bucket and threw its contents into his face. Julian took a shocked intake of breath which almost choked him. Both men laughed loudly. They threw the rags at him then turned and left the room, locking the door behind them.

Once they'd gone Julian slumped back into the corner. After he got his breath back, he began to rub the blood from his hands, wrists and face with the rags which smelt disgusting. He tried his best not to think about what they had been used for previously.

He attempted to straighten up his clothes and make the most of his appearance for no other reason than to make himself feel better. He didn't touch his lower legs as the pain had subsided, and he had no wish to aggravate the wounds. He did, however, draw up his jeans and could see the swellings above and below the ligature. There was a mixture of dried and fresh blood around both ankles. He slid the trouser legs back down, rested his head back against the wall and closed his eyes. Exhausted, he slept for what was left of Tuesday night.

CHAPTER 15

Wednesday 5.30 AM - 2019

Adam and his team headed for the airport where they met up with Harry. After the necessary introductions, they boarded the small private jet. Adam deliberately pointed Michelle towards the seat next to Charlie, hoping that she could soften his attitude towards her during the flight, he sat next to Harry. He felt he owed him a bit more of an explanation as to why they were going out there. He also thought that Harry may have picked up some local info since they last spoke. Anything would be useful.

After the previous night events, Adam and Michelle kept the knowing looks and smiles to a minimum during the flight, but one or two could not be helped.

It turned out that Harry knew a friendly local, an officer in the Afghan National Army, based at camp Shorabak, Colonel Jamil Karak. He gave Adam the contact details.

'Colonel Karak knows of a large arms deal that's expected to happen in Helmand province shortly,' said Harry. 'Of course, Helmand is a big place with plenty of mountains to hide in. You're going to need some luck locating the transfer spot. At least you know which direction to head. Colonel Karak will be keen to stop any further arms going to the Taliban. After all, it would be his men that they're used against, so you should find him helpful, at least to a point.

'Can I contact this guy for more info?' Asked Adam

'Not only can you, but you'll also have to. Don't forget we Brits no longer have an active military presence in his country. Apart from the occasional covert stuff that your old muckers get up to and some training support, there is no British military presence. You'll need to arrange a meet up to pay your dues ASAP, or you might find that they kick you out,' said Harry emphatically.

'Point taken Harry. How much does he know?'

'I'm not really sure. He's a good guy but plays his cards close to his chest. He certainly knows about the shipment and the hostage situation. He'd dearly like to know who is buying these weapons. I guess he'll have more info by the time you get to him.'

'Let's hope so,' Adam replied.

Turning his head, Adam could see how Michelle was getting on with Charlie. He was relieved to find that she was working her magic on him as they were both chuckling at something. That's good news, he thought I don't need any additional tension in the team.

Having chatted to Harry Adam then left his seat to join Matt, who was sitting on his own. They hadn't had much time to talk, so it was an excellent opportunity for a little bonding.

'Hi Matt, sorry I haven't had much of a chance to chat with everything happening so quickly.'

'That's alright boss, it sounds like you've had a crazy few days.'

'That's true, Matt, but I'd like to thank you for your loyalty in just jumping in like this. Just so you know you and Charlie will get full merc's rates for the job.'

'I appreciate that boss, and I can't deny that the money will come in handy, but that's not really why I came along. I just don't fit life in Civi Street, and I'm not a natural for the mercenaries, so I'm at a bit of a loose end.'

Adam knew exactly what he meant. This was a common difficulty. So many men and women had risked their lives for their country only to arrive home as misfits to society. The training and way of life that had conditioned them into becoming such effective fighting machines often prevented them from re-joining the very people and community they were defending. A cruel irony and a sad comment on the human condition that not enough is done to correct the problem.

'We'll have a chat after this job Matt and see what can be done, I work with Harry in the security industry, so you never know.'

'Thanks, boss, we'll do that.'

'Back to the job though Matt, we need a good Armoured Personnel Carrier for this. I don't suppose Jack Taylor will supply us with a Titan 6x6, but we need something similar. When we get to the mercenary base camp, I want you to have a good look around and get the best available vehicle.'

'You know me, boss, if it's there we will have it and at the right price.'

'I know Matt, I can rely on you. I think I'll try for a kip we've got another two hours yet.'

'Me to,' agreed Matt.

They both put their seats back and closed their eyes.

Adams mind wandered to the difficulties and dangers that lay before them, he knew that the lads could look after themselves. Still, he was going to have to keep Michelle close by when things got heated. He was very fond of her and found it difficult to separate his emotions and retain a professional detachment. This distraction was new to him and not a situation that he was comfortable with.

It was not going to be easy discovering Bolton's destination, and god knows what Julian was being subjected to during all of this time. He thought of his friend being beaten up, and he knew that Julian would not do well. But Julian was a strong-willed character, which would help him survive, depending on the ordeal's severity. He was going to have to harden himself to the personal considerations of both Michelle and Julian, to ensure that his decision making was not compromised.

He hoped that the men Jack Taylor was sending would be good quality as some mercenaries can be nothing more than trained thugs. He needed people that could think for themselves.

Locating Julian was going to be tricky, but Colonel Karak may be able to help with that. His first job would be to call him and see if there was an update on the convoy's position and get any pointers on potential handover locations. It was also worth trying to get some manpower support although he didn't really expect to. The Afghan military was not always well disposed to assisting British troops, especially unofficial ones. The Afghan army was already spread pretty thin as the Taliban had increased its power and presence in the area ever since the British had left.

For their mission to be a complete success, they could not afford to alert Bolton or Gorton-Hyde to their presence. Gorton-Hyde was obviously the organiser and profiteer. It was a safe bet that the arms were coming from Ukraine. There must also be a string of corrupt civil servants from government offices to the Police and Military involved in making this thing happen.

Adam dozed off but was awoken fifteen minutes later. The monotonous drone of the twin jets changed in tone when the plane began its descent into Qala Nau airport.

He sat up in his seat and turned to his three colleagues, noting that Michelle and Charlie seemed to have become firm friends, and were still chatting away.

'Is everybody wide awake and ready to go?' Before anyone could answer, he said 'Charlie what's the form on landing?'

'The plane will stay out on the strip and a fuel truck will approach to replenish the tanks accompanied by a covered wagon for security. The tanker will hook up to the plane, and the other vehicle will park next to it. We'll disembark to the wagon's side, keeping out of view from the main building and climb in the back. No one will speak to us we'll simply be driven to the outskirts of the airfield. The truck stops, and we jump out. Then we exit through a pre-formed gap in the perimeter wire where some of Jack's men will pick us up and take us to their HQ.'

'Sounds nice and simple, I like it. Is everybody clear?'

They all nodded although Michelle was a little wide-eyed.

'Just stay next to me,' he muttered to her and winked reassuringly. She smiled back at him.

Adam went over to Harry's seat, thanked him for all that he had done and promised that he would be back to work next week.

'Let's hope so,' Harry replied and slipped a small package to him surreptitiously. 'Just in case.'

'We'll be fine,' said Adam and put the package in his jacket pocket.

Once on the ground everyone removed their seat belts and looked out of the windows for a sight of the refuelling tanker and its companion. It would be fair to say that they were all a little tense waiting for them to appear even Harry, who wasn't even on the mission.

The trucks came into view, and once they had pulled up, Harry got out to speak to the refueller. Whilst talking to him, he gestured behind his back to the others to get over to the truck.

'Charlie and Matt first. Go,' Adam said quietly

and grabbed Michelle's elbow, steering her towards the steps to exit the plane.

The sudden heat came as no surprise to the three men. Still, Michelle felt the change from a rainy 10 degrees in England to the oppressively sunny 40 degrees on the airstrip. It was like opening an oven door and sticking your head in it.

She followed her instructions and stuck to Adam as they quickly walked to the rear of the truck. The door was held open by an Afghan airport employee, who'd presumably been well paid, and they climbed inside. They sat quietly as the truck set off across the airfield in no particular hurry. Tension returned to the team, listening for any external shouts or, god forbid, gunfire as they progressed to the perimeter.

They arrived without incident and swiftly disembarked the truck. A few yards away, one of Jack Taylor's men could be seen waving them over to the gap in the perimeter fence. The four of them approached in silence and passed through.

'Go down the hill and get into the 4X4 that's waiting there,' instructed the mercenary soldier.

The four made their way down the reddish-brown rocks that were typical of the Arabian terrain. Adam gestured to Michelle to stay behind him as the footing could be a little insecure. To his surprise, she simply ran passed him. She negotiated the rocky hill with the speed and agility of a mountain goat arriving at the bottom before any of them. 'Point taken,' he muttered to himself.

They all scrambled into the sandy coloured Military Personnel Vehicle, and it sped off towards the distant hills. Once clear of the airfield introductions were made. All on a first name basis apart from Adam. Who was still referred to as Captain even in this unregulated force.

The three men that had joined them were Carl, Wayne and Mark, all of whom seemed to be on the ball and amiable. Carl was the team leader.

'Wayne, Mark and I will be sticking with you for the mission, and we'll pick three more guys when we get to the camp Captain Crest,' said Carl.

'Sounds good, Carl. We can drop the Captain, I was never that keen on it. I always thought it sounded like a character from a comic book.'

'Will do Sir.' Carl smiled, still unable to remove all deference.

Wayne turned around from the front passenger seat and addressing Adam said 'We were told that you were all ex-service, is that the case?' he made a point of looking at Michelle.

'Charlie, Matt and I are ex SAS, and Michelle is a mission investor,' replied Adam. Wayne did not display Carl's polite deference. He continued ', and she's well able to take care of herself. Is that a problem Wayne?'

Wayne continued to look at Michelle, and she glared back at him.

'Not a problem for me,' he said, shrugging his shoulders' just need to be sure of the team strength that's all,' he turned back to face the front.

One to watch, thought Adam as he looked across at Michelle and winked. She did not return a smile this time.

The next twenty minutes passed in silence as they travelled along the dusty road. They came to a gap in the rocky hills just wide enough to fit the 4X4 through and drove down a corridor through the hillside which eventually opened out into a large circular clearing. This was surrounded by the hills on all sides. There was only one way in and an exit corridor on the opposite side. *A pretty good place for a base camp* thought Adam.

Around the edges of the circular clearing were several large tents and a variety of armoured vehicles. Adam estimated that the camp could accommodate up to 200 personnel for a sustained period. The 4X4 continued across to the far side of the camp and stopped outside the largest tent.

'Here we are guys, let's go and see the boss,' announced Carl.

For the second time that day, Michelle felt the dramatic temperature difference when moving from the air-conditioned environment of the 4X4 to the extreme heat in the dust bowl of a base camp. She did not show any reaction and followed the others into the tent.

Inside was a mobile military headquarters with uniformed personnel working in cubicles. At the end of the room there appeared to be the archetypal mercenary soldier sitting behind a desk. His large physique was topped with a weather-worn face and a dark stubbled beard.

'All that's missing is an eye patch and a cigar,' Michelle whispered to Adam.

'Any other time that might be funny,' he whispered back.

'Sorry,' she said contritely.

The six-foot four-inch mercenary stood up from his desk and came around to greet them 'Hi Charlie good to see you again care to do the intros?'

'Good to see you again Jack,' said Charlie 'this is Matt Waring and Adam Crest both ex SAS and Michelle, our mission funding partner.'

He nodded at Matt then said 'Ahh Captain Crest although we've never met you're reputation precedes you,' he offered his hand to Adam.

Adam equalled the firmness of his handshake and replied 'Same goes for me, Jack.'

Taylor then turned to Michelle, smiling and offered his hand 'Hello Michelle. I note that Matt has taken care not to mention your surname. I will respect that and not enquire any further. This is not the easiest environment for a female non-pro but, that's not really any of my business.' The smile disappeared from his face. 'As long as my men are not put at risk because of it.'

'Your men need not be frightened Mr Taylor,' she replied with a hint of sarcasm and gripped his hand firmly whilst holding his gaze defiantly.

'Hmmm,' he murmured as he released her hand and returned to the other side of his desk.

Taylor sat down again 'Well, you've met Carl, Wayne and Mark. Gavin, Paul and Henri are outside and will be joining you to form the complement of six men as requested. Your kit and vehicle are also outside as listed. I already received the fifty per cent deposit so if you could now arrange payment of the other fifty per cent we can all get on with our day.'

'Of course Jack,' Adam replied and turning to his team said 'Matt, can you go outside and check off the inventory and vehicle then do the intros with the other guys. Charlie, could you and Michelle arrange the transfer of funds with the admin team over there?'

'Will do,' replied Charlie, and they all went off to their tasks.

Adam returned to Taylor' Perhaps we could have five minutes while things are being sorted?'

'Yes, of course, Adam, take a seat. Fancy a drink?' he said as he pulled a half-empty bottle of whisky from a drawer.

'No thanks Jack but a bottle of water wouldn't go amiss.'

'Please yourself,' he said, grabbing a bottle of Highland Spring from a case next to his desk and tossing it to Adam. He poured a large whisky for himself. 'What can I do for you?'

Whilst Jack Taylor's appearance was that of a rough and ready fighting man, his demeanour showed him to be a more educated and intelligent man. His speech and manners revealing the traits of a public school in his distant past. However, Adam sensed that this charm only aided his devious nature, and he felt an immediate distrust of the man. Taylor was definitely not a man who fought for Queen and country. The almighty dollar was his only motivation, and Adam needed to take care.

'A brief background on the six guys would help,' said Adam.

Taylor thought for a moment before replying 'Carl and Gavin are your best two if you are splitting they would be your team leaders and they both speak enough Pashto to get by. Mark and Paul work well with them, but you might have to watch Wayne and Henri, both of whom can be insubordinate. Still, they are all bloody good in a firefight, especially Henri, he's French ex-Foreign Legion. He found the regime to be too strict,' Taylor raised an eyebrow. 'The rest are all ex British military with excellent desert craft and well trained.'

'Thanks for that, Jack. What do you know of our mission?' asked Adam.

'Only the initial information that Charlie gave me, something about chasing an arms dealer across Helmand province.'

'There's a little bit more to it than that.'

'I guessed there might be hence the attractive blonde team member, eh,' he smirked.

'Michelle has some grassroots connections with the mission,' Adam confirmed cautiously. 'But there's also a civilian kidnapping involved which may end up as murder if we don't get to them in time.'

'It sounds like you have a task on your hands,' Taylor said more seriously but with little genuine interest.

'We have to get to the intended destination for the handover of the cargo. We don't know where it is or even where the transport vehicles are.' Adam was not happy about revealing the fullness of the situation, but as he was desperate for information, there was little choice.

'I see,' said Taylor with a little more interest. 'What's their strength?'

'Ten men flew over plus any locals that may have joined them at this side, probably the same again, with no shortage of firepower.'

'Sounds like your only advantage is going to be surprise. As long as they don't find out you're here. Of course, your men are better trained as well. It should be good fun,' he said with a wry smile.

'We'll sort it,' said Adam. 'But any additional Intel would be gratefully received.'

'I'll make a call and see what can be done,' he said, picking up the sat phone.

Taylor spoke to someone in a dialect that Adam

could not understand. Still, it sounded as though he was getting some information.

He put down the sat phone and said 'It seems that you've had a bit of luck, your weapons shipment ran into a problem. The pneumatics failed on one set of the Hercules landing gear, causing a somewhat messy arrival at Darwai airport. They're still unloading the cargo. That gives you a bit of a head start, I would say. Although you'll have to go some if the hand-off is in Helmand province.'

Taylor had not volunteered his contacts details, and Adam knew better than to ask. Similarly, Adam did not reveal the fact that he intended to meet with Colonel Karak, where he hoped to get some more detailed information.

'Many thanks, Jack, we may have caught a break for once.'

'I notice from your kit list that there is an L115. That's a very expensive weapon?' he questioned.

'It's a weapon that I am very familiar with, and it may come in useful,' Adam replied non committally.

'None of my business, of course,' said Taylor smiling at him.

Adam smiled back and said nothing but thought to himself, *to right pal it isn't any of your business.*

Charlie and Michelle came over from the other side of the tent. Charlie said 'All done Sir, Matt has checked off the inventory and loaded a Mastiff 2 Armoured Personnel Carrier and trailer.'

'The transfer of funds is also completed, Adam,' reported Michelle.

Taylor looked over to one of his admin team who gave a nod of confirmation that the funds were transferred.

'Thanks, Michelle,' Adam said. 'Charlie, please can you ensure that the L115 and sighting scope is in the main vehicle?'

'Will do.'

'Right,' said Adam turning to Taylor. 'We'll change into our work clothes, could we use your latrine, Jack?'

'Of course, believe it or not, we have both genders. We sometimes recruit women to the ranks, and I wouldn't want your 'lady' to feel uncomfortable, Adam,' said Taylor with a smirk.

Adam could see Michelle revving up to say something, so he quickly stepped in 'That's great thanks Jack we'll get changed then get out of your hair.'

Was he being paranoid or had there been a particular emphasis on the word lady. Adam wondering how much Taylor really knew.

'No problem,' said Taylor returning to his chair and whisky. 'We have each other's contact numbers. Good luck. Oh, and by the way, if you manage to bring the Mastiff back in one piece I'll give you some money back.' Taylor grinned.

'Good to know,' replied Adam.

The three left the tent and met up with Matt to collect their uniforms which they changed into in the, less than alpine fresh, latrines. Michelle removed several cases of beer and bottled water from the ladies facilities before doing the same. They all re-joined the Mastiff with the three men feeling less comfortable but much happier in their combat gear. Michelle just felt less comfortable.

Matt waved the six men over and introduced the three they had not already met, and they all shook hands. Henri held on to Michelle's hand a little longer than necessary, which was noted by Adam. As Jack Taylor had said, Henri and Wayne displayed a different attitude to the other guys. He wondered how long it would be before he needed to mark their respective cards. There would be an opportunity to get to know them all the better during the next few hours in the Mastiff.

'Mount up everyone, Matt can you take the first stint driving with Michelle as a passenger then

I can brief the guys in the back. Head for Shorabak.'

'Will do Adam.' Matt felt a little more comfortable using first name terms since their chat on the plane.

Michelle climbed aboard without any difficulty. Despite the step into the vehicle being a meter off the ground. She was immediately relieved to get out of the baking sun. The rest got into the rear and took their seats. Adam checked that the L115 was secured in its case on the rear shelf. The Mastiff 2 was really designed for a crew of eight, so it was a little tight but manageable.

Matt revved the 200 horsepower vehicle engine, which easily pulled the trailer full of weapons, ammunition, tents, and supplies. He headed for the corridor between the rocks that they had entered through earlier that day. Once out of the other side, he followed the sat nav directions for Shorabak. Although it wasn't complicated as there was only one dusty road available through the desert hills.

Michelle stared through the windscreen from the passenger seat as the sand and grit spat at it from the uneven road surface. For the first time since all of this had begun, she was realising what she had gotten into. She was a little apprehensive as to what might be coming next. Turning her head to look into the rear of the cab, she was reassured to see Adam deep in conversation with his men. He seemed very comfortable in control of his natural environment. She smiled to herself, she had not felt this way about a man for many years although that sort of thing would have to wait until this was all over.

Back at the mercenary's camp, Jack Taylor considered making a call to England but decided to leave it until he had a progress report later that afternoon.

In the rear of the Mastiff Adam briefed Taylor's men regarding the mission details, such as they were.

'Essentially, the objectives are to extract a prisoner called Julian, who was abducted in England and maybe in a bad way. The secondary objective is to destroy the arms cargo, which is spread over nine transport containers on the back of three low loaders. This can't be done until I have confirmation that the arms dealer has been arrested in Europe. As far as I know, there are ten men, including Bolton. None have any military training, but it is most likely that he'll have been joined by some locals, possibly Tali's, at Zaranj. We don't know how many at this stage.'

Adam then produced pictures of Julian and Bolton.

'Whatever happens, I'll take care of Bolton, and there'll be a bonus paid to any of you who can put me and this,' he patted the L115 case on the back shelf 'in killing range. Any questions?'

Henri was the first to speak in what seemed a thick French accent 'I don't know what the others think. But it sounds to me like we're walking into the unknown. We don't even know how many men we're up against. It seems a risky enterprise.'

Wayne nodded in agreement.

'That's why you get paid the big bucks,' Adam replied.

'Ha! you must be joking,' scoffed Henri.

Henri was sitting opposite Adam. Adam leaned forward and said quietly, exaggerating the French pronunciation of his name.

'Henri, if you don't want to remain on this mission that's fine by me,' he then turned his gaze on the rest of the mercenaries and raised his voice ', and that goes for all of you. You're welcome to get out now whilst we're still within walking distance of your camp. I don't want any man in this team who is not completely committed. Is that clear?'

Adam stared at each of the mercs, who were all surprised at his challenge. They were quick to say yes or nod in agreement. He knew that none of them would risk losing the money.

Henri simply shrugged his shoulders in true French style and said 'Of course,' as if he had not made his previous comments.

This had obviously been a little test of Adams authority, and he glanced at Charlie who winked at him knowingly.

Adam continued, 'We need intel on the convoy's current whereabouts and destination. Our objective will be to get there before them and set up an ambush. Therefore our first port of call will be Camp Shorabak to pay our respects to Colonel Karak and pick up whatever Intel we can. If we need to split into teams at any point, Charlie will lead one, and I will lead the other. Are we all clear?'

'Yes boss,' came a clear reply from all.

Adam was satisfied with their response for now, although he was not used to the mercenary soldier's independence. He was used to people fighting for a reason other than just financial gain.

Charlie continued the briefing and went through the weapons and kit that they had in the trailer. Adam turned to the front of the vehicle and asked Matt and Michelle if they had got most of what they had said. Michelle turned her head to look at him, and once again, he gave her a reassuring wink and smile which she returned.

Adam instructed Matt to pull up for a few minutes so that they could stretch their legs. This allowed him to make a call to Colonel Karak.

Matt stopped at the next rocky outcrop. Adam disappeared behind it and made the call. Having introduced himself, he explained that Harry had recommended speaking to him. Colonel Karak replied 'Yes Captain Crest, Harry has mentioned you and your team to me and I'm happy to help in your endeavour as long as things do not get out of hand.'

'Of course, Colonel, would it be possible to meet in about one hour?'

'Yes, that would be acceptable. The entrance guards will be notified.'

Adam thanked him then they all got back into the Mastiff.

At 14:00 hours they approached Camp Shorabak which sat amidst the surrounding desert like a mirage, perfectly positioned for long-range visibility. Adam could already see the two tanks at the entrance, one on either side of the swing barrier and the guardhouse. The rest of the camp was surrounded by HESCO barriers and barbed wire fencing for as far as the eye could see. As they drew closer, it was clear to see the staggered concrete blast walls along the inner road leading to the admin block. There were soldiers in the turrets atop the two observation towers on either side of the entrance. Plus 2 men on the ground. As they reached the entrance, all of the guards raised their weapons.

Cautiously Matt slowed and stopped the Mastiff several metres before the barrier. Adam got out. He approached the two guards who stood in their smart combat uniforms. It was rumoured to have cost the American taxpayer $28 million to fit out the Afghan Army. He said to them 'I have spoken to Colonel Karak to arrange a meeting at 14:00. He said that he would notify you to allow us to pass.'

The guards simply stared at Adam, so he repeated himself in his best Pashto. The guards continued to stare at him in silence with weapons raised. Adam was beginning to sweat, and it wasn't only the desert sun that was causing it.

Michelle had sensibly covered her head with a Pashmina and was staring through the windscreen of the vehicle. Everybody was silent, and the tension was palpable. She whispered to Matt. 'What's going on?'

'It's hard to tell, you never know how these guys are going to react, especially now that the British Military has left. But there shouldn't be a problem really,' whispered Matt equally tense and resting his hand on his sidearm.

Suddenly a loud bell rang from the guardhouse, making everybody jump out of their skin except for the Afghan soldiers.

A guard picked up the receiver. After a few words on the phone, he came out with his weapon lowered and approached Adam and said 'Name?'

'Captain Crest,' he thought that he had better use the rank given the situation.

'How many?' said the guard pointing at the Mastiff.

'Nine'

The stone-faced guard walked towards the vehicle with a colleague following behind.

'Open!' he said, pointing the weapon.

Adam opened the driver's side door and instructed the others to open theirs. He was thankful that Michelle had the presence of mind to cover her head. The guards were muttering to each other when they realised that a blonde-haired woman was inside the vehicle. They counted the occupants then returned to the guardhouse phone and after a few words signalled Adam to bring the car through.

One of the guards stood on the running board and held onto the driver's side door as they entered the compound. Matt took things very slowly as he weaved left and right through the mini blast walls until he reached what appeared to be the compound office. The guard jumped off the running board and shouted stop.

Inside the vehicle, Adam said quietly 'I'm not sure whether this is normal or whether it's the Afghans making the point that it's their camp now. Either way, I don't think we're all getting inside, so I'll just try to take Charlie.'

The guard opened the door.

'Out!'

Adam got out and pointed to Charlie inside saying 'Is it okay if I take my second in command?'

Charlie got out, and the guard looked him over.

'You go,' and he pointed to the main doors to a large office block whilst he remained to guard the Mastiff.

'Not exactly welcoming,' Adam murmured to Charlie as they walked towards the building.

Once they got inside things started to improve when a smart adjutant politely asking them to follow him down a corridor which leads to a door with the name Colonel Karak stencilled on it. He knocked, and they all entered.

Colonel Karak immediately jumped up from behind his desk and came around to greet them with a smile on his face and arm outstretched. His equally smart combat uniform emblazoned with the red insignia of the Afghan Army.

'Welcome gentlemen, please take a seat. I'm Colonel Jamil Karak. However, please call me Jamil as we're all friends here. You are not military personnel, at least not officially,' he said with a raised eyebrow.

'Many thanks, Jamil,' said Adam shaking hands and introduced himself and Charlie agreeing first names be used.

'Would you like chi?'

'That would be great,' said Adam, although he would have preferred a pint of water. The adjutant went off to make the tea.

'Whilst I make no apologies for my troop's strict adherence to security procedures during your arrival. I understand that you must have felt less than welcome. Unfortunately, a lot of that is due to, what some Afghanis feel was, the British militaries premature departure in 2015 and the current manoeuvring by the Americans to get out without finishing the job. Many of my men are frustrated and even angry at being left in the lurch shall we say. Especially as the Taliban seem to be increasing in strength.'

Whilst the Colonel was being very pleasant, you might even say friendly, his smile had disappeared. Adam knew that he would have to be careful of what he said.

'I can appreciate the frustration Jamil, but it's difficult for me to comment as I've not had any involvement with operations in Afghanistan for over three years. The only thing I can say is that the reason for our current presence is to prevent a large number of illegal arms from reaching the Taliban. This can only be a good thing.'

His smile returning the Colonel replied 'Of course Adam. I'm also aware of the serious injuries that you sustained whilst fighting the Taliban.'

The adjutant returned and placed a document on the Colonel's desk. He had also brought the Chi pot and glasses. He proceeded to pour the hot sweet liquid raising the pot up and down to create a short-lived frothy head. They all took a sip, and the Colonel continued.

'I've spoken to my good friend Harry. As I understand it, Adam; you have some ambitious objectives in that you need to obtain a civilian prisoner's release and destroy the arms cargo. Whilst ensuring the capture and arrest of the principals involved in this deal, who are meeting somewhere in Europe. I also understand that you don't know the exact whereabouts of your targets, the transfer location, or their team's strength. Is that a correct assessment Adam?'

'That's it in a nutshell,' replied Adam.

'I see,' said the Colonel thoughtfully. He took another sip of his chi whilst perusing the document on his desk.

Adam knew where the Colonel's mind was going, and it was no surprise when he said 'You are well equipped for a small team with a lot of explosives, night vision kit and a sniper rifle.'

The adjutant had been busy rummaging through their trailer whilst waiting for the kettle to boil thought Adam wryly.

The Colonel continued 'you are also using some of Jack Taylor's men, who I know won't be cheap. The men behind this arms deal must be quite big fish to warrant this level of funding Adam.'

It was unspoken but clear that Karak was fishing to see if the funding was government sourced, there might be a bit extra in the pot for him. Adam was going to have to make him realise that there wasn't but without losing his support.

'I should explain Jamil that this mission has come about due to the somewhat bizarre escalation of events beginning with the murder of a personal friend and relative of one of my team. Although substantive, our funding is purely private and limited. This operation is about the rescue of a close friend and ensuring the safety of another by bringing down a group of illegal arms traders.'

'I see,' Karak pondered again then said 'that's a shame,' and closed the document on his desk.

Charlie looked apprehensively at Adam, aware that they were about to be asked to leave with nothing to show from this meeting.

Adam fondled the package that Harry had given him in his pocket. Realising that he had no choice, he said suddenly 'Oh, by the way, Jamil I forgot to tell you Harry sent a box of your favourite cigars.' He handed the package across to Karak.

The Colonel unwrapped the package and took a peek. Without showing any reaction, he put it in his drawer.

The smile returned to Karak's face, and the folder on his desk was re-opened. They both knew what was inside the package. Adam also knew that he would have to work a hell of a lot of overtime to pay for the contents. It seems diamonds are also a Colonels best friend, he thought.

The relief on Charlie's face was clear to see, and although he didn't know what the package contained or where it had come from, he guessed it was something other than cigars.

A more amenable Karak continued 'your quest is both ambitious and admirable Adam. We shall do our very best to advise and support you beginning with the current Intel. I can confirm that the Hercules did land at Darwaz Airport yesterday. However, there was an issue with the hydraulics on the landing gear, causing some unloading delays. The convoy eventually headed east to Tall Kala which is North West of Lashkar Gah. They're being accompanied by a dozen Taliban sympathisers, one of whom provides us with information when suitably rewarded. We understand that your friend is still alive and will be taken to their safe house on the outskirts of Tall Kala, they should be arriving there about now.'

The relief showed on Adam's face as he thought Thank god he's still alive.

Karak raised the palm of his hand from the desk as if to halt Adams thoughts. He looked very seriously at him 'You should be aware that although the Taliban is a terrorist organisation, they do play by certain rules. Unfortunately, these sympathisers are essentially local thugs and do not. The life of a British civilian means less than nothing to them, and his survival will, ironically, be dependent on your English arms dealers keeping him safe. I suspect that will only remain the case whilst he is of some value to them.'

The Colonel wasn't telling Adam anything that he didn't already know. Still, his words accentuated the urgency of getting to Julian.

Trying not to sound too desperate Adam said 'Jamil can you provide the details of the safe house?'

'Yes, I have those in this dossier which I'll give to you before you leave, although we don't know the exact building. It also contains the most likely place for the transfer to take place, it has been used before. It's a canyon at Now Zad which is about 30 miles North East of Tall Kala and will take place early tomorrow morning.'

'Yes, I know exactly where it is,' said Adam.

'Ah, an old hunting ground perhaps?'

'Something like that,' nodded Adam.

'Well now that you have a good idea of their current position and destination, all of which is contained in here,' he handed the dossier to Adam. 'It only remains for me to wish you luck.'

Taking the dossier, Adam said 'We cannot thank you enough, Jamil. Just one question, though. You have all of this information and bearing in mind that if these weapons were to get into the wrong hands, they would most certainly be used against your men. Why don't you carry out this mission?'

'Take a look outside Adam, and you will note that the camp is nearly empty, our forces are spread thinly enough as it is and besides,' he grinned' why should I when you are doing it for me.'

'I suppose so,' said Adam, not returning the grin. 'Thanks for your help.'

The adjutant led them out of the office and back to the Mastiff. He saluted and returned to the admin block. The others stood around the vehicle, all looking at Adam and Charlie expectantly.

'How did it go?' asked Matt.

'We've got what we need. Let's go.' replied Adam bruskly, and they all got into the Mastiff.

Michelle said to Adam 'They went right through the inside of the truck and the trailer you know?'

'Yes, not a very trusting lot,' he replied.

Once inside, Adam said to Matt with some urgency' Head for, Now Zad and put your foot down.'

'Now, Zad!' exclaimed, Matt.

'Yeah, I know. We need to get a move on.'

CHAPTER 16

Wednesday 11.00 AM - 2019

Sir Lawrence Gorton-Hyde marched into his office in Whitehall with a look on his face that signified to all around him that he was in a worse mood than usual. Needless to say, his staff gave him a wide birth and were relieved when he went into his office, slamming the door behind him. He grabbed at the telephone 'Get me, Naylor,' he barked. Twenty seconds later, the phone rang.

'Ralph, where the hell are you?' he barked once again.

'I've just got off the plane from Ukraine, what's wrong, Sir?' Ralph Naylor asked.

'I will tell you 'what's wrong'. Crest is becoming a real liability. Someone is leaking information to him, and he knows all about the shipment'.

Ralph knew better than to interrupt as there was a further rant coming.

'Even worse,' he continued 'the information is spreading. Ayesha caught him on camera talking to his pal from the Home Office outside a hotel on Monday afternoon. Mellors tells me that he was on his way to the airfield yesterday morning. Fortunately, the flight has taken off, and we have his chap safely in our custody, but we've no idea where Crest is. I wouldn't mind, but I've had tabs on Crest for over two years ever since the fiasco at Now Zad until that idiot Braden lost his grip on him. I could not believe it when he turned up at that garage last week, the cheeky bastard gave me a false name as well.'

Whilst the volume had reduced, Ralph knew what was coming next.

'You know Ralph I blame you for this mess, you're supposed to have my back and make sure that this sort of thing doesn't happen. Now get yourself back here straight away so that we can sort this mess out.'

A dejected Ralph replied 'Will do Sir, I'll be there in one hour.'

'See that you are.'

There's no doubting Naylor's loyalty, but he's nowhere near as sharp as Tom Riley was, thought Gorton-Hyde.

He pressed the intercom 'Coffee Alice, now!'

He sat back in his leather swivel chair, his temper beginning to wane having exercised it on Ralph. He started to consider Crests motives, likely next actions and ultimately his whereabouts.

Maybe he was a friend of Frank bloody Patterson's

and is out for revenge. If only that idiot Bolton hadn't made such a hash of disposing of Patterson, we wouldn't be in this mess. But that doesn't explain how he knows about the shipment contents, there must be a mole, his thoughts continued, *unless Patterson was still alive when Crest got to him. Although Bolton was confident that he could not be. Either way, he knows now. The question is, does he have the determination and the wherewithal to follow the cargo to its destination. If he does, we have his pal as a hostage. He'll also be looking for some assistance from the local paramilitary.* A steely grin crossed Gorton-Hyde's face as he picked up the phone and made a phone call to an old acquaintance in Afghanistan, just in case.

After speaking to Taylor, Gorton-Hyde felt a little happier knowing that if Crest were to venture into Afghanistan, he would be informed.

The next task was to hunt down the mole in their midst, whoever it was would pay dearly for their treachery. However, Ralph would have to sort out that as he would be out of the country. Dealing with the arrangements for the financial transaction.

Alice brought the coffee in.

'Tell Ralph to come straight in as soon as he gets here.'

'Certainly, Sir,' replied Alice and left the room as

quickly as possible.

He knew that extra caution would be needed whilst Crest was on the loose, and his meeting with Kamal would have to be very discreet. Once again, he pressed the intercom button.

'Alice, on Monday did you book a flight to Paris for this evening and reserve a room at the George Cinque?'

'Yes, Sir.'

'Got something right for once,' came the short reply, and the intercom disconnected abruptly.

Alice had given up wishing hateful things about her boss long ago. Still, she did satisfy herself with a private smile.

A little pleased with his subterfuge, Gorton-Hyde opened a desk drawer and felt along the inside for the small sliding panel. Once located, he moved it to the side and removed the burner phone. He pushed the button, and a man's voice answered.

Gorton-Hyde said quietly 'Completion 7.00 am tomorrow at the Raffles Istanbul?'

'Agreed,' replied the voice.

Gorton-Hyde replaced the phone and took a sip from his coffee cup, feeling confident in his arrangements.

Moments later there was a knock at his office door 'Come!'

Ralph Naylor entered appearing a little weary after his overnight flight and subsequent dash to Whitehall. He had the gruff appearance of a professional wrestler and his 6 feet 4-inch frame had proved useful when Gorton-Hyde needed someone intimidating.

'About time, Ralph,' said Gorton-Hyde looking up from his newspaper. 'You look like shit, man. For god's sake get yourself tidied up I want you to go to Paris and hang around the George Cinque lobby. Watch out for anyone asking for me this evening and let me know immediately. If my guess is right, you'll see a couple of our finest plain clothes bobbies blundering around in the dark as usual. Book the flight yourself on one of the cheap airlines and keep a low profile.'

'Will do Sir,' replied Ralph pretty much standing to attention.

'Now, in your spare time,' he said sarcastically, 'I want you to find out who this bloody informant is. I will not tolerate disloyalty and betrayal is that clear?'

'Yes Sir, do we have anything more on Crest?'

'Don't worry about Crest for the moment I've taken measures to block his progress. How are things with Yuri?'

'He was his usual cheerful self,' replied Ralph 'he says that he'll have another shipment ready in six months. As ever he wants to re-negotiate the price.'

'Of course, he does, that greedy Russian is never happy. We'll have to arrange a new place for holding storage which is a bloody shame really. Patterson's barns were useful for that purpose. You'd better start looking for an alternative.' Gorton-Hyde paused thoughtfully then continued 'unfortunately our future operations are threatened by the knowledge that Crest and his pal possess. They will both have to be eliminated. We have Lycett, but we need to locate Crest. I want you to deal with this carefully Ralph, use Bolton but make sure that there are no loose ends this time.'

'Understood Sir, I'll get Bolton to deal with it as soon as he returns from Afghanistan,' said Ralph.

'I suspect Crest may very well be on his way to Afghanistan not least because Bolton has Lycett. Bolton would welcome his arrival. He's wanted a showdown with Crest for some time. He would have finished him off at the weekend if I hadn't stopped him.'

Unsure of what Bolton's issue might be Ralph replied 'It would work out well if they were both dealt with out there, Sir.'

'Indeed it would, but as I've said I don't want any slip up's so keep on top of things. I have a meeting with Joint Intelligence to get to before heading off to Istanbul so you'd better get going. For god's sake find that leak,' was Gorton-Hyde's parting shot.

'Sir,' replied Ralph and left the office.

Not entirely convinced of either Naylor's or Bolton's competence Gorton-Hyde once again removed the phone from his desk drawer and made one more call this time to someone more local in case things were not resolved in Afghanistan. Satisfied that he'd now covered all eventualities, he returned to his preparations for the afternoons meeting with the joint Chiefs.

Later that afternoon, Gorton-Hyde sat in the meeting listening to the self-important heads of the various intelligence agencies droning on. Mostly about how difficult it was to fight the war against terrorism in the UK and abroad and then complaining to the minister that they needed more money. None of them even bothered to ask his opinion. He consoled himself with smug thoughts of how he was making millions in illegal arms deals right under their collective noses.

He had put his phone inside the inner pocket of

his black suit jacket, and he suddenly felt it vibrate against his chest. Damn, he thought I need to answer this. But there was no way he could leave the meeting just for a phone call, so he sat in frustrated silence until eventually, the vibration stopped. Five minutes later, it started again, and he became more and more frustrated at not being able to answer the call. This must-have shown on his face as the Minister sitting opposite suddenly said in concerned tone 'Larry, are you alright? You look a bit off colour.'

Seizing the opportunity, Gorton-Hyde replied 'Oh, I've been a bit under the weather recently Sir, it will pass I'm sure.'

'Nothing serious I hope, well we are overdue for a comfort break anyway. Ladies and gentlemen, I suggest we break and resume in fifteen minutes. Agreed?'

They all got up from the table, and Gorton-Hyde left the room quickly and headed down the nearest corridor to an anteroom. Once he had closed the door and ensured that nobody else was in the room, he took out his phone and looked at the text message which simply said 'T' he immediately rang Taylor. The phone connected at the other end and he said 'You called.'

"C' is here with a small team on his way to intercept the transfer.'

'OK,' replied Gorton-Hyde thinking that it was no bad thing as long as Bolton took care of him.

'One more thing, there is an attractive blonde woman with him of your close acquaintance,' a mischievous grin appeared on Taylor's face before he pushed the 'end' button.

Gorton-Hyde froze with the phone to his ear, and his face turned bright red with fury as the information sank in. He then spat out the words 'The Bitch ….The Bitch'. His anger turned towards the people who were supposed to be guarding her, he rang Ralph Naylor.

Ralph answered 'Yes, Sir.'

'Get hold of 'B' urgently and tell him to contact me on a secure line, and I mean urgently.'

Ralph could hear the anger in his voice and responded immediately 'Will do Sir.' He didn't bother to mention the difficulties of getting hold of Bolton in the Afghan desert as he knew what the reply would be.

Gorton-Hyde then called his home number which he knew would be a waste of time, as expected there was no reply. Similarly, he tried Michelle's mobile, again to no avail. Bolton will bloody pay for his incompetence, he thought. As his temper dissipated, his thoughts turned cold, and he considered that there might be a benefit to the situation as long as Bolton didn't screw things up again. His phone vibrated in his jacket pocket.

'Is this line secure?' said Gorton-Hyde gruffly.

'As secure as any Larry,' came a somewhat cheerful reply from Bolton which only served to re-ignite Gorton-Hyde's temper.

'Don't use my name, you idiot.'

'Oh right,' replied Bolton, who was taken aback by the sudden aggression.

'Get hold of the clowns you sent to guard my 'package' as it seems that the 'package' is now in your vicinity along with 'C' and his crew.'

'WHAT THE ......,' exclaimed Bolton' Er right ….. let me make a couple of calls and come straight back to you.'

'Yes, you had better do that,' said the venomous voice 'and make it bloody quick.'

Then one of the secretarial lackeys opened the anti-room door and said 'I hope you are feeling better Sir Lawrence. But we need to reconvene now.'

'Right, Yes, I will be there in five minutes.' he replied irritably.

His phone vibrated again 'Speak.'

A contrite voice at the other end said 'I must

apologise, but it looks like my team have dropped the ball, and the 'package' has been removed to foreign parts. Removal took place last night, and it is suspected that 'C' was involved.'

'Yes .... yes .... You are only telling me what I already know, and an apology will not cut it. There's only one way that you can redeem yourself, and that is to make sure that 'C' and his team are eliminated including the 'package'. I don't want any uncertainties. Do I make myself absolutely crystal bloody clear?'

The nervous voice replied 'Yes Sir. I understand that they're on their way to us so we will be ready for them.'

'Contact me when it's done and make sure that it's before I finalise the exchange tomorrow morning.' He ended the call and returned to the meeting.

He took his seat after making his apologies. The rest of the discussions past him by, he was preoccupied with his mutinous wife and the possible ramifications if Bolton didn't get the job done.

The meeting finally ended in its usual non-resolute manner. He got a taxi to Heathrow Airport as quickly as possible.

He had grown tired of Michelle's insubordination many years ago, some found her confident spirit alluring. He did not. Whilst in the back of the taxi he thought to himself All I have done for that women, she was nothing when I found her, and this is how she repays me, well I hope she doesn't die too quickly. He then considered the most important thing. Which was to make sure that he had a secure 'back door' just in case things went wrong.

CHAPTER 17

Wednesday 6.00 AM - 2019

Julian awoke from a fitful sleep at dawn. The constant pain from his legs and face coupled with the shouting from the Arabs downstairs for most of the night had meant that he didn't get much rest. He surveyed the room only to discover that there was nothing in it. Just a door and a three feet by two feet hole in the rear wall, which he supposed could be called a window if it had any glass. The floor surface was made from more ill-fitting rough wood timbers.

He closed his eyes again but this time tried to concentrate on what information he had. He didn't know what country he was in except that it was in the Middle East, most likely Afghanistan. He estimated that there were around 18 men here. A mixture of Bolton's men and the Afghanis that he'd seen. He'd heard what he presumed was Bolton talk about Now Zad and Tall Kala. He could assume that all 3 trucks were here with the cargo. He could only hope that Adam had somehow managed to follow them out here. He didn't allow himself to consider the alternative.

Later that morning, he heard the bolt being slid across the wooden door and braced himself for more abuse, but a young Arab boy came in with another bucket of water. This time it was not thrown in his face just placed by his side, and two chunks of bread were put next to it. The boy, who was about 10 years old, stared with what seemed to be concern at the man's bloody and bruised face. Julian did his utmost to smile through his badly damaged nose, and mouth and holding out his hand said softly 'Hello, my name is Julian, what is your name?'

The boy's large brown eyes widened at the sound of his voice, and his lips parted to speak. He screamed at the top of his voice 'ALLAHU AKBAR!!'. He then swiftly drew a short curved dagger from his belt and plunged it deep into Julian's right shoulder, turned the blade, and then ripped it out.

'Aaaaagh!' Julian cried out in agony and rolled away to the left just in time to miss the second blow from the boy's knife. By the time the boy was ready to wield another blow, Brad had burst in through the door and lifted the child, kicking and screaming, off his feet and cast him bodily from the room. The boy hit the landing floor and ran off down the corridor.

Brad turned Julian around and checked the wound muttering under his breath 'Bloody hell, I really don't need this shit.' He ripped away Julian's shirt. Although blood was flowing copiously from the wound, he considered that it was not life-threatening. 'Crazy fuckin Arabs,' he muttered, trying to stem the flow with one of the dirty rags.

Bolton's unmistakeable spiked white hair appeared at the top of the stairs. He shouted down the corridor as he progressed to the doorway 'For Christ's sake Brad, I told you to keep him safe, I might have known you'd screw up'.

As Bolton entered the room, Brad opened his mouth to defend himself, but before he could say anything, Bolton continued 'I don't want to hear your bullshit. Just get down to my Range Rover and grab the first aid kit from the glove box, quickly.'

Brad scuttled off down the corridor to do his masters bidding without saying a word. Bolton stood over Julians pathetic and whimpering form and said 'you're really not built for this sort of thing are you, buddy. Have you any idea what these Taliban lads like to do to gay boys, it really doesn't bear thinking about. Well, I promise that once you have served your purpose and I've completed our business here, we'll make it quick for you.'

Julian slowly raised his head from his chest. With tears in his eyes and through gritted teeth glared at Bolton and said vehemently 'You are very much mistaken if you think that this will end well for you Bolton.'

Bolton laughed loudly and said 'Maybe I was wrong, perhaps you have got some bollocks after all.'

Brad returned with the first aid kit, and Bolton said to him 'Sort him out. I don't want any more cock up's so either you or one of our guys stay on this door just in case any more of our local friends decided to finish him off.' He lowered his voice and murmured 'If you have any trouble, tell them that they can have him when we've finished our business.' Brad grinned and nodded his agreement. 'I'll be back to check on him this afternoon,' said Bolton then left the room.

Brad proceeded to clean Julian's wound with some water from the bucket and made a reasonably decent job applying a dressing to the stab wound. He said, half to himself 'I'm buggered if I am going to babysit you mate so I'll send Petrov up. You'll like him,' he said sarcastically.

He left, and 10 minutes later, one of the wagon drivers arrived with a wooden chair and sat against the rear wall under the window. Julian recognised him from the petrol station, which now seemed a lifetime ago. With his holstered side-arm dangling from his waist on one side and a mobile phone in its belt pouch on the other, he folded his arms and closed his eyes then dozed off without saying a word.

As the day progressed into the afternoon, the heat in the room increased to unbearable temperatures. Julian scooped out what little remained of the filthy water from the bucket until it was dry. He dare not ask for any more, so just lay on the floor sweating and bleeding.

Later that afternoon Bolton returned as promised and was in a much less cheerful mood having received a phone call from Gorton-Hyde. Petrov immediately stood up as he entered the room. Bolton went over to look at Julian. He bent down and put his face an inch away from Julians. Julian was very conscious of the sickly sweet smell of stale alcohol and sweat that emanated from Bolton's presence as he spat out the words.

'Don't think for one second that your buddy is going to save your gay arse boy,' he drew his side-arm and pushed the barrel hard into Julian's cheek. 'We know he's coming and we'll be ready. I'll take great pleasure in putting a bullet from this into the head of my brother's killer. I just thought that you should know that.' Bolton nodded at Petrov and walked out.

Julian was filled with mixed emotions. Elated to think that Adam was on his way to rescue him from this hell hole but desperate to find a way to warn him that Bolton knew he was coming. He wondered what on earth Bolton's brother had to do with anything.

Apart from the loud Arabic voices from downstairs, (they only seemed to communicate at high volume), Julian was left in peace with his pain and thoughts. He lay there for several hours as Petrov dozed off again.

The guard did not stir, his head slumped forward on his chest apart from emitting the occasional snore he seemed to be soundly asleep. It was around 7.00 pm when Julian began to hatch a plan. He was about 5 feet away from the guard. A dangerous and possibly reckless idea formed in his head.

Petrov's phone pouch was on the side of his waist nearest to Julian. He'd seen phones in use by some of the Taliban downstairs so he knew that there must be a signal. If he could drag himself across without waking him, he may be able to remove the phone and contact Adam. He just had to pray that Adam still had the burner phone on him and of course hope that Petrov did not wake up.

Julian was undoubtedly not physically built for desert warfare (or any warfare for that matter), but he was not short on courage. He made some movements to position his body so that he could drag himself across the floor. There was no chance of him being able to stand, and no reaction from the guard as Petrov continued to sleep. He decided to try it.

He waited for the perpetually arguing voices downstairs to increase in volume, which did not seem to disturb his guard. He used his good, left arm to drag his body slowly across the rough wooden floor, making as little noise as possible. It worked well, and although painful, he reached Petrov in three drags.

A little out of breath, he waited a moment. He was sweating, and his heart was racing as he sat himself up and raised his hand towards the phone pouch which had a magnetic flap. He lifted the flap carefully. He nipped the top of the phone with his thumb and forefinger and began to ease it out. It felt like forever before it cleared the pouch. It was then that he realised he'd been holding his breath, so he slowly and quietly released the air from his lungs.

He dragged himself across to the opposite side of the room as far from Petrov as he could and turned his back to him to muffle the sound of the phone call. There was a lull in the voices from downstairs, so he had to wait, a few moments. The guttural bickering soon began again, and Julian pressed the call button.

Another lifetime passed as he waited for an answer. Suddenly, Adams unmistakable voice came on at the other end 'Who's that?' was all he heard.

'Oh thank god Adam, it's Julian,' he whispered into the phone trying not to sound too desperate.

'Julian!!' exclaimed Adam. 'I can hardly hear you. Where the hell are you?'

'Don't speak just listen, dear boy,' he said with urgency in his voice. 'I'm a captive but have stolen this phone from my sleeping guard. I am at a place called Tall Kala in a single-story walled house outside the town. Bolton and his crew know that you're coming somehow and will ambush you either here or at their transfer site in a place call Now Zad. He said something about avenging his brother's killer.'

With equal urgency, Adam replied quietly so that his voice did not carry to loudly from the speaker at Julians end 'OK, I understand. How many men are there and where about's, are you in the building? How many doors and windows are there?'

Julian understood quickly what Adam needed and why. He replied 'Bolton and 9 of his men plus 8 or 9 Afghans, I'm in a room at the rear and farthest left looking from the front of the building with one wooden door and one 3 feet wide window to the rear wall.'

'What shape are you in?'

Julian paused before replying and looked down at his now bluish-black feet. Not wishing to cause Adam too much concern said 'I will need some assistance.'

Adam had noted the pause and guessed that Julian was in a bad way. He replied with concerned determination 'Julian I promise that I'll get you out of there by tomorrow morning. Now you'd better get that phone back to the guard.'

Julian was about to reply when the heavy metal butt of an automatic pistol smashed across the back of his skull and darkness ensued.

'Vybliadok,' came the expletive as Petrov grabbed his phone from Julian then dragged his unconscious body back to where he had been lying. Not wishing to have to explain how his phone had been stolen to Bolton he sat back down. If anyone asked the prisoner was just sleeping as far as he was concerned.

CHAPTER 18

Wednesday 3.00 PM - 2019

After leaving camp Shorabak, Adam and his team were progressing through the Helmand province towards Now Zad.

Sitting in the rear of the Mastiff, he briefed his team on Karak's information and an update to their plan of action. He kept his voice loud enough so that Charlie and Michelle could listen from the front.

'It's pretty certain that Bolton and team are overnighting in Tall Kala. They'll deliver the shipment at Now Zad canyon tomorrow morning. We also know that Julian is with them. We don't know whether they'll take him to the trade-off or leave him in Tall Kala until after their business is completed. What do you think, Charlie?'

'It could go either way. They may do as you say then finish him off on their return to Tall Kala, once he has no value. Or they could decide to use him as a show of bravado and execute him in front of their terrorist colleagues at Now Zad,' said Charlie.

'Agreed. If we continue our current pace, we should have time visit Now Zad first and carry out a recce. We'll split into two teams, and one will continue to Tall Kala and assess the situation there. Whilst the primary objective is to extract the hostage in an ideal world, we'll be able to wait until the transfer takes place in the morning. This will allow for things to be brought to a head at the European end. Then we can rescue Julian and destroy the shipment along with Bolton's team at the same time. However, don't forget that Bolton is mine. Understood?'

'Yes boss,' came the group reply. Michelle was particularly keen on the last bit and was eager to be involved in Bolton's demise.

'It's now 16:00 hours, and our ETA is currently 18:00 hours so you'd better organise your kit whilst we have the time. Charlie can you pull over then everyone can grab their automatic rifles and do the necessary in the back of the APC whilst we are on the move. I know it's a bit tight, but I don't want to lose our time advantage. I'll take over the driving so that you can join in.' Adam did not say that this would give him some time with Michelle as he wanted to talk to her.

Charlie pulled up near a convenient rocky outcrop, keeping the Mastiff out of view as much as possible. They all climbed out and stretched their legs. The rocks also provided for other conveniences which all but Michelle took advantage of. Once relieved, they grabbed their weapons from the trailer and climbed back in. Adam joined Michelle in the front. He checked the fuel and temp gauges then they set off again with a cloud of dust and sand spouting from the wheels of the big Mastiff.

Once they were comfortably on their way, Adam looked across at Michelle and smiled. With his voice pitched at a low level he said 'I'm sorry that I haven't had a chance to talk to you, but I'm sure you understand.'

She returned his smile saying 'Of course Adam, whilst I very much want to talk to you, that is of secondary importance to the mission. Besides, we'll have plenty of time to talk afterwards.'

Adam was pleased by her professional attitude and happy to hear that there was going to be an 'afterwards' with her. The tone in his voice changed. He knew that what he was going to say wouldn't be well received. He had to say it anyway.

'You couldn't have known what this was going to be like Michelle, yet you insisted on coming anyway. You have also provided financial support, which means this mission is much more likely to succeed.'

'Where is this going Adam?' Her smile had gone.

'Things are going to get a thousand times more

dangerous once we confront the enemy. You cannot possibly know how to deal with a firefight in the desert most likely in darkness. We're all experienced professionals and well used to desert warfare. Still, not one of us is going into this without the full understanding that we may not come out of it without serious injury or worse. That said it would make a lot of sense to drop you off just before Now Zad in some sheltered area with a tent and supplies. We'll pick you up later tomorrow after mission completion.' The last sentence was more of a statement than a question, but he knew that she would not accept it as such. He was correct.

'I'm well aware that I am a burden and mission risk. I also know that I'm only here because of your understanding of my need to see justice for my brother. But I think that I've already demonstrated my ability to deal with the heat and terrain and I'm no stranger to firearms. I have also made my peace with the fact that I may well have to take another human beings life or lives. My conscience will never be clear, but I can live with it. As far as the practicalities go, you are, of course, correct. I've no idea what to expect, but I am surrounded by a team of professionals as you point out. I'm happy to trust you with my life.' She knew it wasn't much of an argument but made it as passionately as she could.

Once again, Adam knew that he was not going to

win. Still, he couldn't allow sentiment to compromise safety and mission success.

'OK Michelle, I don't disagree with the points you've made but there have to be some rules. We stop at the next area of rocky cover, and you must demonstrate to me that you can handle both the side arms and automatic weapons. You must never remove your vest and helmet. Most importantly, you stick to my side regardless of what happens, unless I tell you not to. Then you do whatever I do tell you immediately and without question.'

'Absolutely Sir,' she said without levity.

Adam allowed the mood to lighten saying 'I think we will keep the 'Sir' long term I quite like it.' He grinned.

'In your dreams,' she muttered, smiling back at him.

They soon came across some rocky cover and stopped. Adam and Michelle took an SA80 automatic rifle and H&K sidearm around the back of the rocks. Adam went through the loading, cocking and safety procedures then he fired off a few rounds. Michelle picked up the SA80 to fire, and Adam immediately grabbed it from her before she could pull the trigger.

'For Christ's sake, you didn't say you were left-handed.'

'I didn't think it was important, she replied a bit taken aback at Adam's behaviour.

'It is if you don't want a face full of, hot shell casing. The SA80 only ejects from the right.

'Oh, right. Well, it's just as well I am ambidextrous.'

With that she grabbed the weapon back, cocked and fired.

'No one likes a smart arse,' said Adam.

Finally, he showed her how to use a grenade.

He wasn't entirely surprised at how good she was, and it was comforting to know that she could defend herself. He went back to the APC with a lady who was deservedly much chuffed with herself. Once Michelle had come down from her firearms driven high, she went quiet. Adam suggested 'You'd better take a nap, it could be a very long night.'

'I guess so,' she said, resting her head back against the seat.

The men in the back had also become quiet, with the weapons prep done they would no doubt be contemplating the forthcoming events.

Dusk was a very sudden affair in the desert and day turned to night in the space of about ten minutes. It was not great for driving when headlights had to be kept shaded. Adam bumped along the dusty road, which had become more of a rocky track and allowed his thoughts to wander to his team.

He'd noticed that during both of the stops most of the men had disappeared behind the rocks together, but Henri and Wayne had headed to different area's each on their own. Nothing wrong with a bit of privacy thought Adam but I Must remember to have a word with Charlie and Matt anyway. He certainly didn't trust Taylor, and they were his people.

He wondered how Ben Gifford was getting on with plans to trap Gorton-Hyde in Paris. He hoped that Ben had been careful who he confided in at the Foreign Office and the security services. You never know who is bent nowadays, he thought.

Julian crossed his mind, and he had to wonder how he was holding up in captivity. He wasn't sure who was the biggest threat, the morons from Europe or the Taliban, they had no regard for human life, including their own. 'I've got to get him out,' he muttered in frustration.

Suddenly the Mastiffs dashboard lit up with warning lights. Smoke and flames burst from the bonnet. Adam instinctively hit the brakes throwing everyone forward and providing a rude awakening for Michelle.

'WHAT THE HELL!!' he shouted as the tyres dug into the sand bringing the vehicle to an abrupt halt.

To Adams surprise, Michelle had grabbed the fire extinguisher from the footwell and was out of the cab in seconds. Quick as a flash she was spraying the bonnet with the white foam and had the fire out in minutes. The others were surrounding the vehicle with cocked weapons, assuming that they had been hit by some sort of rocket or grenade.

'What do you reckon, boss?' questioned Charlie coolly.

'It's OK, Charlie, you can stand down. This is vehicle-related, not external. All of the dashboard warning lights came on before the fire, suggesting some sort of electrical failure. Stay alert just in case. I'm going to pop the bonnet in the hope that it doesn't re-ignite. Stand back, everyone.'

Adam released the catch, Matt and Wayne lifted the lid slowly.

Wayne said 'Can you give it another squirt Michelle just to be safe?'

Michelle obliged emptying the rest of the canister into the engine bay.

Matt looked at Michelle and said 'that was

bloody good reactions, Michelle, I have to be honest I didn't even know where the extinguisher was.'

The other men all nodded and muttered 'Well done.'

'Safety first boys,' she said a little pleased with herself.

Adam said 'Matt, can you have a look and see what the damage is? Find out what caused it if you can and how quickly it can be repaired?'

'Will do boss'.

'I'll give you a hand,' suggested Wayne. 'I've worked on Mastiff's before.'

'Righto,' replied Matt surprised at Wayne's helpful attitude.

'Gavin, can you get them some lights from the trailer? The rest of you stay on watch and be alert,' said Adam.

Adam walked across to Michelle and gently took her elbow, directing her away from the vehicle. Once they had been swallowed up in the darkness, he stopped and kissed her, they parted, and he said 'That was bloody amazing.'

'It was only a Kiss Adam, given the right time and place. I am sure we can do much better.'

'No, I mean your reaction speed in the Mastiff.'

'Well I just saw a fire and put it out really,' she replied modestly. 'I wouldn't have even known where the extinguisher was if I hadn't seen Wayne checking it before we set off.'

'Wayne?' said Adam in surprise.

'Yes he was quite helpful, he explained that you always check that the pin is in the lever if not it means that it's been discharged and would be useless.'

'Just as well it was then.'

'Just as well he checked though, the one in his other hand had the pin removed. I guess he had just swapped them.'

'Or maybe he was about to. Has he spoken to you since?'

'No, not a word.'

Adam thought for a moment then said 'Quickly. We need to get back to the Mastiff. Wayne is working on it with Matt. I want to know exactly what he is doing to help if you know what I mean.'

Michelle hadn't worked it out yet, but she ran after Adam.

As they emerged from the darkness towards the portable spotlights which were clipped to the charred bonnet. Adam could see Matt standing next to the vehicle and Wayne's legs poking out of the engine bay. As he approached Matt, he said quietly 'What's he doing?'

'He's just finishing off cleaning away the extinguisher foam,' Matt replied.

Adam moved around to the front saying 'How's it going, Wayne? Have you found the cause of the fire yet?'

Wayne immediately pulled himself out from under the bonnet. He stood with his hands in his pockets and said 'It's hard to tell boss, I've cleared the foam away, but there's a lot of fire damage, my guess would be an electrical fault in the wiring loom.'

'Yes, I suppose that would be favourite,' replied Adam and looked at Matt 'a bit unusual with this build quality though wouldn't you think Matt?'

'That's true Boss. I've never heard of anything like this happening to theses Mastiffs before they're pretty bombproof. Literally.'

Looking pointedly at Matt, Adam continued 'Can you finish this on your own Matt? I need Wayne to join the watch team, we're spread pretty thin out there, and it's a big desert. If you need an extra pair of hands, Michelle and I can help.'

Matt caught Adams drift and replied 'No problem boss, but it's going to take a while, and I can't promise full functionality.'

'Do your best. As long as we can get to our destinations, that's all that matters. Wayne, you take the rear watch.'

Wayne was about to object but seeing the look on Adam's face he thought better of it. He went off to the trailer, grabbed a weapon before proceeding into the darkness at the back of the vehicle.

Once again, with lowered voice, Adam said to Matt 'Do not let him out of your sight for the remainder of the mission and let me know of any unusual behaviour. Have a good look around this engine for any evidence of an incendiary device. However, I think we might be too late now.'

'Will do boss,' replied Matt, realising what Adam was inferring.

Adam nodded to Michelle to join him as he headed off in front of the stricken vehicle to find Charlie. As agreed, she stuck to him like glue. The men had formed a ten-meter perimeter, and as they approached Charlie in his Night Vision Goggles, Adam called 'We come in peace Charlie.'

Charlie raised his NVG's 'Boss. How's it looking back there?'

'Matt's working on it. The damage is mainly

to hosing, and wiring so should be repairable. Still, it'll probably take a couple of hours, which means that we've eroded our time advantage and could lose the element of surprise. We'll need to get the first team installed at Now Zad. It's another hour's drive to Tall Kala, and we still don't know Julian's exact location.'

Adam moved closer to Charlie and lowered his voice 'I think we have another problem. I have an uneasy feeling about Wayne and Henri. Neither seems particularly keen on being here. Whenever we have stopped for a break, they head off on their own in separate directions. I'm also struggling to believe that the Mastiff would spontaneously combust. Wayne was very quick to get involved in cleaning up the engine after the fire. Maybe I'm becoming paranoid, but I've got Matt marking Wayne. I'd like you to keep an eye on Henri.'

'Understood Boss, I'll let you know of anything odd. I guess the trade-off will be around first light tomorrow.'

'Dawn is just after 06:00 hours so we can estimate something between then and 08:00 hours, but I should get confirmation from Ben Gifford tonight sometime. The timing will have to be pretty slick if we are going to nail Gorton-Hyde and Bolton at the same time. I don't want Taylor's boys to know any of this until the time comes. OK, Charlie?'

'Of course boss, just the four of us aye,' and he smiled and nodded to Michelle who returned the smile.

'I'm off to check on Matt's progress and then pay a visit to Wayne.'

Charlie dropped the NVG's back over his eyes and continued his vigil as Adam and Michelle turned back. Adam pulled out both his burner phone and his smartphone. He checked the signals which were both low but usable considering their position.

'How are you getting on?' Adam enquired of Matt.

'We should be back on the road in an hour or so, the fire was put out before there was too much damage,' said Matt nodding an acknowledgement to Michelle.

'Let me know as soon as,' Adam replied. 'Michelle, you wait in the cab.'

Michelle obeyed immediately as agreed. Adam wandered passed and out towards the darkness at the rear. He approached the position where Wayne should be, his movements became stealthier on the off chance that he might catch Wayne up to something. Of course, he also risked getting a bullet through the head. It is unwise to sneak up on these guys in the dark.

The caution and risk paid off as he could hear murmuring through the darkness from Wayne's position. The next man was at least ten meters along, so he was either talking to himself, which was unlikely or using his phone.

Adam froze and strained to hear what he was saying. He could just make out, 'Now Zad……. about 21:00 ………. he's suspicious………….. woman is still here………..'.

All went quiet, which presumably meant that the conversation was over. Adam loosened his sidearm in its leg holster but resisted the temptation to whack Wayne over the head. Instead, he stayed frozen for a few moments and cautiously made his way back to the APC.

Adam was sure that he was talking to Taylor. The few words that he had picked up were enough to confirm his treachery and that he was aware of Adam's suspicions. The question was, who was Taylor relaying this information to? There were two possibilities, and neither was good news. He made his way back to Matt and Michelle thoughtfully. Matt was still up to his elbows in burnt engine parts.

'It seems that my suspicions were correct, I'm certain that he is passing our mission details to Taylor. I've just overheard bits of a call and have to assume that his previous disappearances at earlier stops were to make similar calls. Someone's been made aware of our positions all afternoon. See if you can 'accidentally' break or remove his phone. At least then we can keep him around. I guess he's only doing it for the money and he may still be useful in a fight. The mystery is, what is Henri is up to if he's not working with Wayne? Unless he just likes his latrine privacy and enjoys being belligerent.'

'Odd buggers, the French boss but we'll see what Charlie can find out.'

Adam felt the vibration of his burner phone I'm expecting comms from Ben so I'll take this in the cab,' he said and went around to the driver's side. He got in next to Michelle. Once seated, he pushed the answer button and listened.

He sat up straight in the seat as he recognised the voice at the other end and immediately replied 'Julian!! I can hardly hear you. Where the hell are you?'

Michelle turned her head sharply to listen as Adam conversed with Julian, observing his face's concern as the conversation ended abruptly. Adam looked at the disconnected phone 'Shit! …. bloody shit!' he said.

'What's happened? Was that Julian?'

'Yes, the call ended with the unmistakable sound

of someone being hit over the head,' he said with anger in his voice. 'Well, at least we know where he is.'

'Where?' asked Michelle.

'Under guard in a room at a house just outside Tall Kala. He sounded like shit even before someone battered him.'

'Don't worry Adam, we will get him out,' said Michelle with a comforting pat in his leg.

'To bloody right, we will,' said Adam. 'The trick is how we get him out when we don't know if they're taking him with them to the trade-off or leaving him where he is.'

'We've to get to Tall Kala before they leave,' observed Michelle.

Adam nodded agreement and said 'I also know where our treacherous friend Wayne's information regarding our progress ended up. With bloody Bolton.'

'I guess we have lost the element of surprise.'

'Yes, I'll have to rethink things.'

They both became quiet and thoughtful.

Adam spoke first, 'You know, this might work to our advantage. Bolton may know that we're on our way, but he doesn't know that we're aware of the Tall Kala house. He'll presume that we'll tackle him at Now Zad in which case we can be pretty sure that he'll leave Julian at Tall Kala, preventing us from getting to him.'

Michelle said quietly 'I suppose if you hadn't come to rescue me on Monday night, then Julian would not be in this position.'

Adam turned to look at her and replied 'if I hadn't come to get you on Monday night the likelihood is that you would by now be the captive, or worse. There are a lot of people responsible for Julian's capture. None of them is you. If I hadn't contacted him regarding this in the first place, he would be at home listening to his classical music. If Mellors hadn't turned out to be a treacherous bastard, Julian would never have been put on that plane, so please don't blame yourself.'

'OK Adam I understand what you are saying,' she replied, looking away but they both knew that she would not be able to forgive herself if they didn't get him out safely.

'The good thing is, thanks to Colonel Karak and my conversation with Julian, we've a decent idea where he is. If we get there in time, there should be an opportunity to get him out.'

Both returned to their thoughts. Suddenly Adam shouted out of the open driver's side window 'For God's sake Matt, is this thing fixed yet?'

Recognising Adams frustration, he replied 'Two minutes boss, and you can try the ignition.'

'Thank God for that.'

Matt tightened up the last few makeshift hoses then gave Adam the thumbs up saying 'There'll still be some warning lights on the dash but just ignore them.'

'Oh right,' said Adam a little apprehensively and pushed the starter button.

The Mastiff engine coughed and spluttered, seeming to complain at being put back to work after its recent abuse but quickly settled into a rhythmic idling speed.

'Well done Matt, can you call the guys back and don't forget what I said about our friend, will you?'

'Will do on both counts Boss.'

'Right, let's get back on the road,' said Adam clapping his hands together 'Michelle can you do me a favour and swap with Charlie, I need to bring him up to speed and discuss tactics.'

'Gotcha Boss,' she said, got out of the passenger seat and into the rear.

Once on the road again Adam told Charlie about his eavesdropping on Wayne and also the call from Julian.

It took a lot to worry Charlie, and he looked a little worried. 'This is going to be tight Boss, have you got a strategy?'

'I have Charlie, but it is far from ideal. We have to assume that Bolton knows our strength and when we're coming. He doesn't know that we're aware of Tall Kala. My guess is that he won't make it easy for us by having both Julian and the shipment in the same location, which means that he'll keep Julian in Tall Kala and of course he'll have to take the weapons to Now Zad for the handover. Agreed?'

'Makes sense, Boss.'

'We are going to be much more dependent on stealth and brute force now we've lost the element of surprise. On the plus side, we know the canyon layout. I guess the ideal base position will be the same as a couple of years ago, on the rocky outcrop above the house and compound. Last time we went around the back and across the top of the hills in the APC. We won't have time for that tonight as we'll need the APC to go on to Tall Kala. We'll have to go on foot into the bottleneck of the canyon from the front. Work our way along the canyon floor at the base of the rocks on the right of the opening. Then head down the side to the walled house and compound. Once there we can set the explosives then scale the cliff to the position on the rocky outcrop above. We can pick off any survivors as and when. We have a dozen Claymores which we can 'daisy chain' and command-detonate. That'll take care of the building and compound. We've a dozen magnetic C4 mines and radio detonators, for the containers and trucks. There were no lookouts last time, but of course, that could have changed bearing in mind what happened. We won't know for certain until we get there.'

'That works in theory. What about the split?'

'I'm thinking 6 and 4. You take Matt and Wayne of course plus Gavin, Mark and Paul. I'll take Michelle, Carl and Henri to Tall Kala.'

'Sounds good,' said Charlie casting a look over his shoulder and grinned when he saw Matt squashed up next to Wayne. The latter looked less than cheerful as he was no doubt being treated to a blow by blow account of Matt's last rugby match for his beloved Unicorns. He won't be getting up to any mischief, he thought then he turned his attention back to Adam' What about Tall Kala?'

'Hard to say really, I have to assume that Bolton will go with the containers and leave a small contingent to guard Julian. It's about an hour from one place to the other, so I'm hoping that he'll leave before daylight, we're going to need the cover of darkness to get in there. We have 40 grenades, so we'll take 10. We know whereabouts he is inside the building, we just don't know for sure where the building is,' he said wryly. 'Still, Tall Kala is only a small place. I've looked on Google terrain and spotted a couple of likely areas that fit both Colonel Karak's directions and Julian's sketchy description'.

'Almost sounds like a plan,' said Charlie doubtfully. 'I wonder how things are going on the other side of the Med, have you heard from Ben Gifford yet?'

'No, but I'm expecting a call any time now. Anyway, I'd better get my foot down as time is starting to become an issue.'

The dust and sand plumed up from the Mastiff's tyres unseen in desert darkness as they hastened to the Now Zad canyon.

CHAPTER 19

Wednesday 4.00 PM - 2019

Ben Gifford settled back in his window seat on the Turkish Airlines flight from Gatwick to Istanbul having finished his G&T and tub of Pringles. He preferred salted peanuts, but you can't get them any more health and safety gone mad, he thought to himself.

His four-man team were seated nearby, two from his department and two from MI5. They had all been briefed on the mission. After arriving at the airport, they would split up and make their way individually to the Raffles hotel checking in separately. Later they would meet to finalise the details of their early morning trap for Gorton-Hyde.

MI5 had proved particularly helpful and knowledgeable regarding Gorton-Hyde's activities, in fact, Ben got the feeling that he might be helping them out rather than the other way around. It was made clear to him that some fringe members of the Saudi royal family were involved. So there would need to be diplomacy in handling any arrests. He had also discovered that similar illegal arms dealing had been going on for some years.

He put his head back, closed his eyes and considered the events of the last couple of days. If it hadn't been for the bitter but helpful Alice, they would all be in the wrong place. Instead, it was just the two men he had deliberately instructed, that had gone to Paris.

After his conversation with Adam on Tuesday, it had been easy to discover Gorton-Hyde's plans for the week with a phone call to his PA, Alice. It appeared that he planned to go to Paris after a meeting with the JIC on Wednesday and was booked into the George Cinque. It all seemed a bit too easy to Ben, so he called a chap in the F.O. that Julian had mentioned, Charles Renton. The latter was very informative regarding rumours about Gorton-Hyde's extracurricular activities. He had no time for Sir Lawrence but was clearly terrified of him. Most of Gorton-Hyde's own staff felt the same, especially Alice.

Later on Tuesday, he called into Gorton-Hyde's office and shared a pot of tea with Alice, a friendly lady and quite comfortable chatting with him. She also made no bones about her dislike for her bullying employer and would be pleased to see him come to a sticky end. So when asked if she was prepared to enable a bit of snooping, she was happy to help the police. She handed Ben the keys to his unoccupied office. Gorton-Hyde was not due back in until the Wednesday morning.

Ben proceeded to install an illegal microphone, he knew that he'd never get a warrant for a legitimate one. This meant that he would not be able to use anything that he gained from it in evidence, but then it was information rather than evidence that he was after. He locked up the office and walked back out through the administration area winking at Alice on the way out, she responded with an equally cheeky wink.

The strategy paid off handsomely as the following day Gorton-Hyde's conversation with Naylor in his office was overheard by Ben and his team. Along with his arrangements for Istanbul and subsequent meeting on Thursday morning.

Ben arranged for two of his men to go to Paris that evening and make some very obvious inquiries in the George Cinque Hotel's lobby regarding Sir Lawrence. That should keep Ralph Naylor happy at least until his arrest. This would also prevent any suspicions from getting back to Gorton-Hyde.

Ben managed an hour-long snooze before landing at Istanbul. As he disembarked, he was greeted by the pleasantly warm evening air, which was a stark contrast to the cold and wet weather that he had left behind in Gatwick. He got a taxi and took a little satisfaction from requesting the Raffles as his destination. The last time he and Mrs Gifford had been in Turkey the best they could do was an all-inclusive in Bodrum.

On arrival he was surprised at how modern looking the Raffles was, he had expected something more traditional. Inside it was spectacular with masses of chandelier lighting reflecting off the glistening marble and a colossal bronze sculpture. He made his way to the check-in desk and whilst signing in he casually said to the receptionist 'Has Sir Lawrence already checked in?'

'Yes sir, about half an hour ago, do you wish me to call his room?' replied the beautiful darkskinned receptionist her long straight black hair cascading down to the small of her back.

'No thanks we will be meeting later,' replied Ben, not wishing to make anything more of the enquiry.

Well at least he's here, let's hope the other fellow is as well, he thought as he made his way up to his room.

He threw his cabin case on the bed, his only piece of luggage. Then took out his smartphone and sent an email to Adam saying 'Team in position and target confirmed on-site, how are things at your end?'

❋ ❋ ❋

Half an hour earlier, Gorton-Hyde had arrived and was in his hotel room, though the Urban Suite was much plusher than Ben's smaller deluxe room. He poured himself a glass of Champagne from the complimentary chilled bottle, his mobile phone rang.

'Naylor.'

'Sir, I'm in the George Cinque lobby, and as you expected, I've just seen to dark-suited men asking if you're staying here. I have to say these boys are not very good at this sort of thing. They were easy to spot.'

Gorton-Hyde chuckled 'Yes, England's finest Ralph.'

Pleased and somewhat relieved to hear his master in good humour he agreed 'Quite Sir, what's next?'

The tone changed immediately 'What do you mean 'what's next'. I found your 'leak' for you now get hold of Bolton and make bloody sure that he's dealing with the problem out there or this whole thing could collapse. Call me as soon as you hear anything.'

Gorton-Hyde sat back feeling quite pleased with himself the buffoons have taken the bait, he thought smugly, all I have to do is clinch the deal with Kamal tomorrow. He knew that Kamal was still nervous, it had taken two years to get him back to the table after his cousin's death at the last aborted deal.

He was confident that the ace he had up his sleeve would sweeten the deal enough to see it through. Content with his plan, he went downstairs to the restaurant for his evening meal.

Enjoying his Chateaubriand and a passable bottle of Pinot Noir. In a quiet corner of the restaurant, he was blissfully unaware of the five sets of eyes watching him surreptitiously from various positions in the bar and restaurant.

❋ ❋ ❋

Despite his boss's abrupt ending to their telephone conversation, Ralph Naylor was feeling quite chuffed with himself. He had carried out his part of the plan perfectly so he thought he'd treat himself to a meal at the George Cinque restaurant. It was not something that he could generally afford, but he reckoned that he had earned it and would put it on expenses. Of course, he would have to make sure that Gorton-Hyde didn't find out.

After his expensive indulgence, Ralph went outside to wander back to his budget hotel. He considered who he would butter up to get the 150 euro receipt through expenses.

Heading towards the Metro, he turned left onto one of the quieter streets without noticing the two men following him. He suddenly remembered his boss's instructions and reached into his pocket for his phone. While he was studying the screen for Bolton's number, he didn't notice that the two men had caught him up.

One of them drew a cosh from the pocket of his black Crombie overcoat and having to reach high, due to Ralph's physique, he brought it down onto the back of his head as hard as he could.

Ralph stood frozen.

'Hit him again,' the other man said hurriedly.

Another brutal blow was reigned down onto Ralph's skull, and this time he dropped. They waved to a car across the road which sped towards them. It took both men to manhandle the substantial form into the back of the vehicle. Both men clambered in and slammed the doors shut. The car drove off towards the rear entrance of the British Embassy on Rue du Faubourg Saint-Honore.

Ralph was carried into a room with a fold-out bed in the corner. They dropped him on the bed with some relief and left, locking the door behind them. One of the men said 'You'd better ring the boss.'

The other officer pushed the call button on his phone.

'Stage one complete boss.'

Ben Gifford's voice came from the other end.

'Well done lads, any problems?'

'No, it went like a breeze, Sir. He's a big fella though it took two blows to drop him.'

'Good. Better make sure that he is alright. Let's hope that the rest of this goes as smoothly.'

Gifford tucked into his Istanbul style MacDonald's cheeseburger.

CHAPTER 20

Wednesday 6.00 PM - 2019

The Mastiff continued to thunder along the desert track, showing no weakening signs despite the dashboard's red warning lights. Adam focused on the road ahead, which was dimly lit by the shaded headlights. All was quiet in the cab as most of the team were getting forty winks.

The smartphone buzzed in his pocket with Ben's email. He read it. Ben was not aware of the information leak and that the cat was out of the bag regarding their presence in Afghanistan. He had better call him. It wouldn't do any harm to stop and get them all woken up, they were only three miles from Now Zad.

He pulled over and said 'Right, everybody out for the last stop, take a pee if you need one and get your kit ready.'

As they all dismounted Adam gave Matt a knowing look, he replied with an almost imperceptible nod. Charlie was already following Henri behind a rock. Matt stood fiddling around with the trailer cover, waiting to see where Wayne went. As expected, he headed off into the darkness behind the trailer. Matt waited a moment then followed quietly at a distance keeping Wayne's form identifiable in the gloom.

After he'd walked twenty yards or so he saw the unmistakable light from the screen of a mobile phone. He quickened his pace and walked forcefully straight into the back of Wayne, causing the phone to spring from his hands and fall to the ground. Feigning a trip forward Matt slammed his booted foot onto the still lit mobile phone screen making sure that he had crushed it beyond use.

'Bloody hell, sorry mate. I didn't see you there, I'm dying for a piss.' They both looked down at the now-useless phone.

'Fucking hell! Look what you've done,' exclaimed Wayne.

'Oh shit, never mind you can use mine if you need to ring your old mum or something,' he said innocently offering his phone to Wayne.

Thinking better of making a fuss, Wayne replied 'I was just using the screen light to look out for scorpions that's all.'

'Yeah, of course,' replied Matt and wandered back to the truck smiling to himself.

In the meantime, Adam had taken a different direction and was making a call.

'Ben?'

'Yes, Adam, how's it going?'

'OK but we've a leak at my end. We have it under control, but Bolton knows that we're coming. He will be expecting us at Now Zad. This means that Gorton-Hyde also knows.

'Oh shit, do you know where Julian is yet?'

'Yes, he's at the Taliban safe house somewhere in Tall Kala. The bloody fool managed to call me on a phone that he stole from his guard. It didn't end well.'

'That doesn't sound good 'Adam. Do you have a plan to get him out?'

'We're about three miles from Now Zad canyon where we'll install team A ready to deal with Bolton and the shipment in the morning. I'll lead team B to Tala Kala to extract Julian. Hopefully, Bolton will not have left to many men there. We can make all the preparations during the night, but I guess we can't bring things to a conclusion until you've closed the trap on Gorton-Hyde.'

'You're right Adam. Gorton-Hyde must not get a sniff of our plans at this end. From what you have told me, he knows that you're out there so he must be confident that his team can deal with you. Their' ace in the hole' is that they're holding Julian as a hostage. But his Saudi pal must receive some confirmation that the transfer is ready to go at your end or he will walk away from the table, then we'll have nothing. I'll let you know the second that they start the money transfer, sorry that's the best I can do.'

'Yes, I know Ben. It's just that we don't know how many 'Terris' there are in the compound at Now Zad. Ideally, I didn't want to split the team. I'll just have to extract Julian, then we'll get back to Charlie as quickly as possible.'

'OK, I'll be in touch.'

Adam pocketed his phone and got everybody back in the truck. He looked at Charlie who said 'He just took a piss and didn't say a word but as I said he is French. Probably just doesn't like the English.'

Adam laughed and cast a look back to Matt, who grinned and nodded slightly to confirm that the leak had been dealt with. That's some good news, thought Adam as they set off once again for the final leg.

Approaching the Now Zad canyon, Adam could see the rocky hills' shadow against the full moonlight. It was as he remembered, like a funnel with the rock face forming the sides. It curved inwards along the canyon then thinned towards the end where the house and compound sat. Behind which was a cliff face, he knew that there would be a rocky outcrop above and to the right where Colin Gooding had died. He had nearly joined him, his blood ran cold just thinking about it.

The vehicle lights were now turned off as they slowly crept towards the Eastern side's canyon opening. He stopped the Mastiff, and they silently got out, carrying their automatic weapons. Adam tapped Charlie's shoulder, they could see each other in the bright moonlight and pointed to the trailer, indicating that they should unload the explosives and share out the grenades. Charlie passed the instruction equally silently to Mark and Paul, who stacked the cases against the hillside.

Adam and Charlie crept around the edge of the rocks until they looked further into the canyon using their night vision binoculars. They could see the whitewashed outer walls of the compound about 1,000 meters away. They were surprised to see a new addition to the compound's defences.

'Oh shit,' murmured Charlie as he viewed a newly built 5 meter high, thick wire fence. It ran across the canyon floor from one rock face to the other. There was a watchtower at each end and double gates in the middle. They both suddenly jerked back against the rock face when they caught sight of movement at the top of one of the watchtowers. Looking at each other, Adam signalled to go back around the rocks until they could talk. The others followed wondering what the problem was.

Once far enough away, they spoke in whispers, and Adam explained the new addition to the defences.

'This doesn't work if we can't get to the compound and up to the outcrop above undetected. We haven't got the time to drive around the mount to come in from the other side. We have to go in from the front,' Adam went quiet as he considered options.

After a few moments, Charlie whispered 'The fence isn't much of an obstacle. It doesn't appear to be electrified, and there isn't any spotlighting. It's 5 meters high, but it's made of easily climbable thick wire mesh. To be honest, our only real issues are the guards at each end. If we can remove and replace them without discovery, we can still go ahead as planned.' He looked around 'Who speaks the best Pashto?'

They all looked at each other. Paul whispered 'I don't know about you and Matt, but I guess me and Gav might be the best. We've been out here a long time and become nearly fluent.'

Charlie replied 'Good enough. Matt and I only speak enough to give orders. Well, we've the best shooter I know with us, so what do you think Adam. Can it be done?'

'I guess if I can close the proximity a bit and get

a smooth swing on the stand I could do them both, using the suppressor to muffle the sound and kill the muzzle flash. Of course, it just depends on how the first one falls as to whether it alerts the other. I guess the plan is for Gavin and Paul to replace them and stay up there until the balloon goes up,' he looked at the two men 'you'll need some bottle lads. If they decide to change the watch, you'll be buggered.'

The two men nodded.

'It's the best plan we've got. Let's get on with it. Matt can you pass me the L115 and Michelle could you remove the camouflage tarp from the trailer I'll need it for cover.'

Michelle stood mesmerised for a moment listening to the matter-of-fact manner in which these men went about their business.

'Michelle!' said Adam.

'Oh … yes … sorry, of course, I'll get it now.'

Adam frowned a little as she went off. He unpacked the L115 rifle and fitted the night sights and suppressor.

Once Michelle had returned with the tarp, Charlie took it and followed Adam back around the edge of the rocks. They both hit the ground and Charlie covered Adam from head to feet with camouflage tarp.

Adam continued to crawl forward with his rifle crooked in his elbows across the front of his chest. He was almost invisible to the eye from any reasonable distance. Although the full moon was not doing him any favours. He estimated that the watchtowers were about seven hundred meters away. If he could get the shot down to six hundred that would improve his chances.

After a slow and near-silent crawl, he reckoned it was as good as it was going to get. He cautiously extended and placed the feet of the rifle stand firmly on the ground. The tarp covered him like a blanket reaching over his head and most of the weapon. From above, his entire body was camouflaged. He placed his eye at the other end of the sights and peered up at the nearest tower on the left end of the fence.

The tower was a wooden construction positioned on the other side of the fence. The turret sides overlapped the top, which shouldn't be too difficult to climb into from this side in Adams' view. He studied the top of the open turret. He found that he had a clear view of the Taliban sentry leaning on the edge, smoking a cigarette. He could have taken him there and then but needed to check the other one. The other sentry was leaning against the turret wall with the back of his head towards Adam. With a bit of luck he might be having 40 winks, he thought. It would be best to take the right-hand side first. The left side was a closer shot and therefore less margin for error on the swing back.

He put the right-hand guard in his crosshairs and paused then swung the weapon smoothly but quickly across to the man in the other turret stopping the crosshairs on his head. Having completed the dress rehearsal, Adam decided that he had better take the shots before either man changed position. He swung the barrel back towards the right tower. The moment the sights settled on the centre of his head Adam took a breath then slowly released the air from his lungs as he squeezed the trigger. There was a distinct thud, but no muzzle flash and the sentry sank to the floor of his turret. He swung the sights across to the left and smoothly chambered the next round then squeezed the trigger once again before the guard had a chance to react to the muffled sound of the first shot. There was a dull thud, and the man's head fell forward over the edge of the tower.

Adam prayed that his body would not continue forward and drop out of the turret to the floor. It didn't. The body just hung over the edge. Not bad, he thought. Considering that he hadn't picked up a rifle in over twelve months.

He knew that Gavin and Paul would have been waiting for the second shot. They came whistling past Adam on either side of him heading for their respective towers. Adam stayed in position and kept his sights on the front entrance to the house just in case.

The two men made short work of scaling the fence and climbing into the turrets, they removed the dead Taliban fighter's baggy clothes and put them on. Plus the sandy coloured Pakol caps. As both men were dark-haired and well-tanned, they would easily pass for the two guards from a distance. They unravelled the ropes they were carrying and dropped one end down the fence's front to the ground.

It was almost eerie in the silent moonlit canyon as Adam pushed the comms button on his radio and whispered 'Go, Charlie.'

Charlie and Matt were the next to fly past Adam, and they both carried two holdalls. Each filled with the Claymores. Once they reached their respective corners, they attached the bags to the ropes, which were then hauled up to the top and secreted in the turrets.

They scaled the fence, collected the bags in silence and descended the tower stairs on the other side. Once at the bottom, they made their way along opposite sides of the canyon walls to the compound's outer wall and waited for their companions.

Wayne and Mark were the next to head for the fence carrying the remaining kit including the C4 charges. They followed the same procedure, and Wayne joined Matt on the left end of the perimeter wall, and Mark joined Charlie at the other end.

Charlie's whispering voice came over Adams radio. 'Once the Claymores are in place, we will get up to the ridge above, and I will contact you to confirm that we are in position'.

'OK, Charlie I'll update you on our progress then.'

Before leaving, Adam took a moment to move the rifle sights up and to the right to view the rocky outcrop where he had been over two years previously. He couldn't help but feel a twinge in his leg. There was no sign of any movement from the house he cautiously got to a crouch and made his way back to the others.

'You three get in the truck it's 03:30, and we'd better get going. Carl, can you stow the L115?'

'Will do boss.'

Michelle got into the passenger seat, and the other two got into the rear of the Mastiff. Once underway, Michelle asked Adam 'How do we know where Julian is?'

'We don't exactly, I've looked on Google Earth, and there are two places that look both remote and large enough to take the container lorries. One is north of the village, and the other is east so we'll try the Northern site first. There's also some rocky terrain close to it which will help with a discreet approach. Some raised ground should allow us to get a look over any perimeter walls to the house and spot the trucks.' Adam then cast his voice towards the back of the cab saying 'Carl, do you know this area at all?'

'No, I haven't been in this neck of the woods before.' Carl looked across at Henri' What about you Henri?'

The sullen Frenchman replied 'Yes I've passed through Tall Kala several times. There's a large remote house to the North with a walled compound which is the most likely place for the enemy base.'

Adam said 'Really Henri, why on earth didn't you mention this before?'

'Nobody asked,' came the short and disinterested reply.

Adam could not see him in the back of the vehicle, but he knew that Henri's reply was no doubt accompanied by a dismissive shrug of the shoulders. A little frustrated by his attitude Adam continued 'What's the terrain like around the building and do you know how high the wall is?'

'You're correct, there is a small hill 700 meters to the right of the house, but the rest of the terrain is open flat desert. The perimeter wall is about three meters high,' he said flatly. Then volunteered 'we would have to approach on foot as zee truck would be too noisy and visible in zis moonlight.'

'OK thanks for that Henri, we'll stop as near as we can then plan from there,' Adam replied feeling a bit happier that Henri had engaged. His accent didn't seem to be as thick as it had been earlier.

Adam switched off the headlamps as the full moon provided enough light to drive through the open terrain. He put his foot down. Time was now becoming an issue as it would be nearly 04:30 before they got to Tall Kala. Without knowing how much manpower they were going to encounter, it might take some time to extract Julian. They'd have to wait until Bolton, and the wagons had set off to Now Zad before getting him out.

Most importantly, they must ensure that nobody could contact Bolton and alert him to their actions. He could easily turn round and come back, which could blow the whole mission. Every single one of Bolton's men in the house would have to be swiftly silenced one way or another!

Adam was deep in thought, and it was almost too late when he saw the convoy lead by the Range Rover approaching him in the distance. He quickly yanked the steering wheel to the left swerving off the track and into the desert. He stamped on the accelerator pedal, kicking up sand and stone from all four wheels and barrelled across the open desert. He prayed that he'd been quick enough and they hadn't been spotted.

Michelle ended up in the footwell, having been smashed against the passenger door by the sudden lurch to the left. The guys in the back were better prepared and were both on their knees with automatic weapons cocked and pointing out of opposite rear side windows. Adam kept going at full tilt until he was sure that they would be out of view then stopped the Mastiff.

'Sorry about that, I probably should have foreseen the possibility of us crossing paths. Bolton obviously wants to be punctual, and I guess those trucks travel quite slowly. Carl, can you have a look with the night vision binoculars and see if there's any sign that they saw us?'

'Already on it boss. They haven't moved off the track so I think we might've got away with it,' said Carl scanning the terrain.

'More good luck than good management,' said

Adam' either way, I'll take it. We'd better get going again. On the plus side, it means that we can get on with the extraction without waiting for Bolton to leave as long as he doesn't find out.' He looked across at Michelle, who managed to get herself back into the passenger seat. Adam noticed the trickle of blood from her forehead.

'You OK?'

Michelle turned to him and realised that he was looking at her head, she wiped her hand across it and looked at the smear of blood but simply rubbed it on her combat trousers.

'Fine apart from a bruised head and ego. I guess that's what seat belts are for,' she grinned. 'Ten out of ten for quick reactions, though.'

Adam grinned as they headed back towards the track at a less frantic pace. They reached the outskirts of Tall Kala just after 04:30.

Guided by Henri's local knowledge, they approached the vicinity of the house and compound. Just as Henri had described the immediate area around it was far to open to use the Mastiff. The nearest cover turned out to be a sand dune about 650 meters away, they stopped the truck behind it, all four of them got out and cautiously crawled up the dune. They peeked over the top edge of the sand using binoculars to examine the house for any tell-tale signs of occupancy.

Speaking quietly as voices would carry even at that distance, Adam said to Michelle 'Can you go back to the truck and get your sighting scope? It's in the case with the L115, we need to get a better look.'

'Will do boss,' she replied.

Quickly returning, she offered the scope to Adam, who gestured that she should use it. She nodded appreciatively and set it up on top of the dune. Peering into the compound over the top of the patchy white wall, the Axion scope had a range of up to 1200 meters. Allowing for a better view than the glasses.

Adam said quietly 'Take a slow pass across the entire compound and building. Talk us through every detail. We are looking for signs that will confirm that this is the right place, such as anything that shows Bolton and his men were here and who's still here.'

With a rock, steady hand, Michelle began the pass from right to left. 'The outer wall is three meters high and surrounds the building with a double gate entrance to the front wall. The gates are metal and appear substantive. There's space in the compound on the right-hand side for three low-loaders and the Range Rover. The only vehicle there at the moment is parked in the right-hand corner, a battered old Jeep which might be usable.' She paused. 'Moving across the grounds to the left, there are a dozen old wooden chairs and a table,' her voice tightened. 'One military-aged male is sitting at the table smoking and talking on a mobile phone. There's an automatic weapon resting against the back of his chair.'

Adam interrupted 'Is he a local?'

'I would say not as he's wearing a tan leather jacket and blue jeans which would suggest European or American.'

Adam interrupted again 'Let me have a look, Michelle?'

'Of course,' she replied. Without disturbing the scope, she moved her body down and across the dune. Adam did the opposite and peered through the sight.

His fist clenched as he recognised the man from the Norfolk airfield. It was Bolton's second in command. Julian was too important to leave with just anyone, at least for the moment anyway. 'Gotcha you bastard,' muttered Adam and signalled Michelle to resume her position.

'We've got the right place,' announced Adam quietly. 'The chap sitting in the compound is Bolton's number two, which also means Julian is likely to be on site. Carry on with your recce

Michelle.'

Michelle resumed her narrative 'The house is set back three meters from the inside of the perimeter wall. There are several window openings all with shutters but only 1 closed. I can see that the perimeter wall is set much closer to the rear of the building, about a meter apart. There are four people in the room to the right of the front door, in local dress. Nobody is visible on the first floor. The roof is typically flat with a trap door in the middle, nobody about.' Michelle moved her head away from the eyepiece and crawled away from the scope. 'That's about it guys.'

'Well done Michelle,' said Adam.

They moved back down the dune and got into the Mastiff to discuss tactics.

Adam began 'They don't have any lookouts, so they aren't expecting anyone. It would make sense for us to approach from this side as there are no windows. When I spoke to Julian, he said that he was in a first-floor room to rear and left of the building with a window in the rear wall. Once we reach the perimeter wall, we'll skirt around it. Michelle and I will go around the back, and you two run along the front to the far corner.'

'We'll scale the rear wall. The gap between wall and building is short enough at the rear for us to jump across to the first-floor window and grab the ledge in Julian's room. In the meantime, Carl and Henri will scale the far left wall, make their way across the front of the building and take out all of the ground floor personnel. We'll wait upstairs with Julian until you confirm the all-clear downstairs before we bring him down. As far as numbers go, I think it is safe to assume that Bolton would have left the minimum of men behind. Most likely, the four locals plus leather jacket and a guard in Julian's room. But I'm sure that I don't need to tell you not to count on that.'

Carl and Henri nodded their agreement.

Adam continued 'Under no circumstances can any of these guys be allowed to make a phone call. This has to be quick and clean. Best black up and grab ropes and hooks etc, from the truck. I want this wrapped up in one hour so that we can get back to Now Zad before kick-off. Any questions?'

'No boss,' replied Carl and Henri.

Michelle thought, yes about 100, including what if the guard in Julian's room gets us before we get him. But she thought better of asking and followed the others to get ready. She felt like the civilian that she was, among these three professional fighters. Adam had recognised her signs of discomfort during the briefing.

'Michelle, you really don't have to do this. You could be extremely helpful by staying at the Mastiff and bringing it across as soon as we're clear. I can get Julian out on my own.'

The fire returned to Michelle's eyes as she replied 'You must be joking. We've been through all of that. Now please excuse me while I put my make up on.' She slapped the camouflage paint onto her face.

Adam nodded his understanding and climbed the dune again. He took another look through the scope. Leather jacket was still sitting there, and Adam was sorely tempted to get the L115 and put one in his forehead. Instead, he just said to himself softly 'Enjoy your last fag mate, my boys will soon take care of you. Then I'll take care of your boss.' With that, he packed up the scope and joined the others in blacking up.

Once kitted up the four of them left the Mastiff and took a wide route towards the perimeter wall. Conscious that leather jacket may still be sitting in the compound area on the other side. Michelle and Adam followed the wall around to the back, running quietly to the bottom end.

Carl and Henri went the opposite way ran along the front to the other corner. They tossed their respective grappling hooks over the wall and climbed over the top. Once inside the compound, Carl ducked down and ran silently across the house's front, staying low underneath the windows. Reaching the corner near the compound, he took a mirror from his jacket. He carefully angled it along the edge of the house wall. He could see into the compound without detection. As expected, there was leather jacket with a bottle of beer in one hand and a cigarette in the other.

Henri was positioned by the front door near the right-hand window with a grenade in each hand. Both Adam and Carl had comms earpieces. Once they were all in position Carl would say 'go' wait for thirty seconds giving Adam and Michelle time to climb the wall, then take out leather jacket. At the same moment, Henri would throw 2 grenades through the window then the rest for good measure.

At the far end of the rear wall, Adam and Michelle were now standing with ropes in hand, having already tossed the hooks over and pulled them secure. They could see a dim flickering light from the first-floor window which was presumably a candle, hopefully in Julian's room. There were no lights in the other two windows.

The window was less than a meter across the gap from the top of the wall and slightly higher. They would be able to jump across and climb in quite quickly. They could not see or hear any signs of either Julian or a guard. Michelle had mirrored Adam and slung her weapon across her chest, ready to pull around and fire. Truth be told she was absolutely terrified but was not going to let it show.

Suddenly there was a whisper in Adam's ear 'GO!'

Adam began a mental count of thirty seconds whilst heaving himself up the wall. Michelle followed suit next to him, her foot slipping on the crumbling surface. She quickly recovered and soon reached the top perching next to Adam.

Carl stepped out from the shadows at the corner of the house. He fired three shots from his L85 into the head and chest of the unsuspecting Brad. His tan leather jacket turning red as blood burst from his torso.

At the same moment, Henri threw in the grenades, timed to give him a chance to duck down below the window. As soon as the first 2 exploded he threw in the rest. Once they had detonated, he poked the barrel of his weapon through what remained of the window frame and fired off a full magazine in a scattergun style. Carl joined him and did the same.

The moment the first shot was fired, Adam leapt across to the lower ledge of the window and in almost one motion pulled himself up through the gap into the room. He could barely see by the dim candlelight as he desperately looked across the room for Julian. He made out what appeared to be a pile of dirty clothes in the far corner of the floor.

Making to cross the room he suddenly felt the unmistakable cold metal of a gun barrel pressing against the back of his neck. 'Don't move a fucking muscle,' said a thick Eastern European voice.

Adam froze. *Rookie bloody mistake*, he thought. He'd been so preoccupied looking for Julian. On entering through the window, he hadn't checked over his left shoulder.

Suddenly, a loud crack and the gun to Adam's head fell to the ground, quickly followed by the body that had been holding it. Adam turned slowly to see through the window frame, Michelle standing on top of the wall.

She was frozen in position, holding the automatic rifle sights to her eye with the barrel still pointing at the space previously occupied by the guard.

She had hesitated on making the jump across, which was just as well, seen Petrov move across the window to threaten Adam. Instinctively raised her weapon and fired the deadly headshot.

'You bloody star,' said Adam 'are you OK?'

He realised that she wasn't and ran across to the

window saying calmly 'Michelle, you must put the weapon down and jump across. I guarantee that I will catch you.'

She did not move.

'Come on, Michelle. I need you to help me with Julian, he's in a bad way.'

The mention of Julian's condition seemed to release her from the petrified state. She lowered the weapon and eventually made the leap into Adams outstretched arms. He dragged her in. Swiftly they moved across the room to Julian.

All hell had broken loose downstairs by now as the boys went about their business with gusto.

Adam and Michelle bent over the dishevelled body in the corner. Julian was lying face down on the floorboards they could see the matted blood across the back of his head and down his shirt.

Nodding across to Petrov lying on the floor Adam said with venom in his voice 'If you have any issues about shooting that bastard, remember he did this to Julian.'

Michelle gave Adam a meaningful look and replied softly 'I don't want to talk about what just happened at the moment.'

'OK.'

They rolled Julian over, and Michelle took a sharp intake of breath when she saw his bruised a battered face, the blood oozing from his stab wound and his still bound feet. They had now turned purple.

Adam simply stared down at his friend, and his jaw visibly hardened as he made a promise to himself.

'I need to check his breathing,' said Michelle.

Suddenly there was the sound of running up the stairs, Adam grabbed his weapon and swung it round to point it down the landing. Before reaching the top of the stairs, the person shouted 'Clear boss... Clear boss.'

Adam lowered the L85 and shouted 'Carl! Henri! Get in here now. We've got a man down.'

Both men burst into the room and stopped suddenly at the sight of Julian on the floor Henri said sombrely 'Est-il mort?'

Adam looked at Michelle for an answer. By now she was kneeling on the floor and had Julians head in her lap.

'No. But we need to get him to a hospital quickly. Can you remove the nylon bindings to his legs but be extremely careful. They have cut deep into the flesh and tightened as he has struggled against them. On second thought's it would be better not to remove them, just cut each side so that his legs can separate. We'll extract the ties later when we have some medical equipment, they're too deeply embedded in his muscle tissue. Carl please could you get some water? Henri, can you go and get the Mastiff and find something stretcher like so that we can transport him downstairs?'

Both men replied 'Will do,' and disappeared.

Adam was pleased that she had taken charge.

Once they had gotten some water into Julian, he started to come round and eventually opened his eyes. He croaked 'Oh Adam, dear boy, I knew you'd come for me.'

'Sorry I couldn't get here sooner.'

'That's OK, I know you'll make them pay,' Julian said weakly and looked across at Petrov's body 'It looks like you have already started.'

'I can't take credit for that one, Julian,' replied Adam nodding towards Michelle.

Julian tried to twist his head on Michelle's lap and look up towards her. He winced in pain.

'Don't move anything, for now, Julian,' she said softly.

'My dear lady, I must apologise, have I been lying on your lap all this time and not introduced myself. You must be Michelle, the lady who has stolen my friend's heart and it seems saved his life as well. What a formidable female you……..

mus……..b…..' and he drifted back into unconsciousness.

Michelle looked up at Adam and said 'He has a severe head trauma we must get him to a hospital ASAP.'

Henri had now returned with the Mastiff. He'd ripped off one of the front doors from the house to use as a stretcher. It hadn't taken much doing as there wasn't a lot left of the downstairs area in general. He had strapped some cushions from what remained of the furnishings onto the wood to create some padding. He put the rear seats down in the Mastiff, which worked quite well. Julian's stretcher, along with Michelle and Henri, fitted in quite easily.

They were soon back on the road again heading to Now Zad, and it was 05:30. If it hadn't been for Julian's condition, Adam would have been pleased with himself as they still stood a chance of getting to the trade-off by 06:30. He'd checked that all of the enemies were dead and was confident that no one had been able to get a warning to Bolton.

Coming from this direction, he could drive around the top of the hills to the back of the rocky outcrop, just as he and his team had done 2 years ago. Then join Charlie and the boys. He floored the gas pedal, and they disappeared from Tall Kala in a cloud of dust.

As the Mastiff bumped along the rocky track pretty soon, Michelle was poking his shoulder from the rear seat.

'Adam you can't knock him around like this or he'll never make to a hospital,' she said with real concern 'I can patch him up, but I don't have any medical skills.'

Adam eased off the throttle slightly. He was determined to get to Now Zad in time. Julian was like a brother to him, but he would push things to the limit to achieve his goal.

Glancing at Carl, who was now in the passenger seat next to him, he called over his shoulder 'Michelle, I can't go any slower, or we'll not get to the others in time. Unless you are telling me that we have to give up. You'll just have to do your best, I know that will be more than most. The sooner we get there, the sooner we can get to some better medical kit from the trailer. Plus Charlie has medical training, I can certainly vouch for that.'

Michelle sighed and said 'OK Adam, I understand.' Not happy with his reply, she returned her attention to Julian.

The mention of Charlie reminded Adam that he must make contact and update him on phase one. He grabbed his phone and saw that a text had arrived from him during the excitement in the house. Adam was pleased to know they were in position, but he had to let them know that Bolton would be early. He pushed the call button.

CHAPTER 21

Wednesday 9.00 PM - 2019

After Adam and his team had left Tall Kala Charlie and Mark scaled the perimeter wall whilst Matt and Wayne did the same at the other end. Both teams hauled over their equipment quickly and quietly. Once on the other side, they crouched in the corners concealed in the shadows created by the two external sodium lights on the house. They waited to see if there were any signs of movement inside. They were all professionals, but heart rates still rose as they crouched against the wall and waited to move.

On scanning the area to the side of the house. Charlie was surprised to find that there had been an addition to the compound below. In the form of a large storage building which was easily big enough to take the three trucks and containers. He contemplated placing some of the Claymore mines on the new building but thought better of it as it was doubtless empty and the mines would be better used in dealing with the personnel in the house.

Once they were certain that they had not been detected, Matt and Wayne went to work placing the Claymores mounting spears into the earth. Ensuring that the backs were firmly against the inside of the perimeter wall. The curved blast panels were facing slightly upwards towards the front of the house.

The mines would release 700 ball bearings at 4,000 feet per second decimating anybody within 50 meters of a 60-degree arc. Matt and Wayne covered the mines with sand and dirt until they were barely visible standing only five inches above the ground.

They connected all six creating a 'daisy chain' leading to one firing wire. Which was covered with sand and run across to Charlie and Mark. The two men had been covering them with weapons targeted at the front of the house.

'All in position,' whispered Matt in Charlie's ear.

Matt and Wayne then took over. Providing cover for Charlie and Mark as they made their crouched approach to the house's right-hand side wall, avoiding the illumination from the external lights. They fitted their six Claymores directionally facing the pathway leading from the house's rear and into the compound.

Once again they were linked and the single firing wire buried in the sand leading across the compound and back to Matt and Wayne in the shadowy corner.

Now came the tricky bit as they'd have to climb the steep rock face to the right of the compound and up to the ledge above. They were also carrying the remainder of their kit and had to ensure the two firing wires' integrity. At the edge of the compound, they found the rock face, there was an upward slope which provided a starting point for the climb.

Silently Charlie tapped Matt on the shoulder and signalled him to go first and the others to follow. He would bring up the rear with the firing wires, ensuring that nobody could damage them accidentally.

The route up the mount-side to the ledge was deceptive. It initially took them in the opposite direction, away from the shelf above. Then doubling back and ending with an almost sheer twenty-foot climb none of which was much fun in the darkness. Extra care had to be taken not to dislodge rocks or stones which might fall to the ground and alert the enemy inside the house.

When they reached the last section, Wayne began to mutter words of complaint, as he looked up at the twenty-foot climbing challenge.

Matt turned on him and whispered harshly. 'It can't be that hard it's only twenty feet, a bleeding 'Terri' managed it easily, before killing my mate and stabbing the boss in the leg.' Not waiting for a reply he turned and began the ascent. Wayne took careful note of the footholds that

Matt was using.

Once Matt had gotten to the top and safely climbed onto the ledge, Wayne made his way up. Matt leant over the edge and took Wayne's weapon and kit back from him to make it easier.

Once all four men were on the top of the outcrop, they set up their firing point for the Claymores. They had pre-tested the detonators integrity. As long as the connections had held, they should fire using the two M57 'Clackers', connected to the other ends of the 2 firing wires. They also set up their individual shooting positions ready to deal with Bolton's men and any survivors from the house below.

When they were all installed, they sat back against the rock away from the ledge's edge and took on some water. Charlie took out his phone and sent a text to Adam.

'A'

04:30. All in position.

'C'

Charlie put the phone away and took the opportunity to rest his eyes. One thing you learnt to do in combat was to take any moments of rest that you could, you never knew when the next opportunity might arise. He rested his head against the same rock that Adam had used two years previously and considered recent events.

Like Adam, he had enjoyed being back in action, and like Matt, he had struggled to fit into civi street. He had been pleased to receive Adams call to arms. It was good to have the three of them back together.

He had resented Michelle's presence at first. There was a risk that her complete lack of experience would put the whole team in danger. He also held the outdated view that females should not be in combat. However, after hearing her story on the plane and spending some time with her over the last couple of days, he developed a healthy respect.

Initially, he was a little disconcerted by the boss's obvious romantic attraction to her. But he had also come to terms with that and considered that she was a good person who might also be good for Adam. In fact, they made a great team.

His phone vibrated in his pocket, and he pulled it out. Answering quietly 'Adam. We're ready to go once Bolton arrives.'

'Good Charlie, we've got Julian, but he's in a bad way and needs medical attention ASAP. We're on our way to you now, and ETA is 06:45. We passed Bolton when we were on the way here so he'll arrive about 06:00 hours, which is good news as you may benefit from a little pre-dawn darkness. You'll need to be ready to install the C4 explosives at the first opportunity.'

'No problem, Adam. We're ready to go, just get yourselves over here as quick as you can, I presume you'll come around the back of the hills to our position?'

'Yes. Advise when Bolton has arrived.'

'Will do Boss.'

Charlie updated the rest of the team with Adams info and laid out the proposed plan for C4 install.

'Assuming Bolton and his crew will initially park up the trucks on the other side of the fence, at least until the financial end of the deal is done. We'll have to go back over via the watchtower and attach the explosives to the containers. Then get back over here undetected. We can detonate remotely at zero hours. Mark and I will do the job. You and Wayne can cover us from here, Matt.'

'Will do Charlie,' said Matt.

Wayne nodded his agreement, happy not to be taking on the risky job.

Charlie and Mark busied themselves checking the magnetic attachments and the signal receiver on the detonators, a small box about the size of a cigarette packet with a guarded on/off switch. It was secured to the block of C4 explosives which was in turn fixed to a magnetic plate with a removable plastic cover. All twelve of the bombs could be activated simultaneously from the wireless firing device. Charlie would do this from their base position back on the ledge.

They packed six each of the explosives, each about the size of a house brick, into their backpacks.

Charlie continued 'Dawn will be just after 06:00 hours, so hopefully we'll have a bit of night cover. Either way, the sun won't get over these hills until about 08:00 hours so the canyon edges will be in shadow. If they park right down the middle, we'll have a problem and have to rethink things. But we'll cross that bridge if we come to it. Bolton and his crew will have been travelling for at least two hours so they'll be keen to stretch their legs. Once they wander away from the vehicles, we'll take the available opportunity to place one block under each of the wagon cabins then one block on the rear of every container. The intention is to ensure that the wagons are disabled and as much destruction as possible is caused to the container contents. Any questions?'

'No, that's all pretty clear,' Mark replied.

'Matt and Wayne will cover us from the ledge, but ideally, we will get this done without any shots fired and remain covert.'

Charlie knew that this would depend very much on when the trucks arrived and where they were parked. It would require some skill and initiative, but Mark seemed to be a bright and steady guy. He had to leave Matt to keep an eye on Wayne anyway, so there was no choice. A climbing rope was anchored and dropped over the ledge to speed up the passage down to the ground. They sat and waited in the darkness.

At 05:50 the rumble of distant lorries became audible as they approached the canyon's mouth from the left. They entered slowly following the line of the rock face to the left, led by Bolton's Black Range Rover. It pulled across the front of the fence and stopped. The three trucks were lined up neatly against the canyon wall.

Charlie thought to himself that couldn't be better, I just hope that Paul and Gavin can pull this off.

Bolton got out if his car and shouted up to the guards in the towers ignoring the fact that they were both pointing automatic weapons at him 'Hey you. Tell your boss that we've arrived.'

Gavin shouted back form the turret using a thick Afghani accent 'He knows! …. you wait!'

Lights had already started to appear in the windows of the house.

'Yeah ..yeah I know we're early anyway,' said Bolton dismissively and walked away towards the trucks waving his arms at the occupants to get out.

Eagerly three men exited each cabin, some of them hurrying across to the canyon's opposite side to take a leak and others lighting up cigarettes.

This is it, Charlie thought and gave the thumbs up. He disappeared down the rope quickly followed by Mark. Once at the bottom, both men scuttled along the rocks, their backpacks heavy with explosives. Reaching the perimeter wall, they scaled it with the help of a rope and hook, then continued to the guard tower. Quickly the two men climbed the stairs to reach Paul at the top who had already lowered a rope down the other side of the fence.

Without passing a comment, they grabbed the rope and lowered themselves swiftly back to the ground on the other side of the fence just in front of the first lorry cabin. Moving to the driver's side, between the canyon wall and the vehicle. They entered a handy corridor that had been created by all three of the trucks and their trailers.

Charlie looked at Mark and gestured firmly towards the far end of the corridor. Silently Mark gave Charlie the thumbs up in agreement then set off for the back of the third truck.

Charlie selected the first bomb from his backpack, removed the thick plastic cover from the magnetic surface and flicked the activation switch. The red LED showed that the detonator was now live. Reaching underneath the cabin, he felt for the engine oil-sump cover. Once found, he allowed the powerful magnet to attach to the engine. He tested the firmness of the hold and once satisfied, moved on to the rear of the first container. Reaching up once again and attaching the magnetic plate this time to the metal body of the container. He carried out the same process on the next 2 containers and was ready to cross to the next truck.

There was plenty of chatter going on in the middle of the canyon where Bolton's men had gathered to drink water and smoke. One of them began to walk back towards the trucks, there was a shout in a thick Eastern European accent 'Where you go Radko?'

'Take a peez, what you think?' was the reply.

Charlie stiffened as he heard the man approaching the gap between the two trucks, he crouched as low as possible, hoping that Mark was not approaching from the other end. Radko came through the gap between the two vehicles, thankfully, he turned right to create some privacy behind the middle truck. He answered the call of nature.

Charlie kept his breathing shallow and quiet, it was a mistake to hold your breath in these situations, and you couldn't know how long you would have to continue. You either end up expelling air, which is hard to keep quiet or pass out neither of which would end well. It was just as well as Radko had a lot of fluid to unload.

There was no sound from Mark so Charlie could assume that he'd realised what was happening and done the same as him. Once Radko had completed his task, he returned to his comrades and Charlie moved on to the next truck. After placing his last two bombs, he waited for Mark to meet him.

It was now 06:15, and the sun was up. It hadn't reached their side of the canyon. The hills on the opposite side cast a dark shadow at least for another hour. They were protected from view by the trucks nearly all of the way back to the fence and tower. Once on the other side, they would potentially be visible between the tower base and the perimeter wall.

Mark joined Charlie, and in a crouched run, they made their way back to the front of the vehicles. One at a time, they swiftly ascended the hanging rope and got into the turret with assistance from Paul. Without uttering a sound, they patted Paul on the shoulder and descended the steps.

Both men knew that this was a risky bit and steeled themselves for the dash. When the moment felt right, Charlie set off from the bottom of the turret steps. He soon reached the perimeter wall and grabbed the rope. Quickly he scaled the wall and dropped down the other side swiftly followed by Mark. Neither of them had been detected.

They scuttled across the compound's edge to the bottom of the cliff face and began the ascent. It was much more direct and easier using the climbing line. Charlie soon reached the top. Mark followed suit but found the final section tricky and lost his footing. A shower of loosened rocks cascaded down the hill and clattered into the compound at the bottom. He froze dangling from the rope in mid-air six feet from the edge of the ledge. He waited for the shouting or, worse still, the gunfire.

Charlie listened intently, having moved away from the edge, out of view. The ledge was now bathed in bright sunlight.

Two of the 'Terri's came out of the front door, weapons in hand. They wandered into the compound. Mark tried not to move and prayed that they wouldn't look up.

The two Afghans went across to the big metal gates and looked through a gap at the men milling about on the other side of the fence. If they happened to turn around and look up, they could not have missed Marks form, dangling above.

Charlie had no choice. It was, do or die. He crawled forward and taking a firm hold of the rope heaved Mark up. Mark grabbed the rocky ledge.

Matt and Wayne remained at the back of the ledge with their weapons trained on the men in the compound. Charlie let go of the rope, and clasping Mark's hands pulled him over the top. They both quickly crawled out of view then remained still, waiting for some reaction from below.

Eventually, the Afghans wandered back into the house.

'Sorry about that, Charlie.'

'No problem it could happen to the best of us,' Charlie replied.

Charlie then sat back against the rocks and took a swig of water. Despite a couple of hiccups, they had managed to remain undetected, which was no small thing considering the amount of activity down there. He thought there may be up to a dozen men inside the house. The Claymores, plus their firepower from the ledge, would take care of them. The C4 plus Gavin and Paul could deal with the other dozen on the other side of the fence, from the towers.

All in all, they were in a pretty good position, if Adam and the others could get here before kick-off that should ensure their success. Opportunely his comms phone vibrated as he received Adams text.

'C'

We are parked on the other side of the rocks behind you. Can you get around here and have a look at Julian ASAP.

'A'

Charlie sent back the 'thumbs up' emoji, and he made his way to the exit from the ledge at the back, quietly informing Matt that Adam had arrived.

Matt took up his position with the firing 'clackers' and the remote C4 detonator. The other two men continued to monitor the activity below with their binoculars.

Adam exited the Mastiff as Charlie came around the corner. Carl and Henri grabbed their weapons and nodded to Charlie as they passed him on their way to join Matt and Wayne on the ledge.

'Are they here yet?' said Adam.

'Yes, they got here about three-quarters of an hour ago. You did bloody well to get back here so quickly.'

Adam looked sheepishly towards Michelle who all but glared at him 'Yes I had to give the old Mastiff some hammer. I er, don't think it will have done Julian any good though. Can you take a look at him?'

'Of course,' Charlie replied, sensing some tension between Adam and Michelle. He climbed into the APC to have a look at Julian.

Adam and Michelle stood in silence by the vehicle, waiting for Charlie to finish his examination and treatment. Adams thoughts were in conflict, he desperately wanted to get around to the ledge with the others and assess the situation ready for the final action, but he didn't want to leave until he knew Julian's condition.

Although Michelle had only known Adam for a week, she had learnt enough about him to realise this. Now that her anger at his apparent lack of concern for Julian's condition had subsided she was more sympathetic to his position.

'Adam, there's no point in both of us standing here. You should be with the rest of the team, I'll stay with Julian. Charlie can update you on his condition when he joins you.'

Relieved that Michelle had made his decision for him, Adam replied 'You're a good woman Michelle.'

'Well, you are a good man, despite your reckless driving,' she replied with her endearing smile showing through her black painted face.

With that, Adam grabbed the L115 case, and his automatic rifle then disappeared around the rocks.

Michelle leaned into the vehicle and asked Charlie 'How is he?'

'He's not great, Michelle. I can't really assess the damage to his skull here so I've put a stabilising collar on his head and neck and a field dressing on his stab wound but I can't do much for his legs at the moment. I don't want to remove those ties out here, you've already done a good clean and sterilise job. We'll have to wait until we can get him to a hospital. He's in and out of consciousness. I've given him some morphine for the pain so he'll probably sleep for a while.'

'How far is it to the nearest hospital, Charlie?' said Michelle with grave concern.

'Shorabak is the only place we could go, so it's going to have to wait until this is over I'm afraid.'

Michelle looked at Julian then back at Charlie,

who suddenly realised what she was thinking.

'NO! Michelle. Before you even suggest it. You wouldn't get two miles. The place is crawling with a variety of enemies, of which most are Taliban fighters.'

Her head dropped in resignation 'Yes. I know Charlie.'

'Look, as far as we can tell he's stable, hydrated and not in any pain. You stay here and watch him while we get this mission finished. You won't be discovered up here and even if you are, just drive around that corner and down to the ledge. It's only three hundred meters. You have your weapon, and I'll leave a couple of grenades just in case. Is that OK?'

'Yes, of course, Charlie, you'd better get back to the others,' she said with confidence returning to her voice.

'OK,' said Charlie and gave her the grenades. He patted her on the shoulder then disappeared around the rocks to join the rest.

By now all of Bolton's men had located themselves at the entrance to the canyon. They were expecting Adam and his team to attack from that direction. The ambush was set as far as they were concerned.

It's almost laughable, thought Adam as he positioned himself and set up the L115. He put his eye to the glass, and there was Bolton near to the fence. He was well away from his men and the threat of any action. Adam enjoyed viewing that head through the scope-sights. Tempting as it was to pull the trigger, now was not the time.

For some reason, he suddenly remembered what Julian had said on the phone about Bolton avenging his brothers killer, and it suddenly clicked. 'Of course, the European arms dealer that arrived in the helicopter two years ago,' he murmured. He recalled that he'd taken him out along with the two Arabs. That must have been Bolton's brother, wow he must be pissed off at me. Well, all the more pleasure in putting a bullet through his head, he thought coldly.

Charlie crawled up next to him. 'What's up boss?'

'Nothing important, I'll tell you later. How is he?'

'Stable and out of pain, I've left Michelle to keep an eye on him. I've instructed her to drive down here as a last resort.'

'OK, Charlie.'

Adam's conscience was once again troubled by his concern for both Julian and Michelle being left on their own. Even though they were not far away, they were two innocent civilians that he had been dragged into this battlefield. He pushed the thoughts to the back of his mind and focused on the job at hand.

'That's new,' he said, pointing down at the large building in the compound.

'Yes, they must've built it to accommodate the weapons containers. My guess is that when the time comes, they'll open those double doors and reverse the low loaders into the warehouse, disconnect the cabins and drive them back to Darwai airport.'

'Well that's not going to happen,' said Adam with certainty. 'its 07:00 so we could get the call from Gifford any time over the next hour I guess depending on events at his end. I don't suppose there'll be any contact between Bolton and the 'Terri's until the deal is done,' Adam observed. 'Has Wayne been behaving himself?'

'He's not a happy bunny, and Matt has him on a very short leash. He can either run away or stay and fight. Whatever else he might be I don't have him down as a deserter.'

'We're at full strength then not including Michelle, of course.'

'Yep.'

All seven men lay in the sand on their bellies. In the baking heat of the desert sun. Each with their weapon prone and ready for action. Charlie, with his hand in easy reach of the detonators, just waiting for the call.

CHAPTER 22

Thursday 4.30 AM - 2019

Ben Gifford's phone alarm buzzed and he dragged himself out of bed muttering 'I'm getting too old for this game.' He checked in with his team who were all ready to go. *Fit young buggers*, he thought. He drew the curtains and observed an almost English weather scene of cloud and rain. Glad I'm not paying for this, he thought as he went off to the bathroom.

Once refreshed and dressed, he called one of the MI5 guys in the hope that they had received the necessary intel overnight regarding the venue for Gorton-Hyde's breakfast meeting.

'Thornton, do you have an update?'

'Yes. An accommodating receptionist informed me that a breakfast meeting will take place at 7.00 am. Gorton-Hyde is up and about, and the other party is a Saudi called Kamal. He has four men accompanying him. Also, we have a lot of interest from MI6, someone over there wants a real-time blow by blow on the operation.'

That would explain why some of the 'arrangements' had been so easy to make, he thought. 'Who is it?'

'No idea, beyond my pay grade I expect.'

'Well it will have to wait, I want everyone in my room in five minutes for a final briefing.'

'OK boss I'll tell the others.'

By 5.10 am, all five men were seated in Ben's room. 'Thornton, what's your plan?' asked Ben.

'They're having breakfast served in the Saudi's suite so Parke's and I will knock out the two waiters on their way to the room. We can both speak enough Turkish to get by, but I guess English will be the language of choice anyway. We'll fit the microphone during service then back away, as would be expected but remain in the room. You'll be able to see what's going on via my lapel cam. Once the Saudi confirms transfer from his end, we will deal with the guards.'

Ben addressed his two officers' We'll be in the corridor and burst the front door at the same time and assist with the guards.' Then he turned to include the two MI5 agents' The Saudi is a distant member of the royal family called Kamal bin Sharaf. We do not have the authority to touch him, so everyone focuses on disarming the guards, without gunplay. Gorton-Hyde and Kamal are unlikely to be armed. They're not expecting any trouble. I'll grab Gorton-Hyde and the laptops then we exit and get him out to the car and subsequently to the boat.' Gesturing towards Thornton and Parkes, he said 'You two make your own way back to England through normal channels. We will escort Gorton-Hyde back via Cyprus. Any questions?'

All shook their heads.

'Good, check your weapons are silenced just in case and let's get to our positions it's nearly 6.00am.'

❋ ❋ ❋

Gorton-Hyde awoke at 5.30am feeling refreshed and looking forward to the day. He relished the challenge of making the deal and enjoying the rewards even more. He quickly showered and dressed in his civil service style dark suit as if heading off to Whitehall. Perversely he still considered himself to be a representative of Her Majesty's Government, despite his criminal activities. He presented himself with the pomp and arrogance of old empire.

He helped himself to an Italian blend coffee from the machine in his room and stood in the full-length windows viewing the cloud and rain outside. He checked the crystal face of his Swiss-made Rado watch, which told him it was 6.40 am. Picking up his briefcase which contained the all-important laptop, he made his way up to

Kamal's suite.

At 6.55 am, Gorton-Hyde knocked on the suite door, and a large, square-jawed Saudi Arabian opened it. Without speaking, he gestured him to enter. He followed the guard into the lobby of the suite. The guard then turned and placed a large open palm firmly on his chest halting his movement. There followed a swift and intimate pat-down.

'Is this really necessary?' Gorton-Hyde protested.

The guard did not speak but took the briefcase and opened it. Once satisfied that there was just the laptop inside, he closed and returned it.

'Thank you so much,' said Gorton-Hyde sarcastically 'perhaps now we can get on.'

His sarcasm was wasted as the guard simply turned in silence and proceeded to the large and sumptuously decorated dining room. There another guard was waiting looking equally menacing with the noticeable bulge under his left arm. He was beginning to wish that he had brought Naylor with him for appearance sake if nothing else. He took the seat that was proffered at the highly polished dining table and placed his briefcase on the seat next to him and waited.

A few moments later, the door on the other side of the room opened. Yet 2 more guards entered followed by a good looking Saudi man in his early thirties, dressed in an expensive-looking light grey suit. He walked towards the other side of the table, offering his arm across it, inviting a handshake.

Gorton-Hyde immediately stood and took the outstretched hand' Good morning Kamal, we meet at last. I see you don't take any chances,' he said nodding towards the 4 human statues, now positioned behind Kamal.

'Good morning to you, Sir Lawrence. Yes, we live in difficult times my friend,' he replied as one of his guards drew back the chair in for him to take a seat.

Almost immediately, there was a knock at the external door.

'Ahh bang on time, Breakfast, I hope you're hungry. We'll have a variety of fruits and breads but of course some fried eggs and bacon also. Despite the religious implications having spent my formative years at Eaton and Cambridge, I fully understand the pleasures of a bacon sandwich.'

Both men laughed politely. Two waiters came in with a trolley each and proceeded to unload them onto the table. It was indeed a spread; however, neither men had much of an appetite. They simply took the coffees that the waiters had poured for them. Kamal waved an accustomed dismissive hand, and the two men receded to the back of the room away from the table. Of course, neither Gorton-Hyde nor Kamal and more importantly, the four stooges had noticed the microphone that Thornton had stuck under the edge of the table. This meant that Ben and his men were now observing sight and sound. Using their 'tablet' from the cleaning cupboard at the end of the corridor.

'So far, so good,' whispered Ben.

'Should we get down to business Kamal?' said Gorton-Hyde as politely as possible.

'Certainly, Sir Lawrence.'

Gorton-Hyde made no effort to suggest that he should drop the 'Sir' as he enjoyed the feeling of superiority that it gave him.

Kamal continued 'It has taken two years to rebuild some trust since the utter disaster that your last attempted trade with us brought. I do hope things are better organised this time?'

A little taken aback at the Saudis robust opening comments Gorton-Hyde was on the defensive. He replied 'Absolutely Kamal, I can assure you that I have a much better team dealing with the transfer this time. I can say with absolute certainty that you'll be pleased with the outcome,' he said, thinking that he would save his ace until later.

'That is indeed reassuring to hear Sir Lawrence. However, I do regard this to be a probationary trade, the success of which will influence our future, potentially very lucrative, business deals together. With that in mind, I have reviewed the terms of my offer.'

Kamal took a note pad from the inside pocket of his suit jacket and wrote down a number then passed it across to Gorton-Hyde who took it and very nearly choked on his coffee. Taking a moment to compose himself, he said as calmly as he could 'Ten million dollars. That's half of what we agreed.'

Without flinching and calmly taking a sip from his coffee kamal replied 'That is correct. I am sure that you can appreciate the importance of building a strong business relationship, especially after the previous fiasco. I would consider your acceptance of this price an excellent gesture of goodwill,' he said, ending with a smile.

You slippery bastard. Thought Gorton-Hyde then replied. 'Of course, Kamal, I fully understand that we need to rebuild our trading relationship and value the prospect of our future deals. But if you could just take a look at the inventory on this one. There are sixty Javelin rockets and ten launchers that's ten million alone never mind all the rest.'

Kamal's smile disappeared, and darkness fell across his face as he leaned forward. Glaring at Gorton-Hyde he said almost threateningly 'Lawrence,' (he had dropped the Sir without invitation) 'please do not insult my intelligence. I know exactly what is on the inventory. It's no secret that the Javelin missiles you mention were sent free of charge by the Americans to Ukraine. Your Russian friends stole them and then sold them to you for next to nothing. Even with the rest of the inventory included, your profit will still be substantial. Just not the exorbitant amount that you had expected.' he leaned back in his seat with his eyes not leaving Gorton-Hyde's.

Gorton-Hyde's eyes dropped as he broke the stare in submission, bugger, he thought. He was right of course, even at that price he would clear four million but he still had his ace to play.

His eyes raised to meet Kamal's once again this time framed by a smile 'You win Kamal, I can't disagree with your argument.'

Kamal's smile also returned as did the 'Sir'. 'Excellent Sir Lawrence, then we have a deal.'

'Just before we complete our business.' Gorton-Hyde leaned forward this time. 'What would you pay for the death of your cousin's killer?'

Once again, Kamal's smile disappeared and was

replaced by a look of thunder 'You have the man that murdered my cousin Khaled. Where is he?'

'I don't have him personally, but my team are holding one of his men hostage, and unbeknownst to him they are waiting to ambush him at Now Zad. They will all be dead before the end of the morning. What would that be worth to you?'

Solemnly Kamal said 'I will add another two million to the price.'

'Now, we have a deal, Kamal.'

Both men stood and shook hands. Kamal increased his grip and leaned forward, saying. 'When I have proof that this man is dead, you will have redeemed yourself, and we can look forward to a long and fruitful business relationship.' He paused for effect. 'However, if you fail, I will return for my money and your head,' there was another pause then the smile returned.

Disconcerted Gorton-Hyde replied 'I'm certain that you'll be happy with the outcome. Now should we complete the bank transfer I have my laptop, I trust you have yours?'

'Yes, Sir Lawrence.'

Kamal snapped his fingers, and one of his sentinels placed a gold cased laptop on the table and opened it. Gorton-Hyde removed his much cheaper version from his briefcase and lifted the lid.

Outside in the corridor, Ben and his team had been hanging on every word of this negotiation. They were suddenly galvanised into action as Ben said 'Right. Down to the room and the moment you here Kamal say 'sent' you two hit that door and disarm those goons behind him, I'll take Gorton-Hyde.'

The three men were soon outside the door, and the two agents inside were equally primed.

Everybody waited for what seemed an eternity as Kamal went through his security procedures to access his bank account. Gorton-Hyde stared at his screen and awaited the arrival of twelve million dollars. Kamal then lifted his hand and hovered over the send key, Gorton-Hyde's greedy anticipation was not lost on him. He dropped his finger and said 'SENT.'

Immediately the room exploded with activity as the door burst from its surround. The two officers and the two agents flashed across the room guns pointing threateningly at the guard's heads shouting loudly 'DO NOT MOVE! DO NOT MOVE OR WE WILL FIRE!'

Ben swiftly got to Gorton-Hyde just as he was reaching for his laptop 'Not so fast Sir. We'll need that,' Ben whipped the laptop away. 'Now be a good chap and place your hands behind your back please.'

The guards knew that they were beaten, besides it was evident that their master was not under any threat as nobody had gone near him. They did not have to give their lives to protect him today. They kept their hands raised and allowed their weapons to be removed.

Kamal simply sat still and stared at Gorton-Hyde with fiery rage in his dark brown eyes and waited for the scene to play out.

Gorton-Hyde tried to avoid Kamal's glare and indignantly shouted at Ben 'What the hell do think you are doing, do you know who I am? Who are you anyway?'

Having slipped the wrist ties onto Gorton-Hyde, Ben replied 'I am placing you under arrest for dealing in illegal firearms. I'm sure there'll be lots more by the time we get you back to England, and MI6 show their hand. As to your second question, you are Sir Lawrence Gorton-Hyde I suspect soon to be just Lawrence, and I am DCI Ben Gifford CTC. Now, on your feet, let's go.'

With that, Ben put the laptop in the briefcase, all information securely saved and dragged Gorton-Hyde out of the room. The four men followed walking out backwards with pistols facing the Saudis. Once outside, they dashed for the elevator whilst assisting Ben with the less than helpful Gorton-Hyde.

'Where are you bloody well taking me? This is a kidnap,' he objected.

'You've already been told, back to 'Blighty' of course,' said Thornton with relish.

'You will never get me through an airport I'll scream, kidnap all the way. You lightweights haven't got enough government clout to get Turkish cooperation. That's blindingly obvious.'

'A few days ago, I might have agreed with you. But we seem to have got this far with surprising ease. My guess is you're not very popular back home.'

They exited the elevator and frog marched Gorton-Hyde out of the hotel's front doors to the waiting car. Ben continued 'We've even managed to arrange a special passage for you. You're taking a boat trip first to sunny Cyprus, only it won't be much of a holiday. You'll be going straight to an RAF base. Got the idea?'

Once in the car, Ben got out his phone it was 7.45 am, and he sent a text to Adam.

'A'

Mission accomplished.

'B'

He then sent another to someone in MI6 confirming the same.

CHAPTER 23

Thursday 7.30 AM - 2019

There were a few 'Terri's wandering about in the compound yard, but nobody showed any signs of opening the perimeter wall gates. They were all waiting for a text, email or phone call before taking any action. This included Adam and the six men with him on the hot sandy ledge. They were all focused on their binoculars watching for any signs of discovery, of either their explosives or Gavin and Paul in the watchtowers.

'I wouldn't want to be up there at the moment,' whispered Charlie to Adam.

'Yes, we'll need to sort out some sort of bonus for those 2 boys when this is over.'

'Damn right,' agreed Charlie.

Suddenly, Adams phone vibrated. He took it out and read,

'A'

Mission accomplished.

'B'

'That's it Charlie' Fire'.'

They covered their ears.

Charlie immediately removed the safety bars, squeezed both of the 'Clackers' and pressed the fire button on the remote multiple C4 detonators.

Twenty four explosive devices went off almost simultaneously, and all hell broke loose. Moments later, the live ammunition in the containers went up along with the fuel tanks. The noise was deafening, and the air inside the canyon rocked like a solid mass. There was screaming and shouting everywhere, but nothing could be seen. A massive dust cloud rose into the air, momentarily blocking the sunlight.

As it began to drop back to earth, the seven men strained to make anything out through their glasses. When the remains of the house became visible, they tossed in the rest of the grenades ensuring there weren't any survivors in the ruins.

Eventually, Matt said 'I can see movement at the far end of the canyon. I guess that will be some of Bolton's men who were far enough away to survive the blast.'

Adam said loudly 'There's £500 for the first man to get eyes on Bolton dead or alive.'

Then came the chatter of automatic fire and Henri chirped up 'That will be Gavin and Paul taking out some of Bolton's survivors.'

'Good men,' said Adam, whilst focusing on his glasses.

Flames started to appear through the dust cloud coming from the lorries' fronts as the cabins and tyres burnt.

Suddenly an excited Charlie said 'Adam, I have eyes on Bolton,' and he pointed to the far right side of the fence, which was surprisingly still in one piece.

With his eye glued to the L115 sights, he slowly scanned the area that Charlie had indicated. Visibility was coming and going as the dust cloud blew across the canyon. He caught sight of the unmistakable spiky white hair. You tit, you might as well have an arrow above your head, he thought with disdain, there's a .338 coming your way, arsehole.

His breathing slowed, it was only about six hundred meters, but the conditions weren't great. Bolton was staggering about trying to find his Range Rover. No doubt he was hoping for a getaway.

He was only going to get one shot. Once Bolton was alerted, he would disappear into the smoke and dust. Adam slowly traced the staggering form, keeping the crosshairs firmly in the middle of his head. He knew that his beloved L115 would not fail him. This was all down to him and his skill as a marksman.

Then it happened. For some reason, Bolton stopped moving and slowly turned his face towards Adam, up on the ledge. There was no way that he could possibly see him through the dust cloud, but it seemed as if he was looking right at him.

Ever the professional this did not faze Adam. He exhaled slowly and pulled the trigger. The bullet whistled through the fence and straight into Bolton's forehead. It burst out of the back showering the floor with bits of skull and brain tissue. Adam's eye remained at his sights, he watched the dead man drop to the ground and lay motionless.

'GOTCHA! That's for Frank, Michelle and Julian, you bastard,' he exclaimed.

'Good shot Adam,' said Charlie, who had viewed it through his glasses.

Five minutes had passed. There hadn't been any shouting or movement from what was left of the 'Terri's house. It appeared that the Claymores had also done a thorough job.

Suddenly there was mayhem in the compound below as the warehouse doors burst open. Teams of Taliban fighters ran into the yard. They knew exactly where Adam and the team were, as waves of automatic fire started coming up the cliffside to the ledge.

'GET BACK! GET BACK!' Adam shouted 'back against the cliff everyone.' He looked at Charlie and said 'What the fuck ….?'

Charlie looked back at him, shouting over the gunfire he said 'It's not a warehouse, it's a bloody Taliban fighter training barracks. We need to get out through the back door, quickly while we still can.'

Adam shouted above the constant clatter of the automatic fire 'They'll be up this mount side shortly. Charlie, pull that rope up no point in helping them. Matt, you and Wayne get off the ledge and around the hill to the Mastiff, first.'

'Wayne is long gone boss, lost his bottle and did a runner.'

'Good riddance,' replied Adam. 'Alright, you and Henri go first.'

'Will do,' shouted Matt as loudly as he could. Although the Taliban fighters could not see them at the back of the ledge, their bullets were ricocheting all around them.

The rest of the men returned fire as best they could, shooting blindly over the ledge.

Just as Matt was about to leave, the Mastiff suddenly came careering around the corner, stopping in a cloud of dust, just short of the men on the ledge.

Adam shouted back to Matt, who was nearest the vehicle 'What the hell! Has she come to rescue us, or is there another problem?'

Matt crawled back from the ledge, keeping down he banged on the passenger side door and shouted 'Michelle! Michelle! What's going on?'

Michelle managed to push open the passenger door and shout back to Matt 'There are 2 APC's heading our way at speed across the tops towards us.'

'Oh shit, stay there for the moment. The Mastiff isn't in the firing line. I'll let Adam know. How long before they get here?'

'About 5 minutes, but I'm coming with you.'

With that, she grabbed her weapon and crawled out of the door.

'Bloody hell Michelle,' said Matt, 'keep your head down for Christ's sake.'

The two of them crawled along the back of the ledge until they reached Adam, who didn't bother to question why she had not stayed in the truck. He just grabbed her roughly and pushed her body behind his to protect her from the bullets flying around. Matt told him what she had said about the impending visitors.

'You and Henri set up a rearguard just beyond the

Mastiff, 2 APC's could mean a dozen men so take an extra clip each.'

'Will do boss.'

Charlie and the others continued to blaze away showering bullets indiscriminately over the edge of the ledge. Adam turned his head over his shoulder and shouted to Michelle 'There are 25 possibly 30 young Taliban fighters down there, and they're mad as hell so keep your head down.'

'Are these any good?' she said, producing the two grenades that Charlie had given her.

'Well done you,' Adam smiled at her, 'it won't change the world, but it's better than nothing.'

Adam removed the pins and tossed them over the ledge, the firing ceased for a moment as the 'Terri's were no doubt running away from the falling grenades. There were two loud bangs then the firing recommenced in earnest.

'I think we just made them angry, but we might have got 2 or 3.'

Suddenly the firing stopped, and there was an eerie silence.

'What's happening?' said Michelle.

'They're making the climb up here,' Adam said 'even these guys aren't crazy enough to shoot their own men. They probably think we must be running out of ammo by now.'

Charlie looked up from clip bag at Adam and shrugged 'They would be right.'

'Oh I see,' said Adam.

Michelle was frightened. She whispered into Adam's ear 'whatever happens, please don't let them capture me …. please.'

He just nodded his head, fully understanding her meaning. They were quiet for a moment, then Adam stood up.

'Do you all have ammo for your sidearms?'

They all had at least two clips.

'If we're careful with the ammo I reckon that we can keep these bastards at bay long enough for Matt and Henri to take care of the back door. Then we pile into the Mastiff and make a dash for it. Is everybody clear?' The ledge was silent. 'I SAID IS EVERYBODY CLEAR?'

The reply came back loud and clear, with one voice including Michelle' YES BOSS.'

'Right then, let's make every single shot count.'

They all tossed aside their empty weapons and removed their side arms from their holsters and waited for the Taliban fighters to start appearing over the ledge.

'What's the chance of this working?' asked Michelle quietly

'Every one of us knows the answer to that question, my love. They will likely come over that ledge five and six at a time with grenades and automatic weapons. Matt and Henri will struggle to deal with the rear defence.'

She held him tightly and whispered so that the others couldn't hear 'I'm frightened, Adam.'

He kissed her head then moved her face away from his body, looked at her and said 'There's no shame in that, just don't let it affect your aim.'

They could now hear the sound of rocks being dislodged and falling back down the hill. The 'Terri's were nearing the top of their climb.

'Look out for grenades everyone!' warned Adam.

Pretty soon the first of their heads would appear over the ledge, so they all braced themselves. Eight pistols were pointing at the edge of the shelf as they awaited their fate.

Suddenly there was a loud boom followed by a colossal explosion.

The gates and middle of the perimeter wall disintegrated along with what was left of the house. Thirty seconds later there was another boom, and this time the remainder of the perimeter wall disappeared.

There was a lot of shouting from the Taliban fighters below.

Adam and the team all exchanged quizzical looks. The men were confused because they all recognised the sound of the boom that preceded the destruction below. Still, they couldn't understand why they were hearing the sound of the 125mm cannon from a T-72 tank.

Nobody had appeared over the ledge, and the shooting had stopped. Cautiously peering over the edge Adam could see the Taliban fighters had all dropped their weapons and were standing with their hands in the air.

The dust and smoke dispersed. A beautiful sight began to emerge. Down the middle of the canyon proceeded the T-72. The sound of its V12 diesel engines filling the air. Coupled with the rattle of its huge tracks, under the weight of the 45-tonne vehicle. Rubble and stones were simply crushed beneath. It was flanked on either side by two APC's and behind followed forty Afghan Army soldiers.

'Now there's a sight for sore eyes,' gasped Adam in wonderment.

Matt came dashing around the rocks at the rear of the ledge shouting 'Boss! Boss! we've got company.'

Adam spun around pistol in hand ready to fire.

'No. Not that sort of company,' said Matt quickly

holding up his hand.

Around the corner came Major Wallace Jones accompanied by Colonel Jamil Karak.

Adam's arms fell to his side as he stared in amazement at his old SAS commander 'What the bloody hell?' he eventually managed to say.

'Ah. Captain Crest,' said the major as he approached Adam with outstretched hand' Good to see you.'

Adam took his hand and shook it vigorously but could still only repeat 'What the bloody hell?'

Major Jones looked at him quizzically and said 'Yes … well … you probably have one or two questions that need answering. Let's get you all back to camp Sharobak. We can have a chat then. Colonel Karak's men will clean up the mess down there.'

Suddenly, Adam snapped out of his stupor and blurted 'Sir, I have a badly injured man in the Mastiff. He needs urgent medical attention. Do you also have any idea what happened to my two men in the watchtowers?'

'Colonel Karak has a medic with your colleague now, and they're arranging to transport him by helicopter back to the camp. As for your men in the towers, I understand that they're both casualties but neither life-threatening. Now we really must get on. After you, Lady Gorton-Hyde,' said Major Jones as he gestured towards the exit from the ledge.

A bemused Michelle grabbed Adam's arm and walked off the ledge. The rest of the men followed, all of them a little confused but greatly relieved to be walking out alive.

Five minutes later, the helicopter arrived and carefully loaded Julian on board.

Major Jones said 'Captain Crest. You and Lady Gorton-Hyde come with me in the helicopter the rest of your team can follow in the APC's.'

Adam and Michelle were pleased to be able to travel with Julian but before they left Adam went over to speak to Charlie.

'We're going with Julian in the chopper, and they'll take you and the guys in the APC's. Can you find out what happened to Gavin and Paul and let me know, please? I understand that they're alive but wounded.'

'Will do Adam. Do me a favour and tell me what on earth is going on.'

'I'm not sure myself yet, but I suppose I'll find out once we get to Shorabak. I'll let you know as soon as I do.'

'OK Boss. It'll be good to get some food and a bit of shut-eye everyone's a bit knackered.'

'Just one more thing, Charlie, would you collect the L115 and bring it back to camp with you.'

Charlie grinned and replied 'No problem, Boss.'

Adam, Michelle and Major Jones boarded the chopper, lifted off, then sailed across the desert sky. Colonel Karak drove back around the hillside and down to the canyon floor to see what was left of the weapons shipment. As always a deal had been made, he had a 'finder's keepers' arrangement with Major Jones regarding any surviving arms. He understood that there may be some 'Javelins' in there. Even if some were still usable, he knew that the relationship with the Americans would prevent him from keeping them. But he might get some brownie points and a 'quid pro quo' if he could return some of them.

On the other hand, Crest's team had done a pretty thorough job, so there may be nothing worth having.

About half an hour later, the helicopter landed at Camp Shorabak. Julian was whisked off to the hospital. Major Jones instructed them to head into Colonel Karak's office where they all sat down. There was a knock at the door, and Colonel Karak's officious adjutant entered.

'Bottled water and Chi for all, Corporal?'

'Sir,' replied the adjutant eyeing Michelle as he

left.

Major Jones was very comfortable in Colonel Karak's office.

'Well Captain Crest, I should think you and Lady Gorton-Hyde have a hundred and one questions to ask.'

'We do Sir, but please could I ask that we drop the 'Captain' whilst I'm proud of my service I'm no longer a serving officer.'

'Of course Crest, old habits and all that.'

Michelle then said 'Similarly I've no intention of retaining my title or surname,' she smiled 'please just call me Michelle.'

He returned the smile and said 'Nothing would give me greater pleasure Michelle and you must call me Wallace,' he flashed a look at Adam 'not you though.'

Adam detected the humour in the comment but replied 'Of course not Sir.'

'I'd better start from the beginning, which is over two years ago. You'll recall Crest, the last time that you were perched on that ledge, and the less than professional way we were forced to carry out an operation. Due to interference from Whitehall, it ended in the death of one of my men and yourself becoming a casualty.'

'I do Sir.'

'I raised hell with the MOD and was quickly recalled to England. I attended a meeting with Foreign and Home Office Ministers and joint intelligence who explained the bigger picture. Something that they wouldn't normally bother to do. But they wanted me to work on a problem with them, and I was installed at Vauxhall Bridge. The problem being that illegal arms were being supplied to the Taliban from Russia but brokered and delivered by someone in our own government. The Saudi's were involved in the funding. I was tasked with discovering the man behind it all and uncovering the operation.'

Major Jones stopped talking as the adjutant returned with the drinks. He placed them on the desk and left looking a bit disconcerted by the obvious silence.

'Please help yourselves,' he said before continuing. 'You were unaware Crest. In fact, we were all unaware at the time. That you had successfully taken out the Saudi dealer along with the brother of the English transport organiser. That put a stop to the trade for some time. Our mastermind had to rebuild trust in his supply chain. There was also a strong possibility that you might be a vengeance target. So I arranged for you to be placed under the wing of a good friend and colleague on this project, Major Braden in Defence Intelligence.'

'Good God,' exclaimed Adam.

'Yes, I understand you had a less than, harmonious relationship, but clearly, Braden could not reveal the reason for his insistence that you did not leave. By this time we were suspicious of Gorton-Hyde. Braden was developing a role as a supporter of his and feeding information back to myself. He also had you get rid of two of the Russian dealers along with Gorton-Hyde's chief negotiator to rattle him a bit, a chap called Riley.'

'Ah, now that makes sense,' said Adam.

'For some time, we were looking in the wrong direction for the supply line, i.e. across land via Eastern Europe. Braden had an outstanding agent who managed to infiltrate Gorton-Hyde's organisation and discovered the storage and supply route from England. Incidentally, the same agent, was also watching over you.'

'Do I get to know who this agent is?' asked Adam.

'I'm afraid not as there's still much to be uncovered at our end. I can't say anything that might compromise the agent's position,' he continued 'it was almost unbelievable when you turned up at that petrol station. It took a hell of a lot of delicate and anonymous information delivery to make sure that Gorton-Hyde knew who you were and the potential benefits to keeping you alive. On top of that, Bolton was very keen to avenge his brother and slit your throat once he found out. Hence your twenty-four hours in captivity. You have a lot to thank your guardian angel for one day.'

'So it seems,' said a mystified Adam.

'Once we realised that you had picked up the ball and were running with it, we weren't going to be able to stop you without blowing the investigation. I decided to let you carry on. We kept a close eye on things from a distance just in case anything went wrong. I liaised with Colonel Karak at this end and made sure that Gifford was afforded all he needed at the Turkish end.'

'What happened to Gorton-Hyde?' asked Adam.

'He's under arrest and on his way back to England to face the music via our RAF base in Cyprus. His right-hand man is languishing in a lock-up at the British embassy in Paris. Now that you've taken care of Bolton and his crew, the Saudis may think twice before doing their next illegal arms deal. Once we've routed out the rot in our establishment, we'll go after the Russian end. We owe you and your team a deal of thanks Crest, and I have to say it was a pretty slick operation until the end that is.'

'Yes, we made a pretty good team, Sir,' said Adam as he glanced at Michelle, who nodded agreement.

'Oh, and by the way, the Afghan Army picked up a rogue mercenary making his way across the desert from Now Zad. I'm sure that they'll know what to do with him. Colonel Karak will be paying Jack Taylor a visit to put him straight on a few things as well. I don't think I've missed anything out. Do you have any questions?' Major Jones poured himself a glass of chi and leaned back in his chair.

At the end of this stream of information, Adam and Michelle sat in silence for several minutes. Adam looked at Michelle, who looked bewildered and shrugged her shoulders.

'Not at this time Major, but there's quite a lot to absorb. However, I must thank yourself and Colonel Karak for coming to our aide.'

'No problem Crest, it was the least we could do. We didn't even find out about the Taliban training barracks until yesterday, so we had to move pretty quickly.'

Eventually, Michelle spoke 'What will happen to Lawrence?'

'He'll be charged and subject to the British justice system.'

'That's not what I asked Wallace.'

'Michelle. You know that I cannot speak for our legal system. We all know how it can sometimes be manipulated, especially by people like Gorton-Hyde. All I can say is that I'll be doing everything in my power to ensure that he is locked up for as long as possible.'

'I suppose that's all we can ask for,' she replied resigned to the fact that Lawrence would probably not be made to pay in full for her brother's death.

'Now, I suggest that you get some rest whilst I arrange for your flights home.'

'Thanks again, Major. I need to check on Julian and my men first then we'll do exactly that,' said Adam as they both got up and left the office.

CHAPTER 24

December 2019

Three weeks after their arrival back in England, Julian was well on the road to recovery. However, his head was still in a brace awaiting the healing of a crack in his skull. The doctors did not expect there to be any long term damage from the concussion. He was walking with the aid of a frame and apart from some scarring to his lower legs, the long term prognosis was good. Adam and Michelle had visited every other day and watched Julian quickly return to his flamboyant self.

Gavin and Paul had also left the hospital, having both taken bullets to their arms and legs. They could also expect to make a full recovery.

On a crisp December morning, the sun shone brightly from low in the sky, and a coating of white frost covered the naked trees. Adam and Michelle were busy unloading furniture from a large van. They were ably assisted by Charlie and Matt.

Previously Michelle had made a point of getting back into the house in Kensington before Gorton-Hyde's lawyers arranged for his release on bail. She'd only taken things that she had personally bought and nothing that might remind her of him. She had also made sure that the staff were paid correctly and compensated for their redundancy. Gorton-Hyde would not bother to do it.

After a couple of visits with the van, she eventually shut the front door of the house. She pushed the keys back through the letterbox intending never to set foot in the building again. She climbed into the van and kissed Adam.

'Let's go,' she said.

During the drive back to Reading, they chatted.

'Have you heard any more from Wallace?' asked Michelle.

'I presume you mean the OC,' replied Adam smiling at her use of the Majors first name. 'No not since the debrief. I think he's a permanent fixture at MI6 now as is Braden I suspect. Reward for a successful mission, I suppose.'

'Do you trust them?'

'I trust the OC, but I still don't feel right about Braden even though he turned out to be on our side. Ben Gifford's good guy though, I understand he has got Mellor's old job at the Home Office, which is well deserved. He put his pension at risk going after Gorton-Hyde, especially when he had no idea that MI6 were after him as well.'

'Yes, that's true. How's Harry?'

'Fine. I saw him at the office last week. He's a bit bored at Comm-Sec though, getting sick of selling security systems I guess. Mind you so am I.'

After some thought Michelle said 'The collapse of Guard-Co must have left quite a hole in the security industry?'

'Yes, it was a big company. The Foreign Office is having to rely on MI5 manpower at the moment, which won't go down well.'

'Not just that, I know a lot of important people that used Guard-Co for personal security. All solicited by Lawrence of course.' She paused for a moment. 'Adam, have you never thought about doing your own thing? It's an area you're well-acquainted with.'

Adam glanced across at her, suddenly realising where she was going with this conversation.

'Do you know, that's not a bad idea. I wonder if Harry might be interested as well. There could be an international business potential between his contacts in Asia and Africa and ours in England and Europe. We could recruit our manpower from ex-military personnel providing some much-needed employment.'

Pleased at Adam's enthusiasm, Michelle replied 'Absolutely, I am sure Charlie and Matt would get involved with that.'

'Yes, of course.' Adam paused. 'Am I being presumptuous using the word we? It would cost a fair bit to set this up.'

'Adam, I have plenty of money, and I can't think of a better person to trust with it. Plus I will be your business partner. I'll run the Admin and finance side, and you run the Operational bit.'

'Sounds good. We could call it Security International.'

'What about Crest & Co International Security?'

'Even better,' he agreed.

'One rule, though,' said Michelle.

'What's that?'

'We keep business out of the bedroom.'

'Agreed,' Adam laughed.

An animated discussion continued for the rest of the journey.

They had already gone through the painful but necessary process of removing most of Frank's belongings from the house. Michelle had kept some things to remind her of her beloved brother but not enough to prevent the flourishing of her new beginning in the house. Once the last item had been unloaded, and Charlie and Matt had carried them inside, Adam and Michelle closed the rear doors to the van.

'It's a big house, Michelle,' observed Adam.

'Yes I suppose it is really,' Michelle agreed.

'I mean just for one person that is.'

She knew exactly what Adam was getting at but played along 'Yes, I guess it is.'

'I hope you won't get lonely.'

'There's not much chance of that.'

'Oh, why is that?'

Bringing the playful pretence to an end, Michelle placed her arms around Adam's waist and pulled him towards her. 'Because you and I both know that I will not be living here alone,' then she kissed him.

200 meters down the lane on the opposite side of the road there was a similar detached house which had been empty for some time. In the first-floor front bedroom, a man in a dark suit lay prostrate on his stomach, his legs were splayed for balance. The palm of his left hand was pressed flat against the floor his right arm curved around the form of an L129 marksman's rifle, and his eye peered into the sights. The crosshairs were centred on the head of Adam crest.

The round had been chambered with another waiting for Lady Gorton-Hyde. His right hand was wrapped around the grip with his forefinger stretched out across the guard. He politely waited for them to finish their embrace before pulling the trigger. His concentration was absolute so much so that he did not hear the person enter the room.

The woman behind him in black leather jeans and jacket stood between his splayed legs. She lifted her left leg and place a short but sharp stiletto heel firmly onto the back of the man's left hand. Bending down, she pushed the silenced barrel of her 9mm automatic pistol into the back of his neck.

'Ahhgh,' screamed the man as the heel punctured his skin and penetrated the muscle.

She reduced the pressure on his hand slightly and spoke softly into his ear her voice full of intent 'Take your hand away from the rifle Mr Mellors. I guarantee that I will pull my trigger before you can pull yours.' She increased the pressure on his hand to emphasise the threat.

Mellors screamed in pain again and immediately withdrew his hand from the weapon.

'Hands behind your back,' she commanded, and he obeyed with blood flowing freely from his left hand.

Swiftly the nylon zip ties were in place, and Mellors was helpless.

'Get up,' she commanded.

He got up asking indignantly 'Do you know who I am?'

'Yes, Mr Mellors. I certainly do,' came the trite reply.

'Who the bloody hell are you?'

'That you will never know. Now, get downstairs.'

The woman followed Mellors downstairs to the front door, never removing the pistol barrel from the back of his head.

'Open the door.'

He did as he was told. Outside a black Range Rover drew up. She lowered the pistol to his back, pushed him forward and followed him holding the sniper rifle in the other hand.

From the other side of the road, Adam and Michelle's embrace ended, and they turned to go inside the house. On the way, Adam noticed the Range Rover outside of the house across the road. He could clearly see a man exiting at gunpoint, getting into the back of the car followed by a tall woman with long black hair down to her waist. She was holding a sniper rifle in her left hand. He stared at her. He was sure that he had seen her before.

The woman in black looked straight back at him

and cast an almost imperceptible nod of recognition in his direction then got into the car.

❋ ❋ ❋

Major Wallace Jones's phone rang at his office in London, and he picked up the receiver 'Jones.'

'Sir,' said the female voice 'we have Mellors, but I have some bad news. I'm afraid Gorton-Hyde has jumped bail.'

'Damn!' replied the Major. 'Where is he?'

'Somewhere in Russia, we don't know where exactly.'

'Well bloody well find him. Quickly.'

'We're on it, Sir.'

'You had better increase the security surveillance on Crest and his people. They will be Gorton-Hyde's first target.'

'Will do Sir.'

THE END.

Adam Crest will return in 'Crest & Co'

Printed in Great Britain
by Amazon